By Eliana West

A Paris Walk
Compass of the Heart
Dreidel Date

EMERALD HEARTS
Four Holly Dates
Summer of Noelle
Falling for Joy
Be the Match

MOCKINGBIRD BRIDGE
The Way Forward
The Way Home
The Way Beyond
A Hidden Heart

THE
WAY

MOCKINGBIRD BRIDGE

BOOK TWO

ELIANA WEST

second
press

Published by
SECOND PRESS
info@secondpress.com

The Way Home

Second Edition
First Published by Tule Publishing, May 2021

Cover Art
Cover content is for illustrative purposes only and any person depicted on the cover is
a model.

Trade Paperback ISBN: 9781963011050
Digital ISBN: 9781963011029
Digital eBook published July 2024
v. 2.0

For my Great Aunt Ada Mae—may her memory be a blessing.

ACKNOWLEDGMENTS

I AM honored and humbled to be a part of a wonderful community of authors, and I am thankful for your generosity every day. Anne Turner and Aliyah Burke, I wouldn't have had the courage to tell this story without your encouragement and support. I am so grateful for your friendship and sisterhood.

Donn Thompson Morelli (performing as Donn T) for creating the song "Bird Up Yonder." I will never forget hearing you sing the words for the first time. Thank you for honoring the memory of our ancestors so beautifully.

Thank you, Fire/EMS Officer Dan, for patiently answering all of my questions and explaining everything I need to know about fire and rescue. So proud that I get to call you my friend.

Thank you to my beta readers for your time and wonderful notes.

Neva West, thank you for being a wonderful big sister.

To my husband David, thank you for always believing in my dreams. I am so grateful to have you by my side on this journey. Jackie and Satchel, your strength and compassion inspire me in everything I do. I am proud that I am your mom. Thank you.

Carmen Cook, I can't tell you how much I appreciate your friendship. Your steadfast support and thoughtfulness this past year was key to helping me weather what seemed like an insurmountable storm. It's a wonderful thing to find a friend like that. Thank you for listening and talking me through Taylor and Jo's story and helping me help them find their way home.

CHAPTER ONE

JOSEPHINE MARTIN swatted at the dust bunnies drifting through the air in the attic of her parents' house. The floorboards creaked under her father's feet as he moved another box from the pile in the corner.

"Are you sure it's up here?" she asked, anxiously peering over his shoulder.

"Here, take this," he grunted, handing her another box. "It should be. We haven't gotten rid of anything since we bought the house." He stopped, stretched his back, and looked around the room. "We need to have a garage sale."

"Let's find the trunk first."

Jo tried to keep the impatience out of her voice. She didn't remember the trunk, but after having the same exact dream for the second time, she needed to know if it was real.

Her father looked at her with concern. "I don't mind helping you, sweetheart, but all this work because of a dream?"

"I know it doesn't make sense, but I had to look and see."

Her father put down the box he was holding and gently grasped her arms. "Sweetheart, your mother and I are worried about you. You've lost weight since Oliver broke up with you, and I can see from those dark circles under your eyes you haven't been sleeping."

Jo dropped her chin to her chest. "I'm so embarrassed. I thought he loved me, and the whole time he was just using me."

"I'm so sorry, sweetheart."

"The worst part is that they all knew. My friends, coworkers, supervisors—everyone knew he was seeing my best friend behind my back and didn't say a word to me. There were pictures online of all of them out celebrating Oliver's promotion and their engagement last night." Her voice dropped to a whisper. A fresh wave of anguish washed over her, threatening to take her to her knees. "It hurts so much, Dad."

Her father pulled her into a hug, and she let the tears she'd been fighting fall.

They'd had a whirlwind relationship. Thinking about how excited she was telling her best friend Courtney about her handsome coworker made Jo sick to her stomach. Courtney had insisted on meeting Oliver right away, telling Jo she wanted to make sure he was good enough for her. Looking back now, she could see the lust in Oliver's eyes when Jo introduced him to her best friend. But she had been blinded by what she thought was love. She wanted to believe the fairy-tale lies Oliver was telling her.

She'd met Oliver when a consulting firm where he worked hired her. They bonded over being young Black professionals, working as system architects developing computer systems for companies and organizations. Jo had never been swept off her feet before, and it was thrilling. He was always telling her how beautiful and smart she was. He treated her like an equal in a career dominated by men. Until they were both up for the same promotion.

"I still think you should go back to HR and file an appeal."

Jo stepped out of her father's arms and shook her head. "They've already fired me. They aren't going to take me back."

"If they knew about how Oliver stole your designs and passed them off as his own, they would."

"The head of HR didn't believe me when I told him. I showed them my work and they accused me of stealing from him. The way Oliver framed me, they could prosecute me for theft." Jo bit back a sob. "He said Oliver asked them not to have me arrested, just to fire me instead. As if he was doing me a favor." She shook her head. "Even if I could get them to believe me, I don't want to work for a company that doesn't take their female employees seriously."

Her father wrapped his arm around her. "I know it may be hard to believe it now, but you will be okay, sweetheart."

Jo sniffed and wiped her eyes. "Thanks, Dad."

She could always count on her parents' support. Her dad was her biggest champion. There was never any doubt that if she told him about her dream, he would help her.

She'd had the first dream two weeks ago—the day Oliver shattered her world. It was of an elderly woman standing next to an old trunk in her parents' attic. The woman opened the trunk and pressed her hand to the inside of the lid. "Your future is here," she said.

Jo had the dream again last night. It was so vivid and seemed so real, she got up and drove straight over to her parents' house.

"Now, let's see if we can find this trunk. I know it's back here somewhere."

It was a late summer Saturday morning, and the sun cast a golden shadow through the small attic window while they worked. Together Jo and her father shifted boxes out of the corner until a large trunk appeared. They pushed the piece into the middle of the room. She swiped away the dust on top. The wood glowed a warm golden brown, with dips and grooves that marked handiwork done without benefit of modern tools. The wood was arranged in a chevron pattern on the top. Clearly, whoever had made it put a great deal of care into the project.

"Are you sure about this?" her father asked.

Jo took a deep breath, nodded, and pressed the latch. The hinges creaked, releasing a faint musky smell. Inside, there was an old quilt that looked so fragile she expected it would fall apart if she picked it up. Underneath were pictures, cards, and letters scattered among other small items.

She pressed her hand against the faded floral paper on the inside of the lid the same way the woman in her dream had. There was a tearing sound when a piece of wood popped out behind the paper that covered it.

"Well, I'll be damned," her father whispered as Jo pulled a long thin tin box from its hiding place. She opened the lid and pulled out an envelope and another piece of paper.

Her hands shook as she read the writing on the front. In a bold script, it was addressed to an Ada Mae Colton with A. M. Colton listed for the return addressee.

Her father knelt next to her as she pulled two pieces of paper out of the envelope. She opened the first one and read.

September 7, 1860

Ada Mae,

I will refrain from calling you my dearest, as I know how those endearments upset you.

Halcyon is no longer a home now that you are gone. I can't bear to be in the house with Julia. I have sent her to the house in Jackson and do not plan on ever letting her set foot in Halcyon again. Now I wander this house alone. Thoughts of you and our son haunt my dreams at night. It is the sharpest knife wound to my heart to hear that you have married, but I know it is for the best. I know he is a good man, as you would not settle for anything less, and that assures me he will be a good father to our son.

War is coming, and I will have to fight. You should be safe where you are. I do not believe Illinois will join the Confederacy, but guard your freedom papers closely. Enclosed are enough funds for you and your family to flee as far north as Canada if need be. I have made arrangements with my solicitor that when the time comes for me to depart this earth, Halcyon will pass to you and our son.

You will forever be in my heart,

Absolem

She opened the second piece of paper and drew a sharp breath.

Certificate of Freedom
March 1, 1859

I, Colonel Absolem Madden Colton, do hereby make it known to all that the female slave known as Ada Mae, age to be known as about twenty years, and her son known as Stephen, age six months, are free. They are no longer to be counted as my property nor can they be claimed as property of my wife, Mrs. Julia Colton.

I hereby declare Stephen to be my son and heir. He is entitled to claim such rights and privileges as a free man of the United States of America.

Colonel Absolem Madden Colton
Halcyon Plantation
Colton, Mississippi

"I heard stories, but I didn't believe them," her dad said.
"What stories?"
Her father took a deep breath. "My great-granddaddy used to tell me how we were descended from a freed slave, a woman named Ada Mae Martin. She was free before the Civil War. He said his great-grandfather

was a man named Stephen Martin, and we had mixed blood. Stephen was the son of the man who owned his mama, a confederate general." He shook his head. "I didn't believe him. Who would want to believe that? It would mean...."

Jo wrapped her arm around her father, leaning against him. "It's okay, Dad."

Jo shared her father's anguish, knowing that their ancestor had been forced to bear the child of a man who owned her.

His hand shook when he held the delicate parchment up to the light.

"Dad." Jo spoke softly. "I want to go and see Halcyon."

Her father looked at her with surprise. "It's probably long gone."

"Maybe—either way, I want to go to Mississippi."

His eyes searched hers. "Why? What are you hoping to find?"

"I'm not sure, but I know I need to see it with my own eyes."

"Do you want me to go with you?"

She stood on tiptoe and placed a kiss on her father's cheek. "Thanks, Dad, but I think this is a trip I want to make on my own."

He tucked the letter back in the envelope. "We better go tell your mother about this. Your brother and sister will be here soon, and we can talk about it over dinner."

Jo suppressed a groan. The last thing she wanted to do was share the letter with her brother and sister.

"Thanks, Dad, but I'm going to pass."

"Your brother and sister—"

"You need to stop making excuses for them. I'm tired of putting in the effort and not getting anything in return."

"I hate that you feel that way."

"Just because we're family doesn't mean we have to get along."

"They may not act like it, but they do care."

"Dad, you know that's not true. We've never been close. The twins share a bond that I've just never been a part of."

Her father sighed. "I still don't understand what you're hoping to find when you get to Mississippi."

"Maybe nothing, maybe a little bit of myself... our history."

"You can't run away from your problems, sweetheart."

"You and Mom have always supported us kids and you've always given us a safe place to land. I want to do something different. I can use this trip to heal and figure out what I want to do next. I'm scared if I don't take a chance on something new again, I never will."

LATER THAT night, Jo stood at her dining room table with a glass of wine, looking over the various papers, letters, postcards, and photographs that were in the trunk. Her father's family history was laid out before her. She sorted everything into piles by date. There were WWII letters from her second great-grandfather. A small journal filled with notes detailing army nurses' training from his sister. A registration card for the Pullman Porters' union from Ada Mae's son, Stephen. And other mementos that spanned over a hundred and fifty years of history. But nothing more from Ada Mae.

Jo opened the letter from Colonel Colton again.

War is coming, and I will have to fight. You should be safe where you are. I do not believe Illinois will join the Confederacy but guard your freedom papers closely.

Her pulse quickened as if she were feeling the same fear Ada Mae must have felt on the eve of war, wondering if she and her son would be secure. She looked at the piece of paper that gave Ada Mae and her son their freedom. One aged piece of parchment that had changed her family's history.

She spent the rest of the evening at her computer, learning everything she could about Colton, Mississippi, and the plantation house called Halcyon. She found a grainy black-and-white picture of the plantation house. She leaned forward, studying the image on her screen, and the words in her dream came back to her. "*Your future is here.*" Before she went to bed that night, Jo booked a flight to Mississippi.

A FEW days later, as the plane descended into Jackson, Jo looked out the window. Instead of the vast freshwater ocean of Lake Michigan, she saw just a few small ponds and rivers dotting the landscape. She picked up her rental car and began the drive to Colton. The city quickly dissolved into countryside, with stands of trees separated by farmland. The only crop she recognized was corn. She was a city girl born and raised and already completely out of her element. By the time she made the hour-long drive from Jackson to Colton, she'd convinced herself this was the worst idea she'd ever had. But there wasn't much of a future left for her back in Chicago. Oliver was making sure everyone knew she'd been fired, eliminating almost all her job prospects. She blinked back her tears and focused on the road ahead. Colton might just give her the fresh start she needed.

The green fields gave way to a small cluster of low buildings next to railroad tracks. She drove past an old train depot, following the GPS directions into a town square that looked like something out of a picture book from the 1950s. Downtown Colton was made up of four blocks with a park in the middle. On her way to the town hall, she passed by the smallest library she'd ever seen, with a little bookstore next door. The town hall took up one whole block at the end of the square. Jo pulled into a parking spot right up front and smiled. No one would ever have to circle the block looking for a parking spot in Colton. She got out and looked up at the grand building. This was it, the first step in learning more about Ada Mae and why she didn't get the house she was promised. A bright blue bird swooped down in front of her, hopping alongside her as she climbed the steps. It cocked its head, chattering at her with its bright red beak.

"What do you want?" She laughed at the little bird's antics. "I'm sorry, but you can't come inside with me."

The bird lifted into the air and flew right past her nose before darting away. Jo walked into the building with a smile. She was greeted by the faint musty smell of age combined with antiseptic cleaner that reminded her of her elementary school hallways. From the directory at the entrance, Jo learned that all of the town's services were here, including the jail and a courtroom. She shook her head with a smile. This really was like a town you'd find in an old TV show from the 50s. Looking down the hall, she spotted a sign marked Office and headed in that direction.

An older White woman, her hair cut into a severe bob, sat typing away at an ancient computer when she walked in. She peered at Josephine over the tops of her bright red reading glasses, that matched the lipstick that made the wrinkles on her pale skin stand out.

"Can I help you?" she asked in a tone that suggested she wasn't going to be much help at all.

Before she could answer, a younger woman who shared Jo's same dark brown skin, with close-cropped hair and large eyes that were so dark they were almost black, came through another doorway marked *Mayor*.

"Grace, have you seen the printout for... Oh, hello," she said with a friendly smile.

"Hi, I'm Josephine Martin." Jo extended her hand. "I'm here looking for... well, I'm not exactly sure."

"I'm the mayor, Mae Colton. Come on back to my office and we'll see if we can figure out what you need."

The administrative assistant cleared her throat. "Mayor Colton, I can take care of this for you."

"Grace, I know you're busy looking for the contract from the county for garbage disposal I asked you for two days ago," Mae answered with a raised eyebrow. "This way, Ms. Martin."

Grace pursed her lips and glared at them as Mae led her past the front desk and into her office. Jo looked around and wondered if she had just wandered onto the set of *Mad Men*. Mae took her place behind a huge oak desk that dwarfed her petite frame. There were two chairs covered in dark burgundy vinyl to one side and a smaller version in front of the desk. "Take a seat," she said, gesturing to it.

Jo sat down and pulled the envelope from her bag. "I'm here about Halcyon."

"The old plantation house? What about it?"

She cleared her throat. "I'd like to see it."

"Well, this is interesting." Mae sat back. "Can I ask why?"

Jo handed Mae the envelope. "I recently came across some documents that show my family has a connection to the house."

Mae looked down at the handwriting on the front and drew in a breath. She pulled out the sheaf of paper and started reading. She looked from the letter to Jo and back again. "Holy shit," she whispered. "Grace," she yelled, still looking down at the letter.

Grace popped her head in the door.

"I need all the files you have on Halcyon, including the tax records and current titleholder. If you don't have them, call the county office and have everything sent here."

Grace frowned. "What do you need it for?"

Mae stared the woman down until the older woman stepped back with her lips pressed into a thin line.

"Sorry," she grumbled when Grace left. "I was just appointed as mayor after… well, there was an incident a couple of months ago, and the town was put into receivership. I was asked to serve as interim mayor and"—she held her arms out—"here I am. It's been a bit of an adjustment for some people. We're a small town with limited resources, so there's only one administrative assistant. Grace is used to working with Judge Beaumont and we're struggling a bit to find our footing together." She tilted her head toward the doorway.

Jo gave her a sympathetic smile. She couldn't begin to imagine the challenges of running a small town. She could appreciate what Mae had to deal with as a young Black woman, trying to change the status quo.

Mae carefully folded the letter and put it into the envelope before handing it back to Jo. "You realize what this means, don't you?"

"That we're related?"

"Yes, we must be cousins." She smiled. "The roots of the Colton family tree run deep and are so damn tangled it's hard to figure them out. But if you're Black and you descended from one of the enslaved people who worked on the Colton Plantation, odds are we're related."

Jo held up the letter, pointing to Ada Mae's name in the corner. "She could be your namesake."

Mae tapped her lips. "I was always told Mae was a family name, but I never knew who it was from." She sat up straighter and grabbed her phone. "Are you free for dinner?" Jo nodded as Mae held up a finger. "Hi, Mom, I'm bringing company for dinner tonight. No, not him, it's a surprise." She hung up the phone and rubbed her hands together. "Now that that's taken care of, let's take a drive over to Halcyon."

As they drove out of town, Mae pointed out that the park across the street was named after Colonel Absolem Madden Colton.

"I have to admit it's strange to see a park named after a man who owned our family."

"Parks, monuments, and schools—the South is filled with reminders of the Confederacy," Mae said.

"You'd think they won the war."

"There are still folks out there who have a hard time letting go of the idea of a South that never really existed. They're the same people who think slaves and plantations like Halcyon were just like what they've seen in old movies."

Mae's Jeep zipped down the road toward the mansion. She explained that Halcyon was only ten minutes outside of town, and the way she drove, it was even quicker than that. They turned down the long driveway and Jo got her first glimpse of the plantation. They pulled around a large oak tree that stood at the center of a circular driveway to the front of the house.

"Are you okay?" Mae asked when Jo took a deep breath, hesitating before she got out of the car.

Jo gave her a shaky smile. "I'm good."

"I'm sorry we can't go inside, but we can walk around the exterior."

Wide upper and lower verandas were supported by four large columns on three sides of the house. The shutters that remained hung precariously at different angles, but the front door stood solid under a large arched window. Although worn with time and half overgrown with weeds, the house still had a whisper of how impressive it must have been. How could something that was once so beautiful and grand have been built from so much pain?

When they finished their tour, Mae turned to her. "I don't get it— what do you think you can do with this place?"

"I don't know yet. I can't explain it, but I feel like I'm supposed to be here."

Mae put her arm around Jo's shoulder. "Come on, let's head to my folks' place for dinner. They're going to want to hear all about this."

The wind rustled through the large oak tree on the other side of the driveway, and the scent of eucalyptus filled the air. Jo could have sworn she heard a voice saying *"Your future is here. Welcome home, baby girl,"* in the wind when she walked back to the car.

CHAPTER TWO

PEANUT SHELLS crunched under his boots when Taylor Colton entered the dimly lit juke joint. The Buckthorn was legendary. Mysterious and forbidden when he was a child, now at thirty he crept in as if he were afraid the grown-ups would catch him and throw him out. Mr. Wallace, the owner, gave him a slight nod. He continued popping the tops off beer bottles and pushing them toward the people crowding the bar without breaking his rhythm.

A delayed flight had brought Taylor to Colton later than he'd planned. He'd stopped by the town hall looking for the new mayor and was told she could be found at the Buckthorn. His lips quirked, recalling the way the woman at the reception desk in the mayor's office said the name of the establishment. She looked as if she had just taken a bite out of a lemon. Taylor got the impression the woman didn't approve of the mayor leaving work early on a Friday to have a drink with her friends.

He scanned the picnic tables covered in red-and-white checkered oilcloth, looking for the mayor. It didn't take long to find her, sitting at a table toward the back along with several others, including a stunning Black woman who momentarily distracted him from his task. The woman's hair was parted in the middle and fell in a straight waterfall of deep brown past her shoulders. The style emphasized the high cheekbones of her heart-shaped face. She had large dark eyes and full pink lips. Very kissable lips. Her dark skin glowed against the simple black T-shirt she wore. Taylor zeroed in on the delicate circle of gold on a chain that nestled in the low neckline of her top and was seized by a jolt of attraction he hadn't felt in a very long time. He slowed down, giving himself a minute to admire her, before returning his focus to what he was here for. A few faces around the table were familiar, while others he didn't recognize. Taylor was certain he'd never seen the woman sitting next to the mayor before—he would remember a face like hers.

It had been too long since he'd been back to Colton. His career had taken off at the same time his grandparents who lived in Colton passed away, bringing his summer visits to an end. He nodded and smiled at the people pointing and whispering. He made sure to make eye contact with a couple of women who were practically drooling as he crossed the room. It was a part of the job. Celebrity came with perks, and he enjoyed every single one of them. As the host of one of the most-watched home improvement shows on TV, he was used to being recognized just about everywhere he went.

"Excuse me, Mayor Colton, I don't know if you remember me." Taylor offered his hand when he reached the table.

Colton's new mayor looked up at him with a bright smile. Mae Colton had grown up from the little girl he remembered into a young woman with a welcoming smile.

"I may not remember you, but I think it's safe to say we all know who you are." She tilted her head with a curious expression. "What can I do for you, Mr. Colton?"

"I don't mean to interrupt your evening. I wanted to give you the news before you heard about it from anyone else or the press."

"Have a seat." She gestured toward an empty spot at the table.

"It's good to see you again, Taylor." His cousin Dax Ellis shook his hand. "This is my wife, Callie."

Taylor remembered Dax from when they were kids. They were second cousins once removed or something like that. He'd have to ask his parents to send him a copy of the family tree they'd had a genealogist make a few years ago so he could keep track of everyone. Dax's wife smiled while Dax looked down at her, practically glowing with love.

Taylor sat down and a man approached with a tray of beers.

"And this is my brother Reid," Dax said.

"I'm embarrassed to say this, but I didn't remember you had a brother," he admitted.

"That's okay. I was sent away to military school when you were little. I didn't come back to Colton very often after that," Reid said.

"Until now. Reid moved back to Colton after Callie and I got married." Dax grinned at his brother.

Taylor shook Reid's hand. "I hope I can get to know my cousins again while I'm here."

"What brings you to Colton, and what do you need my help for?" Mae asked.

He cleared his throat, eager for the excited response that would follow his announcement. "I'm going to feature Halcyon on the next season of my show."

There was an awkward silence and a gasp from the woman sitting next to Mae. He often got that response when people realized who he was. But the woman looked anything but delighted.

Taylor looked around the table in confusion. "Is there a problem?"

"I…." Mae sat up and cleared her throat. "Apparently you haven't heard yet. Ms. Martin here has filed a claim on the title for Halcyon," Mae said, gesturing to the woman sitting next to her.

He stared at the mayor in disbelief. "What are you talking about? Our family has owned Halcyon since it was built."

"Taylor, this is Josephine Martin." Mae introduced the woman sitting next to her, who was a lot less appealing than she'd been just a minute ago. "Jo filed a petition of probate to change the title of Halcyon into her name last week. Notice should have been sent out to your family by now."

"This doesn't make any sense. How can you file a claim on Halcyon?"

Mae shifted in her seat, exchanging a look with Callie. "Taylor," Dax said, taking his wife's hand in his. "Jo is a descendant of one of the slaves from the plantation."

"Just like Mae and I are," Callie added quietly.

And there it was: the unavoidable truth of his family legacy. Most of the people in Colton, Mississippi, belonged to two families—one White, one Black, both Coltons. His face heated with shame. He dropped his gaze, unable to look Josephine Martin in the eye.

"She has a letter written by your seventh great-uncle Colonel Colton. He promised the house to Josephine's sixth great-grandmother, named Ada Mae," Dax said.

"I can show you the letter." Josephine lifted her chin with a challenging glint in her eye.

Taylor was finally ready to take on the one project he'd always wanted to do, and this woman could take it all away. He was numb. What could he say?

"I, um… I have some phone calls I need to make," he heard himself say as he got up from the table. He walked out the way he walked in, ignoring the stares and whispers. He slammed his hand on the steering wheel as he drove away from the juke joint. "Dammit," he grumbled.

TAYLOR DROVE straight to Halcyon. The grand house was waiting for him, standing worn but still proud under the moonlight. It was his love of the house that had led him to study design and architecture in college. Taylor craned his neck, looking up at the grand columns that supported the structure. When his grandparents passed away while he was still in school, he'd begged his parents to keep the house until he had the time and money to restore it. He had the money now, more than enough with the success of the show. But the show was a double-edged sword that also meant he never had the time. His parents gave him an ultimatum on his thirtieth birthday—restore Halcyon or they were going to donate it to the state. Now he was out of time.

Passed down through the generations, his great-grandparents were the last members of his family to claim the house as a home. His grandparents preferred to live in town, but they kept the house and five acres of farmland that surrounded it. He'd spent hours exploring the rooms on every visit to Colton as a boy. The memory of playing hide-and-go-seek in the house with his brother brought a smile to his lips.

Headlights bounced off the columns, and a vintage gray pickup pulled up next to his rental car.

"Thought I'd find you here," the older man said, getting out of his truck and pulling his Biloxi Shuckers cap down low over his eyes.

He shook the man's hand. "Uncle Robert, it's good to see you."

Robert Ellis wasn't really his uncle. The family tree would place him firmly in the cousin branch. But just like to everybody else in his family and the town, he was known as Uncle Robert.

"Dax must have called," Taylor said with a grimace.

Uncle Robert nodded and went back to his truck, pulling out a cooler. He gestured to the veranda steps. "I brought us some dinner. I figured you didn't get a chance to eat yet."

His stomach rumbled in confirmation.

They sat down, and Uncle Robert pulled out two beers and a couple of roast beef sandwiches.

"It ain't fancy, but it'll fill you up."

Taylor bit into the sandwich, appreciating the taste of the tender, savory meat with a thick slice of tomato and just the right amount of mayonnaise. A container of potato salad appeared in front of him, and he grunted his appreciation around a mouthful of his sandwich. No one made better potato salad than Uncle Robert. He set aside the empty container a few minutes later with a satisfied sigh. "Thank you, I needed that."

"I know how they fancy-up potato salad in LA. Adding in grapes and kale." He wrinkled his nose. "Those folks put kale in damn near everything."

Taylor smiled. "It's good to be back."

"You haven't been home for a long time. Are you sure this is a project you really want to do?" Uncle Robert asked.

"I've always dreamed of bringing this house back to its original glory. I want people to be able to see it the way it was built. I've spent years thinking about how magnificent it must have been back in the day."

"Be careful, son." Robert frowned.

"I guess you've heard about the other claim on the house."

"I have."

"I can't believe this. All I've ever wanted is to restore Halcyon, and now this woman is going to try to take it away from me."

"She's not trying to take it away from you. Halcyon isn't a toy that someone is trying to steal. You need to realize, what you remember as being magnificent caused other people a whole lot of pain and suffering."

Uncle Robert's reprimand was sharp. Taylor dropped his head, staring down at the weathered floorboards.

"I can't explain it, but I know restoring Halcyon is what I'm supposed to do. It's like a...."

"Like a calling?" Uncle Robert asked.

"It sounds crazy, doesn't it?"

Uncle Robert lifted his cap and ran his hand through his gray hair before setting it back on his head again. "Who am I to question your dreams? If you feel strongly about fixing this place up, then that's what you should do. But—" Uncle Robert held up his hand when Taylor started to speak. "The young lady who filed the claim on the house also has a right to her own aspirations. Who knows, maybe you both have similar ideas of what you want to do with the house once it's restored."

"I haven't thought about it, to be honest. I've only thought about the restoration and nothing more beyond that."

"Maybe you should start."

"Right now, I have to focus on the show. When it's done, Halcyon can be a tourist destination just like a lot of other plantation houses. It will bring tourists to Colton and help the town grow."

Uncle Robert gave Taylor a look that suggested he wasn't very impressed with his idea.

"I guess I'd better call a lawyer," Taylor said, staring into the darkness.

He'd always believed Halcyon was meant to be his. It never even occurred to him that someone else would want it. He didn't have the right words to explain how the house called to him—no one in his family understood it. Halcyon had appeared in his dreams since he was a boy. Hazy, watercolor visions, where he could see the house suspended in time, somewhere between the past and the present.

He took Uncle Robert up on his offer to stay with him instead of at a hotel. When they got to his cabin, he left Taylor on the porch to make his calls. His producer was the first person on his list. She hadn't been enthusiastic about the project to begin with, and the news about another claim on the house wouldn't go over well.

Tessa answered on the first ring. "Did you get everything settled? I'm sure everyone was thrilled when you made your announcement."

"We've hit a bit of a snag."

"What does that mean?"

By the time he finished telling Tessa about what happened at the Buckthorn, he could feel her frustration vibrating through the phone.

"This is totally going to mess up the production schedule." She sighed.

Tessa had never been a big fan of Taylor's pet project, but she knew how important it was to him. Tessa Caldwell wasn't just the producer of his show; they had formed a close friendship over the years. There were always rumors that the two of them were dating, but they never had. Tessa was more like a little sister who acted like a big one. She took on all the mundane details of running the show so that he could do the restoration work he loved.

"I know, but there's nothing we can do."

"I'll call a lawyer, and I'll talk with the PR rep to figure out how to spin this," she said.

"Hold up, Tessa. I don't want to bring the press into this."

"It might be the fastest way to get this woman to drop her claim. We can craft a story about how you've been wanting to restore Halcyon since you were a boy. You know, local boy returns home. And I'll get a PI on her as well. Maybe we can dig up—"

Taylor jumped up and began pacing the length of the porch. "I'm okay with hiring a private investigator, but no press."

"I'm just trying to make sure we do whatever it takes to make this work. Restoring Halcyon could be one of the biggest seasons the show has ever had. The network is very excited about this."

"I know." He'd been pitching this idea since his show debuted. It hadn't been easy to convince the network to agree to feature one house for an entire season, but he'd gradually won them over, and now they were on board with the idea.

It was also his chance to prove his parents wrong. They thought he was wasting his time and money on the crumbling mansion. His parents had never understood his love of architecture. They never said it out loud, but he always felt they were disappointed that he hadn't followed in their footsteps to become a doctor the way his older brother Dylan had.

"Taylor." Tessa's voice softened. "You've talked about this for as long as I've known you. You love that rundown wreck of a house. While I'm not excited as you are about spending months in a small town in Mississippi, I know you'll be devastated if you lose it now."

"Thanks. I know you don't get it, but I appreciate everything you're doing to make this happen for me."

"We'll meet with a lawyer when you get back to LA, and we'll get this figured out," she said.

"Thanks, Tess."

He hung up and paced the porch for a few more minutes before calling out, "Uncle Robert, I'm going for a drive."

He drove back through the town he used to visit and realized it barely existed now. Taylor circled the park that made up the center of the town square. Absolem Madden Colton Park. Named after his seventh great-uncle and the man who'd owned the Colton Plantation and the people enslaved there. The trees were bigger than he remembered, but the gazebo at the center looked exactly the same. It was a fixture of the park, but its most important role was as witness to the many weddings that had taken place there over the years. It was tradition in Colton that a couple who married under the gazebo would have a long and happy life together. He had a hard time picturing himself standing side by side with anyone under its canopy, and certainly none of the women he'd dated over the last few years.

The new sign over the hardware store and the bookstore next to the library were welcome signs of growth. Taylor was happy to see the yellow and red art deco façade of Catfish Café on the corner. He wondered if Tillie was still serving up the pecan pie and hot water corn bread he remembered from his childhood. When he finished his drive through town, he headed back in the direction of Uncle Robert's cabin. He couldn't resist the pull of Halcyon, turning down the dirt driveway where the house waited for him at the end.

He made a circuit of the exterior, making mental notes of the repairs that needed to be made. He patted one of the columns as he walked by. It still felt sturdy and strong under his hand. Unfortunately, that couldn't be said for the rest of the house. He sat down on the front steps, replaying the scene at the Buckthorn in his head.

Headlights blinded him for a second. This time it wasn't Uncle Robert but Josephine Martin pulling up to the house. She got out of the small dark blue SUV, hesitating for just a moment before heading toward him.

"I guess I shouldn't be surprised to find you here," she said as she approached.

He stood up and dusted his hands off. "I suppose I could say the same thing about you."

An awkward silence stretched between them as they faced each other.

"I'm not giving up my claim on this house," she said.

"Neither am I."

Her dark eyes flashed with determination, and that same spark of desire he'd felt the first time he saw her flared to life again. His attraction was an inconvenience he didn't need or want.

"Then I guess I'll see you in court."

He nodded. "I suppose so."

She turned on her heel and walked away with her head held high. He watched her car until the taillights turned out of the driveway and disappeared. He drew in a deep breath, letting the night air cool his frustration.

Taylor started making his way to his car and then stopped, turning back to the house. "I'm never going to let you go."

He didn't hear the way the wind rustling through the trees sounded like a woman weeping as he drove away.

TAYLOR CUT his trip short after learning about Josephine's claim on Halcyon. Back in LA, he threw himself into preparing for filming his show in Colton. He wasn't going to let anyone stop him from making this season of the show a success. Each day that passed with his lawyer unsuccessful in getting Josephine Martin to give up her claim sent his frustration up a notch, until Tessa kicked him out of the production office for the day.

He'd just pulled into his driveway when his phone vibrated in his pocket.

"Taylor, I've got good news," his lawyer announced. "Ms. Martin has agreed to arbitration."

"Good, hopefully we can get this resolved quickly. Going to court could take too much time."

"You'll be meeting with Judge Beaumont in two weeks." Taylor hung up and called Tessa. He headed into his house, grabbing a beer as he made his way out to the back deck.

"I still think you should do some interviews—" she started when he told her the news.

He cut her off before she could start filling his schedule with a bunch of appearances on morning TV shows. "Tessa, we've talked about this. I don't want to do anything that might jeopardize this case, and I don't want a bunch of press hanging around Colton. We have to think of the people who live there. I don't think they would appreciate reporters or paparazzi in their town."

"Fine." Tessa sighed. "Hopefully we'll get the report from the private investigator soon."

"I doubt there's going to be anything in the report that we can use against her."

"That's exactly what you said about Alyssa."

Taylor winced. "That was different."

"How? I'm sorry, Taylor, but she only wanted your money and your fame. If I hadn't hired a private investigator, then you would be in the middle of a very messy divorce right now."

Taylor downed the rest of his beer and walked to the edge of his pool. It was designed to give the false impression that there was no edge at all. It was fake, just like his ex-girlfriend had been. He'd fallen head over heels for her when they met at a party two years ago. She described herself as an aspiring blogger and writer. That part was true; the part where she told him she loved and supported him wasn't. Tessa had always been suspicious, and when she told Taylor she'd hired someone to look into his girlfriend, he'd been furious. But Tessa's instincts had been right. Alyssa was selling stories about him to the tabloids, as well as planning on selling some highly suggestive pictures of the two of them to the highest bidder. He'd been planning to propose when Tessa brought him the news. It turned out she had better instincts than he did.

"You're right; it's better to be safe than sorry."

"I'll never forgive that bitch for breaking your heart."

"I wouldn't say it was broken, just badly bruised. She was never the right person for me—I know that now."

"I'm sorry it had to happen, but I'm glad I was able to expose her for what she really was before it was too late."

"I'll always be thankful to you for that, Tess."

"That's what friends and producers are for."

Taylor finished his phone call and admired the vista of the LA skyline. As much as he'd grown to love the view, he couldn't wait to exchange it for looking out at the giant oak tree from the veranda at Halcyon. In two weeks he'd have Halcyon, and Josephine Martin would be out of his life.

CHAPTER THREE

WIND RUSTLED through the treetops in the park outside the windows of the conference room in Colton Town Hall. Taylor regretted his decision to skip breakfast when his stomach growled for the second time. He turned his attention back to where Josephine Martin sat across from him with her hands folded in front of her, waiting for Judge Beaumont to make an appearance. The black, fitted short-sleeve turtleneck emphasized her long neck and toned arms. Her dark amber-colored eyes watched him warily from across the table.

She leaned over to whisper something to her lawyer while watching Taylor out of the corner of her eye. Judge Beaumont walked in and took a seat at the head of the table, spreading out a small stack of paperwork in front of him. He shuffled through the papers, extending Taylor's anticipation almost to his breaking point. He'd been restless and distracted in the weeks leading up to this moment. For the first time since they agreed to arbitration, his confidence that the judge would rule in his favor faltered. He clenched his hands together under the table to keep himself from reaching up and pressing his hand against his racing heart.

"This is an unusual case," the judge began, peering at a sheaf of papers over the top of his horn-rimmed reading glasses. "Miss Martin, the letter you have provided as evidence of your claim is compelling."

The judge turned to Taylor's side of the table. "Mr. Colton, you have also provided substantial proof of your claim. As the assumption was made that the colonel died childless, and in the absence of a will, the house passed on to his brother, your seventh great-grandfather." Judge Beaumont set the papers down and steepled his hands. "There are some who would say this is a case where reparations are due for the inhuman treatment Miss Martin's ancestors endured."

Taylor bowed his head, blood rushing in his ears. Was he going to lose Halcyon because of the sins of his ancestors? He'd tried to ignore that inconvenient part of his family legacy, but it was sitting across the table from him, staring him in the face. When he saw copies of the letters Josephine had presented as evidence of her claim, he felt physically ill.

He wasn't blind to his family history, but it had all been abstract until that moment. It was the first time he'd ever felt shame about his family heritage.

"However, I can only judge this case based on the law, not social justice. A house of this age and size requires a significant investment of both time and money." The judge sat forward. "This is a project of great magnitude, and although Mr. Colton has the experience, I am not convinced that either of you know what you are taking on." Judge Beaumont clasped his hands. "I've thought long and hard about this. You both have provided enough evidence to support your claim. Therefore, I am going to make the following ruling. I am awarding each of you half of the estate." The judge held up his hand when the lawyers on both sides objected. "You agreed to abide by my decision when you decided to go into arbitration, and this is my final ruling."

Taylor sat in shock. There was no way he was going to share Halcyon with anyone. His lawyer was saying something to him but he didn't hear any of it, trying to process what the judge had just said. His gaze zeroed in on the woman sitting across the table.

"How much?" he asked.

"How much for what?"

She knew exactly what he wanted to know but decided to play innocent, which quickly turned his shock into anger.

"How much do you want for your half of Halcyon?" he said, enunciating each word.

"I'm sorry, Mr. Colton, but my half of Halcyon is not for sale. How much would you take for yours?"

"I'll never sell. Halcyon had been in my family since it was built and it's going to stay that way."

Josephine leaned forward. "Since my ancestors probably built most of Halcyon, I guess I can also say Halcyon has been in my family since it was built."

Judge Beaumont cleared his throat. "Clearly the two of you have some things to work out. Now, if you'll excuse me, I have a meeting I need to get to."

Taylor pushed back from the table and stormed out. He burst through the front door of Town Hall. "Fuck," he shouted.

A woman walking through the park with her little girl jerked her head in his direction with an angry glare.

His lawyer came out followed by Josephine and her legal counsel. "Taylor, Ms. Martin has informed me that she plans to take up residence in Halcyon. We all know that the house needs extensive renovations, and I've explained to Ms. Martin that you planned to film your restoration efforts for your show. Perhaps the two of you can come to an agreement."

Josephine's lawyer looked at her watch. "I'm sorry, I'm afraid I have a plane to catch."

"I have to leave as well," Taylor's lawyer said.

"Thank you, Linda, I appreciate all of your help." Josephine shook her hand.

"Thanks, Sean, I'll be in touch," Taylor said.

"I can't blame them. I'm sure they wanted to get away from this mess as quick as they could," Josephine said, watching as they walked away.

Taylor glanced over at the woman standing next to him. Determination flashed in her gaze.

"You can't move into Halcyon. It's not habitable in the condition it's in right now."

Josephine crossed her arms. "I know that. I've already reached out to get some bids from several contractors in case the judge ruled in my favor."

Taylor shook his head. "Absolutely not—I'm the only contractor who will be working on that house and I'll be filming everything for my show." He grimaced when he heard a loud rumble. "Look, I haven't eaten yet and I'd rather not have this conversation on an empty stomach." He jerked his thumb toward the Catfish Café. "Can I buy you a coffee and a piece of pie and we can talk more?"

"If that will make you less grumpy, sure."

"I'm not—" He snapped his mouth shut when Josephine raised an eyebrow.

He was off his game. There had never been a situation that Taylor couldn't charm his way out of until today. It was just the stress, he told himself. It was just a matter of time before he would win Josephine over and convince her to sell him her half of the house.

They walked down the block and crossed the street to the café. The owner, Tillie Reynolds, greeted them wearing the same gingham shirt and jeans Taylor remembered from his childhood. He was just about to introduce Josephine when Tillie smiled and said, "Go ahead and grab a booth, Jo. I'll be right out with your tea."

They slid into a booth. Josephine sat across from him with her hands folded on the table.

Tillie came over and placed a cup of tea in front of Jo. "I figured chamomile would be good after your meeting with the judge."

Taylor looked at Josephine in surprise at the easy camaraderie she had with the owner of the café.

"Thank you, Tillie, this is perfect."

"Do you want anything to go with that?"

"No, thank you," Josephine said.

Tillie turned to Taylor. "And what would you like, hon?"

"It's good to see you again, Tillie. I'd love a coffee and a piece of pecan pie. Actually, can you make that two slices since you wouldn't send me one?" he said with a smile.

Tillie chuckled. "If you're missing my cooking so bad that you call me and try to get me to ship you a pie overnight, that just means it's time for you to come home for a visit. Welcome back, Mr. Hollywood big-shot," she said, giving him a pat on the shoulder before she walked away.

She returned and set down his coffee and an extra-large slice of pie with a wink before returning to her other customers.

"Ms. Martin—"

"You might as well call me Jo," she interrupted.

"Jo, Halcyon is… well it's a special house and the restoration is a huge project."

She took a sip of her tea, eyeing him over the rim before setting the cup down. "You're not wasting any time trying to get me to give up my half of the house, are you?"

"What in the world do you think you are going to do with half of a plantation house?"

"What are you going to do with it?" she shot back.

"I'm going to restore it back to its original state."

"And then what? What are you going to do with it after that?"

Taylor hesitated. He wasn't about to admit to Josephine or anyone else that he hadn't figured that out yet.

Jo squared her shoulders. "I thought so."

"You still haven't said what you're going to do with it."

"Live in it."

"And exactly what are you going to do to pay for its upkeep? Whatever job you have in Chicago, I guarantee you're probably not going to be able to make the same salary down here."

Jo took another sip of her tea, smiling at him over the rim of the cup. "I'm sorry, but you're not going to be able to use finances to get me to sell my share of the house. I hate to disappoint you, but my dad is an investment banker. He helped me buy my first stock when I turned eighteen. I work as a systems architect. Do you know how much systems architects make? I can work as an independent contractor from anywhere in the world, but Dax Ellis offered me a job at Ellis Technologies. I moved to Colton just over a week ago and I started my new job last week. I may not make the millions that you do, but I have enough to do what needs to be done."

Taylor felt his eyebrow twitch. Jo had planned ahead. She was thoughtful, deliberate, and had already won over Tillie.

"It's not just about money. I'm the one who has the knowledge and experience to do the work that Halcyon needs. I'm sure you've seen my show, so you know I have the resources needed to make sure everything is historically accurate."

Jo shook her head. "Mr. Colton, you've made a lot of assumptions about me. The biggest ones are that I've seen your show and I'm a fan. But—" She held up her hand when he started to interrupt. "—I would be happy to work with you on the restoration."

"Have you really never seen my show?"

"No, I've never seen your show."

He shoved a piece of pie in his mouth, but the buttery concoction offered him no comfort. Taylor didn't think of himself as having a fragile ego, but he found himself oddly disappointed that the woman sitting across from him, whose dark eyes flashed with derision, wasn't familiar with his work. Most women wanted him to like them. Okay, so maybe his ego had gotten a bit overgrown from all the attention over the last few years, he admitted to himself, watching Jo frown at him from the other side of the table. He was good at winning people over; he just needed to act more agreeable and she'd see reason.

"You're right, I apologize. I shouldn't make assumptions. The thing is, I was hoping to film the next season of my show at Halcyon. If you were willing to allow that to happen, I can guarantee that contributions from our sponsors will help offset some of the expenses."

Jo tilted her head. "I'm not interested in being on camera."

"You wouldn't have to be." Taylor tried to keep the eagerness out of his voice. She hadn't refused outright. He took it as a good sign. "There's a lot to be done before either of us can move in, and I am the best person to make sure it gets done properly."

"How will you do that from LA?"

His eye twitched again.

"Everything all right here?" Tillie appeared at their table, coffee pot in hand.

"Everything is fine." Taylor glared at Jo.

"Well, y'all are puttin' on quite a show."

Taylor looked around and realized just about everyone in the café was leaning toward their table, watching the two of them.

"Thank you, Tillie." Jo reached into her bag and pulled out her wallet. "Mr. Colton, perhaps we should continue this discussion outside."

"I'll pay," Taylor offered.

"Yes, you will, for your share," Jo said, handing Tillie a five-dollar bill.

"You know this is too much for a cup of tea."

Jo patted Tillie's arm. "Put it on my tab for breakfast tomorrow."

Taylor put his money on the table and gave Tillie a quick peck on the cheek. "It's good to be home," he said, following Jo out the door.

As soon as they set foot onto the sidewalk, Jo turned toward the Barton Building. The tallest building in town, the three-story former cotton trading office featured large arched windows on its brick façade. Instead of being papered over like they'd been the last time he was home, the windows sparkled in the afternoon sunlight, reflecting the deep green and gold of the leaves in the trees across the street. Taylor admired the restoration work that had been done on the outside. It was good to see signs of progress no matter how few and far between.

"After you left, Judge Beaumont let me know that we can pick up the keys from Grace in the mayor's office. We might as well do a walk-through and see what needs to be done," Jo said.

Jo paused in front of the Barton Building. "I'm just going to run in and change. Do you want to meet me at Halcyon?"

Dax Ellis waved to the two of them from the front window and then got up and poked his head out the door. "Hey, Taylor." He looked between the two of them. "I heard what happened with Judge Beaumont today."

Taylor sighed. News traveled faster than lightning around here.

"If you give me a minute, I'll be right back."

"You seem to be handling this well," Dax said after Jo left.

"I'm still in shock." Taylor ran his hand through his hair. "I assumed I'd be able to come back, start working on Halcyon, and film the show. Now I've got to convince Jo that she has no business trying to take on restoring a mansion and convince her she should sell me her half."

"Just because she doesn't have your experience doesn't mean she's not capable."

"That's not the problem," he said.

"Okay, so what is your problem?"

"Halcyon was always supposed to be mine."

Dax narrowed his eyes. "So the problem is you don't want to share."

"You make me sound like I'm being childish. I know that house inside and out. She has no idea what it's going to take to restore it."

"How do you know? You're making an awful lot of assumptions, don't you think?"

He rolled his shoulders, trying to shake off the tension that was growing every minute. It felt like a coordinated attack, with Dax repeating almost the exact same thing Jo had said.

"Nothing is going how I planned. I think I have the right to be a little frustrated right now," he said.

Jo came down the stairs before Dax could answer. She had changed into jeans cuffed above a pair of work boots and a long-sleeved T-shirt in a shade of yellow that matched the leaves outside. Taylor watched her ponytail sway across her back, admiring the view as she bounced down the stairs toward them.

He realized he'd been staring when Dax cleared his throat. Finding Jo attractive was just one more thing that wasn't planned and a distraction he couldn't afford. He'd waited a long time to prove his parents and his brother wrong about Halcyon. His dad was a highly regarded surgeon and his mom a genetic scientist, and they didn't believe being a TV host was a career that had any value. They often voiced their opinion that if Taylor worked for a prestigious architecture firm, they would be happier with his career choice. Restoring the home that had been passed down for generations from top to bottom would be the biggest project he'd ever taken on, and if he did it right, his family would finally understand that what he did mattered.

Jo shoved her hands in her back pockets. "You ready to go?"

Taylor realized he wasn't ready. He wasn't as prepared as he thought he was for the months of work ahead. Most of all, he wasn't ready for a woman like Jo. But years on TV had taught him a few tricks, including how to look like he was happy when he wasn't.

"Sure," he said with a smile.

CHAPTER FOUR

AFTER A quick stop back at Town Hall to pick up the keys from the mayor's office. Jo followed Taylor to Halcyon.

She took a shaky breath as they pulled into the long driveway. The judge's decision rattled her as much as it had Taylor. But she would rather take half of Halcyon than lose it altogether. She shouldn't have enjoyed ruffling Taylor's feathers as much as she did, but when he walked into the conference room so smug and self-assured, she couldn't help herself. It felt good to see the confident look fall from his face when the judge gave his ruling. She had lied at the café—she had seen his show. She might not be a big fan, but just like the other women who were avid watchers of *History Reborn,* she wasn't immune to Taylor's sparkling blue eyes and winning smile. She gripped the steering wheel tighter. She wasn't going to make the same mistake twice. The next man she trusted would have to bring much more than a handsome face and pretty words to the table. Maybe she didn't know exactly what she was doing with a rundown plantation house, but she knew what she was doing with her heart.

She pulled in behind Taylor and got out of the car. He was pulling off his jacket and tie, unbuttoning his shirt, and rolling up his sleeves. When he caught her staring, his lips quirked. She jerked her gaze away from Taylor's muscled forearms and started toward the house.

"Careful on the veranda—some of these floorboards are rotten straight through," Taylor warned.

"I know," Jo said.

Taylor did a double-take and then sighed. "I guess you've been here quite a few times."

"I have."

She'd been coming out to the house every day since she took the plunge and moved to Colton. After her first visit, where she met Mae and her parents, Jo returned to Chicago and couldn't stop thinking about the little town and the grand house that represented her past and her future. Her brother and sister looked at her like she had sprouted two heads when she made the announcement at their family dinner that she was moving. Her parents were concerned but supportive. Her mom connected her with Linda—one of her sorority sisters from college who specialized in estate law. She'd spent hours poring over finances with her dad and working on a budget. She might not be able to do the work as quickly as Taylor could with his connections and money, but she could get the job done with the savings she had.

He put the key in the lock and turned to her. "Are you ready?"

Her whole body tingled down to her fingertips. Something told her once she set foot across the threshold, her life would be forever changed.

She inhaled a steadying breath and nodded.

The large front door creaked slightly when Taylor pushed it open. Jo followed him in, peering through the dust motes and the light streaming through the window into the dimly lit entryway. A large staircase ran along one side of the hallway, and there were two large arched openings on either side.

"The dining room and kitchen are on this side," Taylor said, pointing to the left next to the staircase.

Jo nodded. "I have a pretty good idea of the downstairs layout from looking through the windows."

"Where would you like to start?"

"How about upstairs, and we can work our way down?"

Jo followed Taylor, careful to step over some of the more dubious-looking stair treads. When they reached the second floor, Taylor gestured toward the end of the hallway.

"There's another staircase that leads to the attic."

"Wow," she said when she walked up the stairs into the massive space that ran the length of the house. A large oval window at one end of the room created more shadows than light. Mountains of furniture covered with sheets were scattered around the room.

"Careful." Taylor grabbed her arm when she took a step deeper into the room. "The floorboards are even worse up here."

Jo looked down at where his hand held her arm. His grasp was firm, and warmth spread from his hand up her arm. She hesitated, giving herself just a second to take in how safe his touch made her feel, before pulling away.

His eyes locked with hers for a heartbeat before he pulled out his phone and turned on the flashlight, sending a beam of light around the room. Taylor's flashlight bounced off several trunks in one of the corners.

They went back downstairs and toured the rooms on the second floor. There were six bedrooms. Each one had a large dressing room. A closet had been turned into the only bathroom on the floor.

"Six bedrooms and only one bathroom—that's not going to work," she said.

"I planned on turning the dressing rooms into bathrooms so each bedroom would have its own attached."

"Trading one bathroom for six? It makes sense, but it's a big undertaking."

"All of the plumbing for the house will have to be replaced anyway."

Jo sighed. "True." The plumbing was just the beginning. Every time she visited the house, she added another item to the growing list of repairs that were needed.

"I'm glad you can see just how big this project is. That's why—"

Jo put her hand up. "Stop, don't try to tell me how you're the better person to have this house."

She turned on her heel and started walking out, ignoring the creaks and groans from the staircase as she made her way back downstairs.

"Jo, wait," Taylor called out.

He started to follow her down the stairs, muttering a curse when his foot went through one of the rotting treads.

She stopped. "Are you okay?"

"I'm fine," he said, poking his finger through a tear in his pants.

"What do I have to do to make you understand I'm not selling my half of Halcyon? Like it or not, we're partners."

Taylor opened his mouth and then snapped it shut again. "Okay, you're right."

They walked through what was once a large, grand dining room and then a butler's pantry on their way to the kitchen.

Taylor rested his hands on his hips and sighed. "This is in worse condition than I expected."

"It didn't seem like it would be usable when I looked through the window. I'm going to have to figure out some kind of temporary kitchen if I'm going to be living here."

"I think you meant to say if we are going to be living here."

Taylor smirked when Jo's jaw dropped.

"I... I thought you would just be working on the show."

Taylor shook his head, his smirk turning into a big smile. "I planned on living in the house during the restoration and filming."

Why hadn't it occurred to her that Taylor might want to live in the house? Her confidence from before evaporated. Living in a rundown mansion by herself was intimidating enough. Living in it with Taylor Colton?

"No, absolutely not," she blurted out.

Taylor folded his arms. "Fifty-fifty, remember?"

"I haven't had a roommate since college."

"I promise I'll leave a sock on the doorknob."

Jo rolled her eyes. "This is serious—we have a lot to figure out. We don't even have a kitchen."

"We can use the butler's pantry as a temporary kitchen."

Jo followed Taylor back into the long narrow space that was bigger than many kitchens in an average Chicago apartment. Floor-to-ceiling cabinets lined one side, and there was a long counter with an opening to the kitchen on the other. A big porcelain sink covered in rust stains sat under a window at the end.

She looked at the stained sink and the dips and grooves on the counter. "I suppose if we got rid of the sink and replaced the countertops, we could make it work."

Taylor's eyes grew wide. "This is Georgia blue granite." He ran his hand over the thick piece of blue-gray stone. "That sink is Victorian. I can restore them; this is what I do."

Dammit, he was right. "I wasn't thinking. Just because something is old doesn't mean it can't be restored."

He nodded, and they continued their tour to look at the other bedrooms and the bathroom at the back of the house.

"The housekeeper's room is the biggest one back here. I thought you might like to have that one," Taylor offered.

Jo looked into the bedroom, with peeling paint on the ceiling and stained wallpaper. It was bigger than her room back in Chicago, and that was the only good thing she could say about it.

"Okay, thanks."

They both stopped in their tracks in the doorway of the bathroom.

"We can't move in without a working bathroom," Jo said, looking around in dismay.

"The floors are in good condition," Taylor said, crouching down to run his hand over the black-and-white hexagon penny tile. "The toilet and sink will need to be replaced."

"What about the tub?" she asked.

"Are you kidding me? A claw-foot tub big enough to fit two." A slow smile spread over his face. "We are definitely keeping this."

The way he was looking at her had her picturing the enormous claw-foot tub cleaned and filled with a hot bubble bath. The next second she pictured Taylor joining her, making her stomach flutter with butterflies.

"A fresh coat of paint and we can make this work."

Taylor was talking to himself more than Jo, his eyes wandering around the room, analyzing each detail. He stood with his hands on his hips, his tan muscled forearms exposed. He was handsome. She wasn't going to pretend he wasn't, but she was here for a fresh start, not to ogle her new roommate.

"It's going to take at least a couple of weeks to get this work done, isn't it?" she asked.

"I have a team of tradesmen who are experienced with this kind of work. I'll make arrangements to get them here as soon as possible."

"Wouldn't it make more sense to use local trades? I want to support the community any way I can, and that means using people from around here to do the work. Mae Colton already gave me the name of a plumber and an electrician. It will be easier for me to oversee the work that needs to be done until you get back from LA."

She could see that her statement hit home when Taylor's smile fell.

"I'm flying back to LA tonight, and I'll be back in a couple of days."

"While you're gone, I'll call the plumber and electrician," Jo said.

Taylor's jaw ticked when he gave her a curt nod.

"Now, I'd like to take a look at the rest of the house, if you don't mind." She was determined to show Taylor that she wasn't afraid or intimidated by the work that needed to be done. It was all an act. Her mind reeled at the scope of the project before them.

Each spot on their tour greeted them with an eerie silence, only broken by the creaking of the floorboards under their feet as they toured the rooms on the other side of the house.

"This is the main parlor," he said, leading her into the first room, "and then the library."

"What a shame all of the books are gone," Jo said looking at the empty shelves that lined the room.

He led her through a room he described as the office and into the last room, a small one with a large set of french doors that led out to an overgrown garden.

"I've never understood why this parlor was here. It's unusual for houses of this kind, and I don't understand why the doors leading to the garden are in this room. They should be in the large parlor."

The minute Jo set foot in the room, she knew it was special, different from any other place in the house. She could feel Ada Mae in the room. The way the sunlight streamed through the french doors felt magical. It was the first room she'd walked into that had life in it. Even with the years of neglect, it felt lived in. She turned in a slow circle, letting the history of the house wash over her. There was sadness that hurt her heart, but she could also sense the hope in this place. She closed her eyes, trying to picture the room the way it once was.

"Jo, are you okay?" Taylor asked. His voice was laced with concern.

She didn't realize Taylor had stayed back while she stood frozen, trying to imagine the past.

She shook herself and gave him a small smile. "I'm fine, I just got a little distracted. It's a lot to take in—that's all."

"It is." He nodded and glanced at his watch. "I have to get going or I'm going to miss my flight."

"I'll have a copy of the key made." She held out her hand.

Taylor hesitated for just a second before giving her the key.

"We should exchange numbers. I'll be back in just a few days, but there will be things we need to discuss before then."

Once they had entered each other's information into their phones, Jo wasn't sure what to say or do next.

After an awkward minute, she thrust her hand out. "Goodbye, Mr. Colton."

His handshake was warm and firm. She'd convinced herself she wasn't going to feel attracted to any man for a very long time. The jolt of electricity she felt when his hand enveloped hers took her by surprise.

As Jo started to pull her hand away, he tightened his hold momentarily. "Do you think by the time I get back you might be willing to call me Taylor?"

She pulled her hand out of his grasp. "I'll see you when you get back."

She watched Taylor back away. He stopped to look at her before he got into his car and drove away. When his taillights disappeared, she took a deep breath and let her shoulders drop.

She turned back to look at the house one more time. There were windows missing that had been boarded up. The paint was peeling, and some of the siding was missing altogether. She shivered, wrapping her arms around herself. She could admit now that she was scared. There was no going back. She had already started to make a future for herself in Colton. She just hadn't pictured Taylor as a part of that future. He was attractive and charming, but he took himself way too seriously. The whole TV celebrity thing wasn't going to work with her. It wasn't something she was attracted to. The way his lips curled into a smile and his eyes darkened into a deep blue when he was frustrated were a different matter.

Before Oliver, maybe she wouldn't have dismissed her attraction, but now…. She straightened her shoulders. Taylor Colton was half owner of the house and nothing more. It didn't matter that her heart beat a little faster when he smiled at her.

"How in the hell am I going to live in the same house with him?" she muttered to herself as she drove away.

CHAPTER FIVE

"So ARE you ready for tomorrow?" Mae asked.

They were hanging out at Mae's apartment, sharing a bottle of wine. It was Sunday night, and Jo would be meeting Taylor at Halcyon in the morning for their first day of work.

"I guess so. I'm not really sure what to expect beyond meeting with the electrician and the plumber." Jo shrugged.

Mae had connected Jo to Sam Riley, the town's electrician who recently retired. It turned out that retirement didn't suit Sam, and he was eager to help. He'd reached out to a plumber friend, and they would be meeting Taylor and Jo at the house in the morning to start work.

Mae grinned. "I love how you put Taylor in his place by insisting on hiring local trades."

"I wouldn't exactly call it that, but it was kind of fun to wipe the confident smirk off his face."

"It's a pretty nice face." Mae waggled her eyebrows. Jo hid her smile, taking another sip of her wine.

"It's going to be kind of weird living there with him isn't it?"

"I hadn't really considered that was something that could happen when the judge made his decision."

"You know that Callie and I will come over and help whenever you need it."

Jo blinked back the tears from her eyes. Mae and Callie had been so kind and generous when she made the move to Colton. Not one of the people she considered a friend had reached out to her since Oliver broke up with her. The friendships she had formed since she moved only magnified how hollow her relationships were back in Chicago.

"Have you heard from Taylor since he left?" Mae asked.

"We've exchanged a few texts. I told him I hired Sam and a plumber, and he let me know he'll be staying with Robert Ellis until we move into the house."

"You might as well call him Uncle Robert—everyone else around here does."

Jo was quickly learning the ins and outs of small-town life. Mainly that just about everybody in Colton was related in some way, and news in town could travel faster than high-speed internet. Everywhere she went, people introduced themselves and had an opinion about Judge Beaumont's decision. She had to bite her tongue when one of the ministers cornered her at Walker's Pharmacy, lecturing her on the sin of cohabitation before marriage when she happened to be standing in front of the condom display. Mae laughed so hard she had tears streaming down her face when Jo told her about it. Mae's amusement also came with a stern warning that Jo should never buy birth control at Walker's or the whole town would know about it before she left the store.

"How are you really feeling about all of this?" Mae asked, her voice tinged with concern.

Jo sighed. She had shared some of what happened back in Chicago, but not all of it. She liked Mae. They had exchanged texts and emails since her first visit to Colton, and since she'd moved in next door a week ago, they'd been hanging out every night.

"Honestly, I go between feeling confident and wondering what in the world I was thinking. I still can't believe I own half of Halcyon and I have Taylor Colton as a roommate."

"He's got a lot of fans who would kill to be in your shoes. Did you see him in *People* magazine's most beautiful people issue last year?" Mae fanned herself.

Of course she had. Just like every other woman in America, she'd ogled the picture of Taylor leaning against a doorframe wearing a tool belt that sat low on his hips. Sunlight highlighted his golden-blond hair. He wore a blue plaid shirt the same shade as his eyes, open at the front revealing a bare chest. Even now the memory of seeing the picture for the first time sent her pulse racing. She reminded herself that looking at a picture was one thing, dealing with Taylor in the flesh was another. That wicked grin would get her into trouble if she wasn't careful.

Jo refilled her glass. "I'm not interested in a good-looking guy with nothing but a sexy smile to offer. I want a man who won't use his charm to get what he wants. I had enough of that with my ex."

"You don't think Taylor has anything else to offer?" Mae gave her a skeptical look.

"He's good at what he does—I'll admit that."

Taylor Colton was really good. Jo didn't share with Mae that she had gone back and re-watched every episode of Taylor's show. It was easy to see why *History Reborn* was a hit. The confidence that annoyed her was put to good use on the show, putting the homeowners he worked with at ease. He patiently explained each step of the work he would do in a way that reassured his clients. He was exactly the kind of contractor she wanted to hire to work on Halcyon. And the kind of man she would be attracted to if her heart wasn't still battered and bruised.

"He seems... genuine, I guess," she admitted.

"We haven't known each other long and I barely remember Taylor from when I was a kid, but neither one of you seem like the kind of person who is going to back down. This is going to be an interesting partnership."

Jo took another sip of wine. "You can say that again."

"It won't to be easy, Jo, but I hope you know I'm here for you if you need me."

"Thanks," she said with a smile.

Moving to Colton had been the best medicine for her broken heart. Her new job and friendships gave her a sense of fulfillment that she didn't realize she had been missing. She reached for the bottle of wine and refilled Mae's glass. "Enough about me, let's talk about why you're always arguing with Jacob Winters."

Mae groaned and got up to retrieve another bottle of wine. "It's a long story."

JO WOKE up the next morning with a headache. She couldn't decide if it was from the wine from the night before or from being anxious about seeing Taylor again. She threw on a pair of jeans with a gray T-shirt and plaited two braids into her hair. She finished her outfit with a pair of work boots she'd decided to invest in and stared at herself in the full-length mirror on the back of the bathroom door. She'd gained some weight back since she moved to Colton. She had Tillie's cooking to thank for that. Her cheeks had a faint pink glow from the daily walks she'd been taking, and the dark circles under her eyes were gone. Her headache faded, and Jo smiled at her reflection. A shiver of excitement ran through her. Today she would start making Halcyon her home.

Jo was laughing so hard her sides hurt while Sam told her a story about Taylor sneaking behind the counter trying to steal a whole pie from Tillie when he was a boy. Her laughter died on her lips when Taylor pulled up. He parked and jumped out, looking just like he did on his show in a pair of jeans with a flannel shirt over a T-shirt and a smile that was much more enticing in person than it was on camera.

He walked toward them, rubbing his hands together. "Good morning. You look like you're ready to get started."

Jo nodded. "Taylor, this is Sam Riley." She gestured to the older Black man.

Taylor glanced at the Riley Electric logo on the pickup truck next to them. "You must be the electrician. Thanks so much for helping us out." Taylor shook his hand.

"I did some work here many years ago. I'm looking forward to seeing what you've got planned. This is my buddy, Minh Nguyen," he said, slapping the shoulder of the slim Vietnamese man standing next to him. "You won't find a better plumber around these parts."

"Good to meet you," Taylor said.

"Same to you." Minh nodded.

"Now that you're here, I guess we should head in," Jo said, pulling the key out of her pocket.

They went inside and gave Sam and Minh a quick tour of the bathroom and kitchen.

"If the two of you can work on the demo, Minh and I will get the supplies we need and we can get started this afternoon."

Jo glanced at Taylor. "Sounds good to me if that's okay with you?"

"I've got a sledgehammer and a crowbar in my car. Do you have a pair of gloves and some safety goggles?"

Jo shook her head. "No, I didn't think about that."

"I brought extra just in case," Taylor said.

Taylor went out to his car and came back with a tool bag in one hand and a crowbar in the other.

"Can I help with anything?" she offered.

"Nope, this is everything. Anything we forget, we can get on our next trip to the hardware store."

"I guess we'll be making a few of those in the next few days."

"Try the next few years." Taylor laughed.

She followed Taylor into the kitchen. He set down the box and pulled out a pair of gloves and safety glasses.

Taylor put on his own gloves and glasses. "You ready?"

She bounced on her toes, unable to contain her excitement. "Let's go."

Together they ripped out the toilet and sink from the bathroom and started tearing out the cabinets in the kitchen. They worked well together and accomplished a lot in a short amount of time. Sam and Minh returned, and while Sam and Taylor worked on the electrical panel, Minh started tearing out the old pipes in the bathroom. Jo offered to start working on the butler's pantry. When Taylor poked his head in to see if Jo was ready for lunch, he drew up short.

"Wow, I can't believe how much better it looks in here already."

Jo had cleaned all of the cabinets; the woodwork glowed and the glass in the cabinets sparkled. Her arms were already starting to ache from all the scrubbing she had done. Who needed a fancy gym membership when all you had to do was find a rundown mansion to restore?

She smiled at him. "I have to admit I was skeptical, but your recipe for a natural wood cleaner is brilliant. Do you really think we can get the rust stains off the sink with vinegar?"

"We'll try it later and you'll see for yourself."

Jo glanced at her watch. "I can't believe how fast the day is going by."

"I came to see if you were ready for some lunch."

"Sounds good."

Jo followed Taylor out to the veranda, where Sam and Minh were waiting with sandwiches and sodas. The two older men were laughing and joking about their latest fishing trip.

"What's noodling?" Jo asked.

Minh grinned. "Noodling is where you catch catfish with your bare hands."

Taylor laughed at the horrified face she made while Minh continued to describe finding a hole underwater and allowing a catfish to grab his hand in order to catch it.

When Sam and Minh offered to take her, she shook her head. "Thanks, but I think I am going to keep my hands out of fish mouths for now."

Sam chuckled. "You don't know what you're missing."

Minh nodded in agreement. "When my family came here from Vietnam, catching catfish was one the few things that was familiar. Some of my cousins run a catfish farm down by Mobile."

"I'd love to see that sometime," Jo said.

"Sounds like a good excuse for a road trip," Taylor added. "We could stop and tour some other plantations on the way. I'd like to see how they handle tourists," he added.

"Maybe," she hedged.

Sam and Minh exchanged a look and then excused themselves.

"Did I say something wrong?" Taylor asked.

Jo hesitated for a minute, clasping and then unclasping her hands in her lap. "I don't want Halcyon to be turned into a pretty backdrop for weddings and parties where no one has to acknowledge the history that happened here."

"Tourism is a good way to generate revenue for the upkeep on a house like this. These houses aren't cheap to maintain, and if Halcyon could be rented out to defray some of those costs, well…" He shrugged. "…is that such a bad thing?"

Jo nodded and got up, dusting her hands on her jeans. "I'm ready to get back to work."

She was quiet around Taylor for the rest of the afternoon. His reaction to her statement about not wanting Halcyon to be used for parties troubled her. His response made it clear that's exactly what he planned, and it left a bitter taste in her mouth.

Taylor was already loading his tool bag into his car when she came outside. "I'll see you tomorrow," he said.

Jo gripped the top of her car door. "I'll see you tomorrow."

"I'm not some redneck racist, you know," he blurted out when Jo started to get in her car.

Jo got back out of the car and leaned against it. "I know that, Taylor. But I also know that we are here with different histories and perspectives. I don't know how I feel about touring other plantations. Yes, it would be good to see other restoration projects, but I'm also uncomfortable."

He took a step toward her. "Do you feel uncomfortable being here?"

Jo looked toward the house. "Sometimes, but it's different here."

Taylor followed her gaze. "This house is special. No one in my family understands why I've always loved this place, and I've never really been able to explain it to them."

"Some things aren't easy to explain," she said, thinking about her dreams of Ada Mae.

"This morning was fun and then after lunch...." He sighed. "Do you think we can start over tomorrow?"

"Yeah, we can do that."

"See you tomorrow, Jo."

"See you tomorrow."

Jo watched Taylor in the rearview mirror as they drove to the end of the driveway, where she turned left and he turned right. *We're two people headed to the same place from different directions,* she realized as he drove away.

MAE WAS just going into her apartment when Jo got back. "Well, how did it go today?" she asked.

"We made good progress."

"On the house or with each other?"

Jo paused. Mae had a way of getting straight to the heart of things. The problem was she didn't have an easy answer. She thought so—they were getting to know each other, and Taylor had asked for a do-over. Yes, they were making progress.

"Maybe a little bit of both. We're definitely getting to know each other better."

Mae studied her for a minute. "You don't sound too happy about that."

"It's easier not to like someone when you don't know them very well," Jo admitted.

Mae opened her door and stepped aside. "Come on, I've got wine and leftovers."

After a dinner of some of the best tamales she'd ever tasted, Jo groaned and rubbed her stomach. "I shouldn't have sat down. I'm so sore I can barely move."

When they finished cleaning up, they took their glasses of wine and sprawled out on Mae's sofa to share the successes and struggles from their day.

"It's nice to have another woman living in the building. I'm going to miss you when you move out. I'll go back to being the only girl in the boys' club."

"They don't seem that bad. Reid is really nice. I've only met Isiah once but... well, he sure makes that sheriff's uniform look good." Jo batted her eyelashes.

Mae threw a pillow at her.

They heard the door open and close to Jacob's apartment across the hall, and Jo looked at Mae with a raised eyebrow.

Mae rolled her eyes. "I don't want to talk about him."

"Okay, fine. How are things going at work?"

"Some days I think I'm making progress, and then I run into another obstacle. The good news is that we got the funding so that Nate can hire another firefighter."

"What's the bad news?"

"We're about a hundred years behind in terms of technology—our computers are antiques."

Jo perked up. "I can help with that."

"I have to admit, I wanted to ask but you have a lot going on and I didn't want to burden you."

"It's not a burden. Colton is my home now and I want to do my part to help."

"I'm afraid we don't have very much money to pay—"

Jo held up her hand. "I'm volunteering my time. Invest the money into updating your equipment."

Mae grinned at her. "Have I told you lately how happy I am that you decided to move here?"

A smile tugged at Jo's lips. "Not nearly as happy as I am."

BEFORE JO finished sliding onto the stool the next morning, Tillie was setting a cup of chamomile tea on the counter in front of her.

"How did it go yesterday, honey?" she asked.

Jo took a deep breath, drawing in the floral aroma. "Thank you, Tillie, this is just what I needed." She took a sip and sighed. "It was okay. It could have been worse, I guess."

Tillie patted her arm. "Let me get you something to eat."

"I'd love a biscuit with honey and butter."

"Coming right up."

Tillie returned just a few minutes later with a couple of biscuits on a plate. She rested her elbows on the counter. "You want to tell me about the good part first or the bad?"

Jo took a bite and thought about her answer. "There wasn't anything bad really; it was just… awkward." Jo went on to tell Tillie about the conversation she and Taylor had over lunch.

"I'm sorry if this makes you uncomfortable." She grimaced.

"What, talkin' about race? Sometimes it's supposed to be uncomfortable. Seems to me we don't talk about it enough." Tillie snorted. "Maybe if we talked about it more, we would be better off."

"Thank you, Tillie."

Tillie handed her a bag. "Here's something for y'all to have for lunch. Tell Mr. Hollywood big-shot he has to share the pie."

Jo laughed and then gave Tillie a quick kiss on the cheek and headed out the door.

CHAPTER SIX

AFTER THAT first day, they had more challenges than successes. Sam ended up rewiring most of the house. They discovered the main plumbing line needed to be replaced. Jo didn't hesitate to jump in, and they spent days digging trenches for new pipes.

If Taylor expected Jo to be intimidated by the work, he was quickly proven wrong. Each day that passed, he became more and more impressed with her. Two weeks later, they were ready to move in. There was no reason to be nervous—he had been spending every day with Jo for the last two weeks—but today was different... permanent.

He'd started moving a few of his things in over the last few days, so all he had left to move in were his clothes. Jo pulled up and Taylor came out and met her at the back of her car.

"Here, I can grab one of those." He gestured to one of her suitcases.

"Thanks. This is all I have."

Taylor wrinkled his forehead. "What about your furniture?"

"I've got a bed being delivered today."

Taylor followed her inside to her room. The house still smelled of fresh paint from the soft white color they'd agreed on for the hallway and bathroom, which allowed the beauty of the mahogany woodwork to shine.

Taylor set her suitcase next to the small stack of boxes in the corner of the empty room. The floors were swept clean but still needed to be refinished.

"It's looking pretty good in here. You did a good job prepping the walls."

"Thank you for taking the time to show me how to do it."

"Have you decided on a color yet?"

"I'm thinking about something blue, maybe a teal color. It's probably not historically accurate."

"This is your room—do whatever will make you happy. I can help if you'd like."

"I'd appreciate that. Callie, Mae, and Emma mentioned something about a painting party, so we might turn it into a girls' night."

"You've made friends quickly."

The twinge of jealousy he felt took him by surprise. He'd thought he'd be able to spend more time with Dax and getting to know Jacob better, but when he wasn't working on getting the house ready to move in, he was working on the logistics of getting ready to start filming his show.

There was a loud knock on the door and someone called out, "Hello."

Jo's lips quirked. People knocking and then walking in was a part of small-town life she was still getting used to. They walked out and found Callie Ellis hovering in the front hall.

"I brought you a housewarming present." She held up a silvery-green plant in a pretty floral pot. She handed the pot to Jo and reached into the tote bag over her shoulder, pulling out a brown labelless bottle. "Taylor, this is from Reid and Dax."

"Is this what I think it is?"

Callie nodded. "Mr. Wallace's private reserve from the Buckthorn."

Taylor gave a low whistle, looking down at the bottle in his hand.

"Is there anything I can help you with?" Callie offered.

Jo shook her head. "I think we're okay for now. Would you like a tour?"

"I'd love to see the house and what you've done so far."

Taylor's phone rang. "I have to take this. Thank you for the housewarming gift, Callie."

Taylor found Jo in the small parlor after his call. She was crouched down in front of the fireplace, studying the intricate carving.

"It's amazing, isn't it?" Taylor said, kneeling down next to her.

Jo reached out to gently caress one of the birds carved into the mantel. "It's extraordinary. Every time I look at it, I see something new."

He pointed to one of the birds. "Have you noticed how they are all pointing in the exact same direction?"

Jo leaned back and cocked her head. Her breath caught and she looked at him with wide eyes. "This is a map."

"What are you talking about?"

"Look—the bottom of this side is Halcyon," she said pointing to where a large oak tree had been carved. Barely distinguishable behind the leaves on the tree was one of the columns from the front porch of the house.

"The bird is flying over a different landscape—the field and flowers change. Look at the stars in the sky at the top. They're scattered. They wanted whoever was looking to think it was just random stars in the sky, but it's here." She reached up and traced the outline of the Big Dipper. "The last bird...." Her voice caught. "The last bird had made it to freedom."

The bird at the opposite end was flying to a nest in what looked like a Christmas tree. Taylor's jaw dropped. He reached out and placed his hand on the carving.

"The bird is a halcyon. I've looked at this a thousand times and I've never seen it," Taylor murmured.

"Sometimes we don't see things until we want to. If a White person looked at it, they would have seen nothing more than beautiful flowers and trees. Someone had to know what they were looking for to see it."

"What other secrets has this house been hiding?" he asked.

Jo looked at him, and he could see the exact same thought he was having reflected in her eyes. They both jumped to their feet and spent the next few hours looking through every inch of the house. But there were no other hidden maps or messages that revealed themselves.

"I still can't believe it," Taylor said when they were standing in front of the fireplace again.

He had brought a sketch pad back with him and was sitting on the floor sketching the mantel while Jo took pictures. When she finished, she stood behind him watching as he sketched, mesmerized by how his hand moved the pencil across the paper.

"You're really good."

Taylor hesitated before he continued to fill in the detail of one of the bird's wings. "My parents weren't very impressed with the As I got in art class compared to the Cs and Ds I always got in science."

"They must be proud of you now."

Taylor put the sketch pad down and stretched. "Not so much—my parents think I'm wasting my time with old houses. They're still disappointed that I didn't follow in their footsteps to become a doctor like my brother."

"I think it would be wonderful if you did some drawings of the house that we could frame and have on display."

Her compliment brought a reluctant smile to his face. He rarely shared his drawings with anyone.

"I doubt I'll have time, but I'll see what I can come up with. I've got some drawings for the kitchen, since that's the room we'll be working on first. Do you want to take a look?"

They left the small parlor and went into the kitchen, where Taylor spread out a set of drawings on the table.

"I made these before...."

"Before I came into the picture," Jo offered.

"I've had years to think about what I would do in this room, but nothing is set in stone."

Jo looked over what he had designed. "These are good."

"Do you have any ideas for what kind of cabinets and finishes you would want to use?" he asked.

"Would brick floors work, maybe in a herringbone pattern? With simple white cabinets, and more of the Georgia blue granite for the countertops. I imagine there would have been a cast-iron stove here when the house was built. Maybe we could use black appliances as sort of a reminder of what was here before."

Taylor stared at her. "You described the room almost exactly the way it used to be before it was remodeled."

Spots of pink appeared on her cheeks. "It just seemed like that's what it would have looked like."

Taylor kept watching Jo out of the corner of his eye while they worked together making lunch. It was easy working alongside Jo. He couldn't quite put his finger on what was so different about her.

Jo sighed, slathering mustard on a piece of bread. "I guess I should get used to sandwiches for a while."

"We could get a Crock-Pot," Taylor offered. "We'll have catering on days when the crew is here, and that will help."

"How many crew members will be here?"

"On a normal shoot we could have as many as thirty, but now that you're here I thought it might be better to work with a smaller crew to begin with, so there'll only be eight for now."

Jo focused on making her sandwich. "Thank you, I appreciate that."

It surprised him how nervous she was about the show. They had a huge backlog of people who wanted to be on *History Reborn*.

"There's nothing to worry about. They're a great group of people, and I'm looking forward to you meeting Tessa."

"She's your producer, right?"

"Producer and closest friend."

They sat down at the table and studied Taylor's plans while they ate.

"I have to admit when we first started working together, I was worried you would want to come in and make everything modern and strip away the old character."

Jo put her sandwich down. "You don't know me very well, do you?"

"I'm getting to know you now. I'll tell you what, how about if I promise not to make assumptions about you if you do the same for me?"

Jo gave him a weary look. "It will make our time together easier if we can be friends," she admitted.

"As your friend, there's something I need to tell you," Taylor said with a serious expression.

"What?"

Taylor's lips quirked. "You have mustard in your hair."

Jo looked down at her ponytail sitting over her shoulder and rolled her eyes with a groan when she saw the bright yellow at the tip.

TAYLOR HAD to deal with another round of emails and phone calls after lunch. When he finished, he joined Jo at the kitchen table where she was working on her laptop.

"Anything I can help with?" he asked when Jo sighed.

"I'm just finishing up the program I created to track the remodel, and soon I'll have all of the code written. I'm sure I'll have some questions when I start entering in the data. I had no idea my list of projects for the house was going to spiral out of control this fast."

"A lot of people start restoration projects thinking they know what they're doing and end up selling a house half-finished because they can't handle it."

Jo snapped her laptop closed and glared at him. "I'm not selling."

"So you've said, but there's no shame in changing your mind."

"What about you? Maybe you'll change your mind."

Taylor wrinkled his forehead. "You don't have to get defensive if you're feeling in over your head. Even with my experience, I'm intimidated by the scope of this project."

"Don't." Jo poked him in the chest. "Stop acting like you know better than me. If I don't know something, I can figure it out. I'm the one who found Sam and made the arrangements for him to work on the electrical, not you."

"It's not that I know better; it's just that I know more—"

"How dare you," she snapped at him. "I can't believe that I'm going to be stuck in this house with a man who thinks he knows better just because he has more testosterone."

"That's not fair!"

They were so focused on each other, neither one of them heard the knocking at the front door.

"Hey, you two are gonna wear each other out. Try to pace yourselves," Tillie announced, standing in the doorway and holding a basket. "Y'all are so busy bickering you didn't even notice you have company. Good Lord, it's even worse than I remembered," she said looking around the room. "It's a good thing I brought y'all something to eat for dinner."

"Thank you, Tillie, that's really nice of you," Taylor said.

Tillie came over and gave Jo a pat on the shoulder. "How's it going, honey?" she asked.

Jo took a breath and shot Taylor an angry glare. "I'm fine."

Tillie started unpacking the basket. "I made a chicken and rice casserole with some greens, and there's cherry hand pies for dessert."

"Would you like to join us?" Jo asked.

"Sorry, honey, I can't run interference for you. You're gonna have to figure this out on your own. I'll see you at the café, or better yet, let's have a girls' day and get manicures."

She turned to Taylor and took his arm. "Come on, handsome, walk me out to my car."

The minute they stepped outside, Tillie smacked him on the back of the head. "What in the world do you think you're doing? You haven't spent one night under the same roof and you're already fighting."

"It's not all my fault, you know. It takes two people to have an argument."

"Men." Tillie rolled her eyes. "Y'all spend half the time not knowing what you're talking about and the other half trying to figure out what you said wrong." When they reached her car, Taylor opened the door for her. She paused before getting in. "You gotta stop acting like you have the advantage here, because I guarantee you a woman like that will bring you to your knees." She reached up and patted his cheek. "I always liked you—you're a good boy. Now remember your manners and go back in there and make nice."

Taylor felt the heat rise in his cheeks. "Yes, ma'am."

Jo was putting the food away when he returned. "I'm sorry, I overreacted," she said quietly.

"I get a little defensive when it comes to Halcyon. The house is what's most important here. I just want to save it before it's lost forever."

"I want the same thing."

"We just need to remember that." He gave her a small smile. "I need to remember that."

Jo would take good care of Halcyon. A part of him knew that. He'd seen how much care she'd put into the work they had done so far. It was both reassuring and unsettling how quickly she'd connected with the house. Then there was the fact that he never thought he'd find a woman who loved this house the way he did. And that was attractive as hell.

"Hey." Taylor grinned at her. "Want to see how many layers of wallpaper are in the big parlor?"

Jo stared at him for a minute before she shook her head, laughing. "Sure, why not."

SEVEN. THERE were seven layers of wallpaper, each more hideous than the last. It took the rest of the afternoon to peel back the layers. They were laughing so hard by the time they reached the final layer on the first wall, Taylor was wiping tears from his eyes. It felt good to laugh like that. When he stopped to think about it, he couldn't remember the last time he had.

"I don't mean to be rude, but your ancestors had terrible taste," Jo said, standing back to look at the red paper with gold and purple flowers.

"I've made a career out of historic preservation, but I don't think anyone would want this to be salvaged. This is going to make a great episode for the show."

"You might need to put up a content warning for people to shield their eyes."

Taylor threw his head back and laughed.

By the time they finished cleaning up, his stomach was starting to rumble. "I don't know about you, but I'm ready to dig into some of that casserole Tillie brought."

"Sounds good to me."

They warmed up the dinner and decided to eat out on the veranda. Jo propped herself against one of the pillars at the top of the stairs with her legs crossed. Taylor mirrored her, sitting against the opposite pillar.

"This is nice. I can see why so many houses have front porches around here," Jo said.

"I always pictured having this veranda lined with rocking chairs and spending summer evenings out here."

He looked over at the long, wide expanse, picturing a row of rocking chairs and ferns hanging above the railing. He blinked and shook his head when Jo sitting next to him, holding his hand, was added to the picture. He opened his eyes. Jo was watching him with a curious expression.

"Sorry," he said. "It's been a long day." He took a bite of the casserole and groaned. "Tillie's food is one of the things I always miss about Colton."

"What about your family?"

"My parents live in Atlanta. Uncle Robert, Dax, and my other cousins are the only family I have here now that my grandparents are gone."

"What about your brother, where does he live?"

"Dylan is an ER doc in Memphis. I'm hoping he'll come down to visit now that I'm here. What about you, do you have any family that will be coming to visit?"

"My parents are excited to come down. My dad is looking forward to connecting with a whole new branch of the family he didn't know about."

"And do you have any brothers or sisters?"

"One of each." She sighed.

"Uh-oh, that doesn't sound good."

She gave him a small smile. "My brother and sister are twins. They have that whole twin-bond thing going on, and I've always been the odd one out."

"Ah." Taylor nodded. "Does that mean they won't be coming for a visit?"

Jo laughed. "They wouldn't be caught dead in a small town, and especially not one in the South."

"There's a lot of stereotypes about the region. Some are justified but a lot aren't true."

"I wasn't sure what to expect when I first came," she ad- mitted. "But I really like it here. There's a sense of community that I didn't really have back in Chicago. I don't know how to explain it but it's… peaceful here."

"I feel the same way—this place is special." He finished his meal and clasped his hands in front of him. "Can I ask you a question?"

She nodded, biting her lip.

He took a deep breath, hoping she wouldn't be angry with him for asking but he needed to know. "Why did you want Halcyon so much? I mean, you'd never been to Colton until just a few months ago. What changed?"

A shadow of sadness passed over her face.

"I grew up in a loving home with great parents, but I never really felt… settled. I wish I could explain it, but the moment I saw a picture of Halcyon, I had to come here. It sparked something in my soul." She bit her lip and looked away. "It's hard to explain, but I thought if I didn't feel a sense of home with my family, maybe I would find it here with my ancestors."

He looked at her in surprise. Jo didn't strike him as the kind of person who felt like an outcast in their own family.

"Would you believe me if I said I know how you feel? I never fit in with my family, but I always felt at home here too."

Their eyes met, and he saw understanding and compassion in her gaze.

She sighed. "Taylor, we both want what's best for Halcyon. We might not always agree on how to move forward, but if we keep that in mind… I don't know, maybe we can figure out a way to make this partnership work."

"Damn it." Taylor ran his hand through his hair. "I didn't want to like you."

Jo smiled. "I didn't want to like you either."

"Just another thing we have in common." He smiled back.

Jo looked at him. Her eyes were way to expressive in the moonlight. He watched, mesmerized, as she took a bite of her pie and then as her tongue darted out to lick a crumb off her full pink lip. He'd lied when he told Jo that he didn't want to like her—it was more than that. He had already moved past being friends with Jo to wanting something more.

CHAPTER SEVEN

THE QUIET that came from it being just the two of them in the house was completely shattered when the film crew arrived. Jo hovered in the doorway for a moment, taking in all of the activity in the kitchen.

Taylor sat on a stool in a corner, sneezing while a young woman dusted powder on his face. There were people scattered all over the room with different types of equipment.

Taylor saw her and waved her over.

"Jo, let me introduce you to Chloe Michaels."

The young woman with a short pixie cut that made her already light amber eyes look even bigger than they were greeted Jo with a friendly smile.

Jo shook her hand. "It's nice to meet you. I hope you all are getting settled in okay."

"Yep, no problems—I wish we didn't have to stay in Greenwood, though. Colton is such a cute little town. I'm looking forward to exploring it more," she said, reaching for the hairspray.

"I have to admit that's one of the things I like about this place, no hotels or big malls," Jo said.

Chloe patted a stray hair on Taylor's head back into place. "Tessa was saying that you might turn this place into a boutique hotel."

Jo stiffened and looked at Taylor in surprise. That wasn't something he'd ever mentioned. Was he making plans behind her back?

Taylor frowned. "That's not something we talked about—you must have misunderstood."

There was a flash of something in Chloe's eyes that looked like she wanted to disagree, but she smiled and said, "I'm sure you're right."

"Nothing is going to happen with the house unless Jo and I agree. We're partners fifty-fifty." Taylor gave her a warm smile that made her heart flutter.

"At least for now," a woman said, walking up with a bright smile. "I'm Taylor's producer, Tessa Caldwell." She shook Jo's hand.

Jo flinched slightly when Tessa tightened her grip a little more than necessary.

She pulled her hand out of Tessa's grasp with a frown and stepped back. "It's nice to meet you."

She looked completely out of place in her silk blouse and high-end jeans. Jo bit back a laugh when she noticed Tessa's high heels. Her hair fell in perfect light brown waves, and her green eyes looked her over with anything but friendliness.

"Excuse me but, Taylor, we need you," Tessa said. "Just a minute." Tessa hesitated for a second before she walked away.

Chloe stepped back. "I'm finished here."

"Thanks, Chloe."

"It was nice to meet you," Jo said.

Chloe gave her a warm smile and said, "I hope we have a chance to get to know each other better."

Taylor turned to her after Chloe left. "Sorry it's so chaotic around here."

"That's okay; it's part of your job."

"Are you going to stay and watch the filming?"

"I was going to go into town to work so I'd be out of your way."

Taylor's face fell. "Oh."

Jo realized he wanted her to be there. She remembered what he said about his parents not approving of his career and began to understand that behind the confidence, Taylor wanted approval.

"I don't have to go in today. I can stay if you want."

"Great." Taylor broke into a smile that lit up his eyes. "We're filming a lot of promo stuff and setup shots. It will be fun."

He called Chloe back over. "Would you mind hanging out with Jo today?"

"Sure."

"Chloe will be able to answer any questions that you have."

He surprised her when he reached out and gave her hand a quick squeeze before he left to go talk to Tessa.

"It always takes a while to get set up for the first shot, so you'll have time before they're ready," Chloe explained.

"How long have you worked for the show?"

"This is my second season. I was really lucky to get this job. The former hair and makeup person is a friend of mine and recommended me. It was a good way to get my foot in the door. I'm hoping to get a position as a production assistant someday."

"Wow, that's really great."

There was a commotion coming from the front hall, and Chloe glanced over her shoulder. "It looks like they're almost ready. The guy with the lights is called a gaffer," Chloe explained.

They were standing off to the side watching while the cameraman set up his shot. Tessa was talking to Taylor, pointing out something on her tablet when she noticed them.

When the cameraman came over to ask Taylor a question, Tessa marched over to where they were standing.

She looked at Jo with an annoyed expression. "We really can't have any distractions. It would be better if you could leave while we're working."

"Taylor asked Jo to stay," Chloe said.

"I'll deal with Taylor. You need to remember you work for me," she snapped.

The last thing Jo wanted to do was to get Chloe into any kind of trouble, but she also didn't want to disappoint Taylor.

She was just about to make an excuse to leave when Taylor came over. "This is great—you'll be able to see everything from here."

Jo couldn't figure out if he didn't see the look of annoyance on Tessa's face or if he was ignoring it. Either way, the look was gone, replaced by a smile that didn't reach her eyes. "Okay, let's get started," she said linking her arm through his and leading Taylor away.

"Sorry about that," Chloe muttered.

Before she could say anything more, someone shouted for quiet.

Taylor stood in the main hallway under the dusty chandelier. He was wearing his trademark outfit, but this time he had a *History Reborn* T-shirt on under a gray plaid shirt.

The moment someone said, "And, action," he broke into the smile that won him a legion of fans and looked directly at the camera.

"Hi, I'm Taylor Colton, and welcome to *History Reborn*." He was good at his job, really good. Jo watched transfixed as he moved around the different rooms in the house, giving his audience a glimpse of the projects he would be featuring on the upcoming season of the show.

"What do you think?" Taylor asked when they stopped for lunch.

"You were great. I don't know how you do it. I'd be flubbing my lines and making all sorts of weird faces instead of having such a nice smile."

Taylor's eyes lit up. "I have a nice smile?"

Jo winced. "I didn't mean it like that. I just meant that you have a good smile for television. I mean, you have a way of smiling at the camera that people like." She slapped her palm on her forehead. "This isn't coming out right."

Taylor's lips quirked. "I'll take the compliment, thanks."

"How much more will you have to do today?"

"Not much, actually—just a few more shots after lunch and then some production meetings to go over the schedule for the rest of the week."

"Thank you for inviting me to watch. I had fun. I'm going to head into town and work for a little while. I promised Mae I'd help her with upgrades to the computers at City Hall with any spare time I have after I finish my projects for Dax."

"Can you have lunch before you go?"

Tessa came into the kitchen. "That would be nice, but I'm afraid Taylor and I have a lot of production notes we need to go over."

Jo fought the urge to roll her eyes. "That's fine—like I said, I have work to do. We can catch up later when I come home." She made sure to look Tessa straight in the eye when she said the word *home*.

"I'll see you tonight," Taylor said.

Since she didn't get to have lunch before she left, Jo stopped at the Catfish Café first.

Tillie was chatting with two Black men. She'd already met Isiah, the town's new sheriff. But she hadn't met the older man wearing a firefighter uniform.

"Well, I wasn't expecting to see you here today," Tillie said when she took a seat at the counter.

"I promised Mae some help with a new computer system for the town."

"How did it go this morning?"

"Pretty good—it's strange having the house full of people all of a sudden."

Tillie nodded. "What can I get you?"

"Can I please have a glass of tea and a meat loaf sandwich?"

"Coming right up."

"Jo, I've been wanting to introduce you to Nate Colton, the head of our one-man fire department," Isiah said.

"Soon to be two men. I've got someone new starting next week," Nate said, holding out his hand.

Jo shook the older man's hand. "It's nice to meet you."

"I've been looking forward to meeting the young lady who is brave enough to take on Halcyon."

Jo ducked her head. "I'm definitely not brave—moving here was kind of an impulse decision."

"What are your plans once you get it fixed up?"

"To be honest, I haven't thought past living in it. I know I don't want to run a bed-and-breakfast. I want this to be a home first, a place for family and friends to gather."

"Fair enough—you're young and you got plenty of time." Nate nodded with a smile.

Jo chatted with Nate and Isiah over lunch. It was eye- opening learning about the challenges of being first responders in a small town with limited resources. She walked over to Mae's office thinking about ways she could help besides working with Mae to select new computer equipment.

"May I help you?" Mae's office assistant, Grace, peered over the top of her reading glasses at Jo when she walked in.

"Hi, I have an appointment to see the mayor."

Grace pursed her lips "And your name is?"

Mae stuck her head out of her office door. "You know who she is, Grace." She smiled and waved Jo toward her office. "Come on back."

Mae shut her door the minute Jo walked in and leaned against it and groaned. "That woman is going to drive me crazy."

"What's going on?"

"She's decided that because I'm young and Black I need to learn how to act"—Mae crooked her fingers into air quotes—"properly."

"Oh no, I'm sorry."

"She insists on running the office like it's Buckingham Palace. Everything has to be so still and formal. That's just not my style."

"Definitely not." Jo chuckled.

"I've been dying to see you and hear about how it went having the film crew at the house this morning."

"It went pretty well, better than I hoped for. It was fun watching Taylor and seeing everything that goes into filming the show."

"Do you think you'll get along with the crew okay?"

"I think so."

Mae cocked her head. "That doesn't sound very confident."

"His producer is…. I just met her, so I don't want to be judgy, but she was kind of a bitch."

"Ugh, that's not good," Mae said.

"The way Taylor described her, I thought she'd be different. She acted almost like a jealous girlfriend."

"Well, is she?"

Jo frowned. "Taylor said she was his best friend, but now that I think about it, I don't think he ever said they *weren't* dating."

Her heart tinged with disappointment. When Taylor had grabbed her hand that morning, she'd thought she felt a spark between them, but maybe she was wrong. She must have misread the signs—it wouldn't be the first time. Oliver had proved she shouldn't trust her instincts when it came to men.

"Taylor's personal life is none of my business." She shrugged.

"Maybe not, but it's not going to make it very pleasant if you've got a jealous girlfriend in the house."

Jo sighed. Mae had a point. She'd have to ask Taylor about it when she got home. It would be better to clear the air now than have things get awkward later on.

She put her thoughts about Taylor and Tessa aside for now. "Enough about that. Let's talk about how we bring this office into the twenty-first century."

Mae glanced at the ancient fax machine in the corner and groaned. "Good luck with that."

They spent the next couple of hours working on a plan to update the ancient equipment and making sure what they planned to purchase would integrate with the county and state systems. It felt good to be needed, like her work mattered. It might not be a big project like she used to take on, but she was getting much more satisfaction knowing what she was doing would make a difference in the lives of the people in Colton. With updated systems, the town would run more efficiently and be able to provide more services to the community.

"I can't believe no one has updated any of this before now," Jo said when they finished.

"Well, the old town council didn't have the town's best interests at heart, and they weren't really interested in growing with the times. It's amazing to me how some people can be so resistant to change."

Just then Grace opened the door. "Mayor Colton, may I remind you that you have an appointment with the county assessor. I am sure Mr. Baker's time is very valuable. We wouldn't want to waste it, now. would we?"

Jo coughed, trying to hide her laugh, while Mae turned her back to Grace and mouthed *You've got to be kidding me.*

"I'm just finishing up with Ms. Martin. I'm well aware of the time, Grace."

The older woman pursed her lips before closing the door again.

"Lord give me strength." Mae rolled her eyes.

Jo said goodbye to Mae and popped her head in the library before she went back to Halcyon. "I'm just checking to see if you received anything from the state archives yet."

Callie shook her head. "No, nothing yet, but I'll let you know as soon as I get anything."

"Hey, while I'm here, any chance you have some books that would have information on garden design from the 1800s?" Jo stepped inside.

"I do have a book about English landscaping that might help."

"Thanks, I want to get some ideas for that garden off the small parlor."

"Let me grab it for you."

Jo left with another book on Southern gardens along with a couple of magazines that Callie found for her in the bookstore. She made plans to check out some garden planning software when she got home. She chewed on her lip when she turned into the driveway. She also needed to ask Taylor about Tessa.

"Hey, good timing. I was just about to get some dinner ready," Taylor greeted her.

He'd set out two plates and a bottle of wine on the makeshift table.

"Oh, I can just grab something and leave."

Taylor looked at her in surprise. "Why would you do that?"

"I thought you and Tessa would like some privacy."

He wrinkled his forehead. "Tessa's at the hotel in Greenwood. This is for us."

"I guess I figured you'd want to have dinner with your girlfriend."

Taylor laughed, shaking his head. "Tessa's not my girlfriend. What in the world even gave you that idea?"

"I just thought… she came across as a bit… possessive about you."

"Tessa? No, our relationship has always been firmly in the friend zone, and that's where it's going to stay. Besides, she's not my type."

Taylor's eyes locked on hers and her mouth became dry. "Oh," she croaked.

He pulled out a chair. "Have a seat."

She put the books on the table and sat down. "You're in a good mood."

Taylor took a chair across from her and poured them each a glass of wine. "We had a good first day of filming, and I just thought we deserved a nice dinner to celebrate."

"This is nice, thank you."

"How was your afternoon?"

Jo told Taylor about her meeting with Mae and her ideas for how she could help the town update their technology while they ate.

"That's really nice of you to volunteer your time," he said.

"I want to help my community."

"What are the books for?"

"I stopped by the library to get some gardening books. I'm going to start weeding the garden outside the small parlor."

"That garden has been neglected for so long. I wish we had some idea of what it used to look like."

"I… I had a dream about it. That's why I wanted to start working out there."

Taylor gave her a skeptical look. "You dreamed about the garden here at Halcyon?"

"I did."

"Will you tell me about it?"

Jo nodded. "Okay."

After they cleaned up the dishes, they headed to the small parlor. They stood in the doorway looking at the moonlit tangle of weeds and overgrown bushes that was once a garden.

"Well, what do you see?" Taylor asked.

"In the dream, the garden was divided into four sections with a brick pathway, and there was a fountain in the center."

The overgrown space faded away as she described the patch the way she'd seen it in her dream.

"There were yellow roses and pretty white flowers that looked like little white stars. They smelled so sweet. There were other flowers, but I don't know what they were."

She stopped. She didn't want to share the other part of the dream, where the garden was surrounded by a high wall and how she saw Ada Mae with the colonel, once again begging for her freedom while they walked arm in arm around the path.

"Are you all right?" Taylor gave her a worried look.

She shook herself. "Sorry, I was just remembering."

"Is there more of the dream?"

"No, that's all I can recall," she lied.

Jo sat down on the top step and Taylor followed her. They sat side by side, watching the lightning bugs dance around the garden.

"Can I ask you a question?" she said.

"Sure, you can ask me anything."

"What do you know about the colonel? Did your family ever tell any stories about him?"

Taylor went still for a second. "I don't know much. I think my family was embarrassed by him… by the past. I do know that he and his wife never had any children. When the colonel died, the house passed to his brother George and eventually down to me."

"Why has the house been empty for so long?"

"I think it's too difficult to afford the upkeep. My grandparents kept a house in town, but they farmed the land." He gave her a sad smile. "I'm sorry I don't know more."

She returned his smile. "We didn't know about Ada Mae until I found the letter."

"This may sound funny, but I've been thinking… maybe we ended up here to make a new future by restoring the past."

Her breath caught. "I don't think it sounds funny at all. I've thought the same thing."

He reached out and gently threaded their fingers together. "I didn't want to share Halcyon with anyone, but now that you're here… I'm glad it was you."

Her pulse started to race. Should she tell him more about her dreams? Could she trust him to share something she'd been guarding so close to her heart? *Yes*, her soul called out. She could trust this man.

"I dreamed about Ada Mae. In my dream she told me my future was here."

Taylor let go of her hand and cupped her cheek. "Did she say if I had any place in your future?" He spoke softly.

Jo shook her head. "I wasn't expecting you," she whispered.

"I wasn't expecting to want to kiss you in an overgrown garden filled with lightning bugs. But lately that's all I've been able to think about."

There was a hint of wonder in his voice and tenderness in his gaze that calmed her racing heart. His head lowered and his lips brushed against her cheek, his warm breath fanning over her skin and sending a shiver of desire through her.

She turned her face until their mouths met. His lips were firm and warm, and her heart thundered in her chest. It had been months since she'd been kissed. Oliver never kissed her like this. He never touched her in a way that made her feel like she was there with him—a part of the moment. This kiss tossed her soul into an unfamiliar sea. And she let the waves of need sweep her away.

Chapter Eight

Taylor became a master thief, stealing kisses from Jo every chance he could. He didn't get to see her during the day as much as he would like, but he made the most of their time together once the film crew left and they had the house to themselves. He quickly tuned in to the fact that Jo wasn't comfortable with any displays of affection when the crew was around, so he saved up each moment that he wanted to kiss or touch her until the end of the day.

They spent a lot of time sitting on the doorstep leading out to the garden or out on the veranda sharing news about their days. He loved listening to Jo talk about designing computer systems, working with Dax, and her volunteer work helping the town update their ancient software. He had friends and the crew members to hang out with, and of course Tessa, but he couldn't remember ever having these quiet hours to just sit and talk with someone.

And then there were the moments when he held her in his arms and they shared so much more than words.

That night they were sitting on the veranda watching the full moon play peekaboo with the clouds.

He kissed her temple. "How was your day today?"

"It was good. I ended up helping Jacob with his new inventory system at the hardware store." She laughed softly. "It was really more of a rescue mission. He was just about to throw his computer out the window when I came in."

"I'm glad you were there to save the day."

She smiled up at him, her eyes bright with amusement. "There's nothing quite like getting paid for my services with gardening tools and seeds."

A sliver of unease went through him. Would Colton be enough for someone as bright and talented as Jo? She could have made a lot more money working in a place like Chicago or another larger city. He didn't want to risk starting a relationship with someone who would get tired of life in the country and eventually want to leave. He'd still have to travel for his show, but Halcyon and Colton were what he wanted to call home.

"Do you miss your old job? Going from working for a large firm to working with a one-man operation in a small town is a pretty big shift."

"No, I don't miss it."

There was a note of sadness in her voice that made him wonder if she was being honest. He felt a twinge of disappointment at the idea of Halcyon without Jo. She was sitting in front of him on the steps. He tightened his arms around her as if that would somehow keep her from leaving. His heart whispered *I'll never let you go.*

"I'd rather work with people who can appreciate my skills and where I don't have to fight so hard to move up in the company," she said.

"Was it that cutthroat at your old company?"

She sighed. "Very."

He kissed the top of her head again. "I'm glad you're here, and I'm certain Jacob is happy to have you here to save him and his computer."

"I talked to him about building the cabinets for the kitchen, and he said he'd stop by with some samples."

"That's great. I'm looking forward to seeing his work."

Jo turned in his arms. "Do you think we could work on the house together this weekend?"

"What do you want to do?"

"It doesn't matter really—I just miss working with you." She hesitated for a moment. "It's been a lot harder to spend time with you since you started filming your show."

"Things are always hectic once we start shooting. I'll make sure this weekend is just for us."

He cupped her face and drew her in for another kiss. She wrapped her arms around his neck, pressing against him. He lost himself for a moment, letting his need drive him. Their kiss deepened and soon Jo was cradled in his lap, his hand splayed against her back, holding her flush against him. He needed to slow down. To stop if he was going to, because he wanted to do much more than make out like a couple of teenagers on the veranda.

He tore his mouth away and searched her face. "Jo, I...."

"I want you too, Taylor, but the last time I was swept off my feet, I paid a price. I promised myself I would take things slow the next time I met someone."

He drew in a deep breath, trying to get his body and his emotions in check. "I want you in my bed, but I'm willing to wait for you. I'm not going anywhere now that I know you're here."

Jo's eyes sparkled in the moonlight. "I didn't think I would find you when I came here."

He pulled her up and wrapped his arm around her waist, pressing his lips to her temple. Arm in arm they made their way through the darkened house, with only the moonlight streaming through the windows to guide them.

When they got to her door, he reached up and stroked her cheek. "I'm going to leave you here. Not because I want to, but because I'm going to respect what you said about taking things slow. I'm willing to wait because you're worth waiting for."

Jo lifted her face to his and he captured her mouth with his, making sure she knew with that last kiss good night how much he wanted her.

HE WAS drifting in that place between sleep and dreams when he heard her call out. Taylor jumped out of bed and ran down the hall when he heard Jo's cries.

"No!" she cried out again when he reached her, the blankets tangled around her as she fought the invisible enemy in her dream.

He pulled her into his arms. "Shhh, Jo, it's okay."

She cried softly in her sleep. "You can't keep her safe."

"Wake up, sweetheart." Taylor wiped the tears from her face and gave her a gentle shake.

Her eyes fluttered open, and she blinked at him for a moment before she buried her face in his chest and cried.

"I saw what she did to her," Jo sobbed.

"Who?"

"I was in her room upstairs and I saw her. Everything in the room was red. The wallpaper and the drapes. The door from the dressing room opened and a tall woman in a deep crimson-red dress with a high lace collar came into the room. She walked over to the dressing table and looked at herself, patting her hair. Everything about her was so severe. She saw my reflection and started screaming, 'Get out of my house.'"

Jo shuddered. "She tried to kill Ada Mae. She pushed her down the stairs, but she didn't die and she didn't lose the baby. I saw it all and I couldn't stop it. It was the colonel's wife, wasn't it?"

He shuddered. "I don't know."

"What do you know about the colonel's wife?"

He shifted so that she was lying against his side with his arm around her. "Not much, actually. No one ever talked about her. I know she was the daughter of a plantation owner in Tennessee, and…" He hesitated. "…she came with a dowry."

Jo closed her eyes and nodded. The truth sat unspoken between them. The dowry would have consisted of enslaved people.

"Are you okay now? Do you want me to get you some water?"

He started to get out of the bed, but she laid her hand on his chest, stopping him. "Don't go."

He gathered her in his arms again, and she sighed. Her breathing began to slow down, and she relaxed against him. He watched the shadows dance over her face in the moonlight that streamed through the window. She sighed and a slight smile played over her lips as she snuggled closer to him. He was quickly losing his heart to this woman, and it scared him.

CHAPTER NINE

TESSA ARRIVED early the next day with a big smile on her face.

"Hey, Tess, what's up?"

"There's something you need to see." Tessa handed him a file folder.

He frowned down at the folder in his hand. "What are you all excited about?"

"Look at the file."

Taylor flipped it open and began scanning the contents.

"It was worth it hiring the private investigator to look into Josephine. It's too bad we didn't get this before you went into arbitration. Now that we have it, you have a good chance to force Josephine to sell."

Taylor scanned the contents of the private investigator's report. "This doesn't make sense."

"What about it doesn't make sense? She's a scam artist."

He looked at the report again. "Jo tried to steal someone's technology?"

Tessa nodded. "I called the guy and spoke to him. She was scheming to take a program for a new algorithm or something." Tessa waved her hand in the air. "I didn't pay much attention to what the program is supposed to do, and that's not important. What matters is that she was trying to take credit for his work. The only reason the company didn't press charges is because he asked them not to. He said in spite of everything, he still had feelings for her and felt sorry that she just couldn't hack it. Coming here and making a claim on Halcyon could be just another scam she's trying to pull. That letter she claims is from the colonel is probably a fake. We need to have it authenticated."

Taylor's stomach soured. Nothing about Jo had given him the impression that she was a devious person. But what did he really know about her? She could be telling him what he wanted to hear to lure him into whatever scheme she'd planned. A heaviness settled in his chest. She'd seemed sincere, but he'd been fooled once before. He hated to admit that what Tessa was always telling him was right. Obviously, he wasn't the best judge of character.

"I really think I should stay at the house with you."

"Tess, I'm a big boy. I don't need you to watch over me. Besides, Jo would have to agree with that."

Tessa heaved a sigh. "Fine, but I'm going to be watching her. And I want someone to look at that letter she claims to be from the colonel." Tessa's expression sobered. "Since we're talking about letters, there was another one, by the way. I got a call from the production office in LA. They received another message from the same fan as before. What if Jo's the one who's been sending the letters?"

Taylor pinched the bridge of his nose. Fan mail came with fame. Most of it was flattering, some of it was funny, and every once in a while, he'd receive hate mail. Most of it wasn't threatening—usually someone who didn't like how he restored a house or didn't like the shirt he wore that day. And there were the few where the threat was disturbing enough that the network would send them to the police for investigation. He'd been receiving messages from the same delusional fan for months now. They weren't threatening, but they were becoming more and more frantic. He felt sorry for whoever could believe that someone they only saw on TV was their soulmate.

"Those started coming long before Jo filed her claim. Anything that involves a threat is forwarded to the authorities. I'm sure they'll find out who it is. Please don't go all conspiracy theory on me; we have enough going on right now."

Nothing was turning out how he had planned. He was already thrown by his growing feelings for Jo. Now he had to face the possibility that her motives might not be as true as she said they were. But his gut told him that wasn't right. Jo had never given him a reason to doubt her intentions.

He put his personal feelings aside for the moment. "Let's just focus on the filming. Jo hasn't caused any trouble, and I don't think she's plotting anything."

Tessa stepped closer, dropping her voice so they wouldn't be overheard. "That's your weakness, Taylor, you never want to see the bad in anyone and that's what got you into trouble with Alyssa. You didn't listen to me then until it was almost too late. You need to listen to me now."

He gritted his teeth. Yes, Tessa had been right about his last girlfriend, but he was getting tired of her reminding him about it.

"I'm not a pushover, Tess. I can handle Jo."

Tessa crossed her arms, clearly skeptical. "I'm just glad I'm here to back you up."

Taylor bit the inside of his cheek. In the past he'd appreciated Tessa running interference for him. But this time he felt like he was being handled, and he didn't like it.

"I don't need backup; I need my producer."

"Have I ever let you down?" Tessa pointed to her chest. "I'm the one who's worked her ass off to help you become a success."

"Yeah, okay, you're right. I just don't need you to treat me like I'm not capable of thinking for myself."

Tessa shook her head. "That wasn't what I was doing."

He knew that look. Tessa wasn't going to back down and he was already tired of arguing about it.

"I have the cabinet samples for you to review today," Tessa said just as Jo came into the kitchen.

Jo's footsteps faltered. "I thought we had agreed we were going to have Jacob Winters make the kitchen cabinets."

"We have a lot of sponsors that are eager to work with us. This is business, Jo."

He didn't mean to snap at her. The private investigator's report was still fresh in his mind, and he resented the position he was being put in. The report brought back the disappointment he'd felt when Alyssa had undermined their relationship with her lies.

"Taylor, what's wrong?"

He picked up the folder. "We hired a private investigator to look into you. What happened at your last job, Jo?"

She drew her shoulders back as she crossed her arms over her chest. "What happened is none of your business. You could have asked me instead of hiring someone to spy on me. How dare you sneak behind my back like this?"

Her voice was low and strained. Her anger was palpable, but her refusal to answer his question brought him another step toward confirming her guilt.

"Maybe not, but we're.... I thought we were getting to know each other. You should have told me."

Her eyes darted toward where Tessa was hovering at his side.

"We know all about you and how you stole from your boyfriend. You have no right to be here. From what I've seen in the report, you should be in jail right now. I had a very interesting chat with Oliver Cox. I'm sure with this new evidence we can appeal the judge's decision." Tessa sneered.

Hurt flashed in Jo's eyes when she looked at him. "You're accusing me of being a fake? This whole time that you've been talking about being friends and all...." She swallowed. "All of the kisses were just part of your act."

"No, I'm not accusing you of anything," he said with a pointed look at Tessa. "I just got the report and I'm trying to make sense of it."

Tessa moved closer to his side with a snide smile. "If we had gotten it sooner, you wouldn't be standing here right now."

"Knock it off, Tess," he growled.

Her lips thinned, and now he was the target of her glare.

"None of it is true." Jo took a deep breath and straightened her shoulders. "Let me ask you a question. If anything in that report were true, do you think Dax Ellis would have hired me? Why would a cybersecurity expert hire a fraud? Ask yourself that, Taylor." Her voice trembled slightly but her gaze was unwavering. "I figured you'd try something to get me to sell my half, but this was...." She shook her head and turned around and walked out of the room.

"Unbelievable." Tessa shook her head. "She's got a lot of nerve, I'll give her that."

"I shouldn't have confronted her like that," he muttered.

Tessa's eyes grew wide. "You aren't going to take her word over the private investigator's report, are you?"

"I think Jo hasn't said or done anything that matches what's in this report. It doesn't add up, Tess."

"Well, you're going to have to figure it out later, because we have work to do."

Taylor pinched the bridge of his nose. "Okay, let's get the filming finished for today."

He had a hard time focusing on work, replaying the scene with Jo over and over again in his head. She hadn't come out of her room, and as the day wore on, he became more worried and anxious about her. After lunch he found Chloe.

"Hey, Chloe, I have a favor to ask."

She frowned at him. "What can I do for you, Mr. Colton?"

Taylor drew back. Chloe had been subdued all day, barely speaking to him.

"Are you okay?" he asked.

"I'm fine. What can I do for you, sir?"

His jaw clenched at her aloofness. This wasn't like her.

"I was wondering if you would mind checking on Jo for me?"

Chloe straightened her shoulders. "That is not part of my job description. I will check on Jo because I like her and I think she deserves better than what happened to her this morning. But I will not report back to you or do anything to make you feel less guilty. And..." There was a tremor in her voice. "...if that means I'll lose my job—"

Taylor held his hand up. "You won't lose your job."

Chloe went into the pantry where lunch had been set up and came out with a plate loaded with food. She walked past Taylor without looking at him and disappeared down the hall to Jo's room.

"What's her problem?" Tessa asked.

"She's just worried about Jo—that's all."

"Is she taking her food from catering?"

"Don't, Tess, I said it was okay."

Tessa folded her arms in front of her. "She needs to watch her step if she wants to keep working here."

Caught off guard, he stared at Tessa. She'd never threatened a member of the crew before.

"I told her she wouldn't get fired. I mean it, Tess, let it go and let me deal with Jo."

He had a hard time forcing any food down while the rest of the crew ate lunch. The mood in the room was somber, and he noticed more than one crew member who wouldn't look him in the eye. He grew increasingly frustrated while he watched for Chloe to return. When she did finally come back into the kitchen, her eyes were red.

By the end of the day, he'd had enough of the worried glances and disapproving looks from the crew.

"Everyone, I'd like your attention," he called out as the crew was preparing to leave. "I want to let you know that despite what happened here this morning, *History Reborn* and Halcyon are my first priority, and I will not allow the co-ownership of this house with Ms. Martin to interfere with the success of the show."

Tessa was the only one who looked happy with his announcement. "I called the lawyer. He's going to look into whether there's any way we can make a case for Judge Beaumont to revise his original decision."

He glared at her, frowning. "That wasn't your decision to make, Tessa."

"I just assumed—"

"Yes, you did," he snapped. "And you shouldn't have. This is my house and my life. I decide what happens next."

Her eyes grew wide. "You're upset. We can talk about this later. Remember, I'm only trying to keep you safe."

After Tessa left, he went to Jo's room. He reached up to knock; his hand hovered in the air for a second before he dropped it. He didn't know what to say. He needed to sort through what he knew about Jo compared to what he saw in the report, because the two didn't add up.

He grabbed the file folder and headed out.

When he pulled up in front of Dax and Callie's house, they were on their porch swing and Taylor got the distinct impression they were waiting for him.

"Taylor." Dax nodded.

"Evening, sorry about dropping by unannounced like this."

Dax and Callie exchanged looks. "We thought you might," Dax said.

"I guess Jo told you what happened today."

"No, Tillie called," Callie said.

He pulled up a chair and sat down, clasping his hands in front of him. "Explain to me how the private investigator's report can be wrong."

Dax leaned forward. "You know I run a cybersecurity firm. Do you honestly think I would hire someone without doing a background check?"

Jo had said almost the exact same thing. He bristled at the twin looks of censure he received from them. "You can't blame me for being cautious. I've waited to restore Halcyon for a long time. I wasn't happy about her claim, but now that I've gotten to know her, I.... It's turned out to be a good partnership. But I can't get sidetracked by someone who isn't being honest with me."

"Do you really think Jo isn't being honest?" Dax's tone was sharp.

"Look, I had a bad experience a couple of years ago with a woman who turned out to be a fraud. If it wasn't for Tess hiring a private investigator back then, I would have made a huge mistake."

Callie shook her head. "I'm sorry that happened to you, but it doesn't mean this situation is the same."

"I know that, and I don't think it is, but I have to be careful. I have enough on my plate right now. I can't deal with a public relations scandal."

"All you need to do is give Jo a chance to defend herself," Dax said.

"Yeah, okay, you're right."

The events of the morning played over and over in his head, and each time he became more uncomfortable with the way he'd behaved. Yes, he could have handled the situation better, but that didn't mean he could ignore what he saw in the report. But then why did he feel so guilty every time he remembered the pained look that flashed in Jo's eyes?

He said good night and drove into town, planning to console himself with a slice of pie.

He didn't even get a chance to set foot over the threshold of the café before Tillie charged him with a thunderous expression.

"You aren't welcome here," she said blocking the doorway.

"Tillie, I don't know what you heard, but—"

"I know all about your private investigator's report. You don't know jack shit about that girl." She poked him in the chest.

"Tillie, you're overreacting."

As soon as the words were out of his mouth, he knew he'd made a mistake. Tillie's face turned so red he thought she was going to have a stroke. He backed up a step and she pushed the door closed.

He got into his car and banged his forehead on the steering wheel. He started the engine and headed toward the one place where he knew he'd get a sympathetic ear and some sage advice.

He wasn't surprised when Uncle Robert was waiting on his front porch when he pulled up.

There was no greeting when he dropped into one of the rocking chairs next to him. He didn't say anything; he just rocked and watched Taylor, waiting.

"I guess you heard what happened."

"This is Colton. Everyone knows by now."

"I'm just trying to understand the discrepancy between the person I've gotten to know and the Josephine Martin who is described in the report. Is that wrong?"

"Did you ask Jo?"

"I haven't had a chance to."

Uncle Robert shook his head. "Let me get this straight. You've been running all over town trying to support your side of the story and you haven't spoken to the one person who matters? Get off my porch and go home."

His jaw dropped. Uncle Robert had never spoken to him so harshly before. He got up and walked back to the car. Kicked out of the Catfish and now out of Uncle Robert's front porch. He got back in his car to make the short drive back to Halcyon. Uncle Robert and Dax were right: he'd been talking to everyone but Jo. He was afraid. He didn't want to find out if the allegations against her were true.

Their relationship was new, but he knew he'd feel its loss more keenly than he had with his past relationships.

The house was dark and quiet when he got back. This time he didn't hesitate to knock on Jo's door.

Her eyes were red-rimmed. "What do you want?"

"I was thinking we should talk."

"Oh, you were thinking we should talk? So now that you're ready to talk, I should just drop everything because it's convenient for you?"

"Maybe now isn't a good time."

"No, it's not."

"Maybe tomorrow...."

"We can talk tomorrow. Right now I'm so angry with you I don't think talking will do any good."

He wedged his foot in the door when she started to close it. "Before I say good night, I just want to say I'm sorry. I didn't handle seeing the private investigator's report well. When you're ready to talk, I can explain why. But for now, I just... I should have told you right away that I believe you."

She gave him a small smile and some of the sadness lifted from her eyes. "Thank you, I appreciate that. We'll talk tomorrow, okay?"

He breathed out a sigh of relief. "Okay."

Restless and unable to stop replaying the disaster of a day in his head, Taylor wandered through the house until he found himself in the attic. The flashlight on his phone swept across the dark expanse. Jo had removed the dust cover from one pile of furniture, a jumble of chairs and small tables. Something glinted when he moved his flashlight over it again. He moved a few chairs, clearing a path until he uncovered a large oval portrait framed under a piece of curved glass.

"Well I'll be," he said softly, swiping away the layer of dust to reveal more of the image.

Taylor crouched down to get a better look at the man in the portrait. Years in a dark attic had preserved much of the color in the piece. Taylor studied the masterful brush strokes that created strands of dark blond hair that was the exact same shade as his own. His own blue eyes looked back at him with a sadness that stole his breath. Taylor stroked his beard. They even shared the same haircut. He'd always wondered what the colonel looked like. The uncanny resemblance sent a chill down his spine. He searched for another painting of his wife. Traditionally portraits like that came in pairs, but he didn't find its mate in any of the piles nearby.

He carefully brought the picture of the colonel downstairs. Propped against the wall in his room, the portrait was even more striking with better lighting. Taylor used one of his T-shirts to carefully wipe away the years of grime until the image was clear. He dropped to the floor in front of the portrait, staring at the man who started all of this.

"What in the hell were you thinking?" he asked.

There was no answer, not that he expected one, but he'd take any help he could get at this point.

He grabbed his phone and called Tess.

"Can you tell me about the conversation you had with Jo's ex again?"

"Why? What's wrong?" Tessa said.

"Nothing's wrong, Tess. I'm just curious, that's all."

"He gave me permission to record our conversation. I can send a copy if you want, and you can hear for yourself. She's a manipulator, Taylor. You've got to be careful."

"Thanks, Mom," he said in a sarcastic tone.

"Okay, fine. I'm just trying to look out for my friend."

"And I appreciate it, I really do." Taylor softened his tone. "I know you've got my best interests at heart."

"I'm sending it over now, and I'll see you tomorrow."

As soon as he hung up, he heard the familiar ding of an email notification. He put on his headphones and listened to the conversation. When the recording was finished, he pulled the headphones off in disgust. Oliver Cox sounded like a pompous jerk. The way he described Jo as an untalented programmer whose success came from professors feeling sorry for her, affirmative action, and her own scheming ways had him grinding his teeth. He hated the spike of jealousy that shot through him hearing Oliver talk about Jo.

The way Tessa had questioned Jo's ex troubled him. It was almost as if she'd encouraged him to say bad things about her. He lay back and sighed, staring up at the cracks in the plaster above. Tomorrow he would explain why he got so rattled and he would apologize again. He closed his eyes and the day drifted away when sleep finally claimed him.

Taylor was trying to shade his eyes against the bright blue sky when he realized there was no sunlight. He slipped further into the dream and could see the room was lit by lamplight reflected in the mirrors on the wall. He saw a woman that he instantly knew was Ada Mae alongside the colonel in the glass. Ada Mae was sitting at the small elegant desk in the corner. The dream was so vivid he could hear the pen as it scratched across the paper. The colonel stood behind her, watching over her shoulder with pride.

"Your penmanship is excellent, my love."

Ada Mae paused. The pen hovered over the paper for just a moment before she continued to write, saying, *"That doesn't matter while I cannot live as a free person. You know this, Absolem, and you must let me go."* Ada Mae put her hand on her rounded belly. *"She won't stop trying to kill us."*

She put the paper she was writing on in the desk drawer and looked at the colonel with desperation in her eyes.

"I won't let that happen. Everything you need for your safety and our children is here."

"You can't keep your promise, you know you can't."

Ada Mae got up from the desk and went to lie down on the bed. *"The baby's coming,"* she said in an urgent whisper.

"You cannot make a sound, my love."

Ada Mae's face contorted in pain and her mouth opened in a silent scream.

CHAPTER TEN

JO JUMPED out of bed and ran toward Taylor's room when she heard him call out. He was tangled in the sheets, doubled over as if he were in pain, moaning.

"Taylor, wake up." She gently shook his shoulder.

Jo climbed in next to him and pulled him into her arms when he let out another low moan.

He shuddered and whispered, "I'll keep you safe."

Her heart softened. She ran her fingers over his forehead, trying to smooth away the furrows. She gave him a firmer shake.

"Taylor, wake up," she said more firmly this time.

He squeezed his eyes tighter for a moment before they popped open.

"Jo?" He looked at her in confusion.

"You were having a bad dream."

"I saw... I.... It was terrible—what he asked her to do."

"It's okay, Taylor."

He shook his head. "No, it's not." He grabbed her hand that had been stroking his forehead and held it in his. "You're not her," he breathed out.

"Who?"

"I was engaged before, and I found out she wasn't being honest with me. When I saw the report from the private investigator, I thought history was repeating." He sucked in a breath. "You're not her and you're not Ada Mae. I don't want to live in the past. I want to be in the present with you."

There was a note of longing in his voice that her heart couldn't ignore. Taylor had been hurt by someone he loved in a similar way she had. Knowing this stripped away any lingering resentment she felt toward him.

"It's late. Go to sleep and we'll talk in the morning."

He tightened his hold on her hand when she tried to get out of his bed. "Will you stay with me?"

She nodded and climbed back in and laid her head on his shoulder. He reached for her hand. Holding it on his chest, he exhaled and his body relaxed.

THE NEXT morning, he handed Jo a cup of coffee. He joined her on the step leading out to the garden, holding his own cup between his hands. He watched the steam mingle with his breath in the brisk morning air for a moment before he spoke.

"I was engaged before. It turned out that Alyssa was selling information to the tabloids. I… I thought we were in love, but I learned…." He shook his head. "It wasn't real, none of it was, even the feelings I felt for her. They weren't anything close to the way I feel about you. When I saw the private investigator's report, I just… I was angry because I thought I'd made the same mistake."

Jo's eyes grew wide at his admission. She set her cup down and turned to face him.

"We've both been betrayed by people we thought we loved."

"I'm sorry."

"I'm not. Sometimes I think I had to lose everything so I could find this," she said, sweeping her hand over the garden. "Before I came here, everything was about work and saying the right things, wearing the right clothes." She sighed. "I was constantly trying to impress people whose opinion of me I thought mattered. Then I came to Colton and learned how to like myself again."

There was a hint of desire in Taylor's eyes when he leaned forward slightly and asked, "Do you think you could learn to like me… again?"

Jo couldn't fight the smile that tugged at her lips. "Maybe…." She pinched her thumb and forefinger together. "But just a little bit."

THERE WAS a tenderness that came from the understanding between them over the days that followed. There was less kissing but a lot more talking. They often sought each other out during the day, just to check in or share something funny that happened.

Unfortunately, those moments came at a cost. Tessa became more and more hostile as the days passed. Nasty looks escalated into nasty comments. At one point Tessa even suggested that Jo had been stealing food from catering. She'd asked Jo to take care of Taylor's laundry and suggested Jo could be paid by the production company as a maid. Every day there was a new comment or snide remark, and each time Taylor came up with an excuse for Tessa's behavior. Jo witnessed Tessa's abusive behavior to the crew with growing concern. She often treated the crew in ways that in any other company would have resulted in a meeting with Human Resources, but no one stood up to her for fear of losing their job. She often made demeaning and outright cruel comments when the crew wasn't around. Jo's attraction to Taylor was tempered with frustration about his refusal to acknowledge Tessa's behavior.

Callie, Dax, and everyone else in town were bending over backward to be nice to Jo after hearing about the private investigator's report. She appreciated the support, but it only made her feel worse. The only person who wasn't looking at her with a sad expression was Tillie, and that's why she found herself sitting at the counter at the Catfish for the third time that week.

Tillie swapped the cold bowl of chili for a fresh one. "Come on, Jo, you need to eat."

Jo picked up the spoon and then set it down again. "I'm sorry, Tillie, I'm just not hungry."

"Starving yourself isn't going to do you any good. I'm not letting you leave here until you've eaten at least half that bowl."

Tillie went to take care of her other customers, coming back to check on her every few minutes. When the last customer left for the night, Tillie came and sat next to Jo.

"What's going on, honey?"

Jo filled her in on the behavior she'd witnessed from Tessa and all of the little digs she'd gotten in over the past week.

"I'm so frustrated," she confessed. "I like the time Taylor and I spend together, but I don't like the way he either doesn't see Tessa's behavior or is choosing to ignore it. Either way, I don't see how a relationship between us can work if he won't…. I'm not asking him to take sides, but I need to know that he…."

"A person wants a partner who they know will have their back. The attraction might be there, but it sounds to me like the trust is missing."

Jo nodded.

"I'm sorry, honey. I wish I had some words of wisdom for you, but I've been without my Fred for so long now I can barely remember what it feels like to be attracted to someone."

Tillie had shared how she married her high school sweetheart, Fred, the day after graduation. They'd worked side by side for eighteen years until cancer took away the love of her life.

Jo took Tillie's hands in hers. "We're strong independent women who deserve to have good men in our lives. And if we can't find them, we'll have just as much fun living our lives without them." She tried to sound more convincing than she felt.

Tillie gave her hands a squeeze. "Damn straight. You hold your head up high when you get back to Halcyon. Taylor's a fool. I just hope he figures it out before it's too late."

When she got back to the house, Taylor was sitting at the makeshift kitchen table with a bottle of whiskey and two glasses. She gave him a brief nod and started unloading the food Tillie had insisted she bring home with her.

He waited for her to finish before he asked, "Is something wrong?"

She leaned against the countertop in the butler's pantry and folded her arms.

"This isn't working, Taylor."

"What do you mean? What isn't working?"

"I can't…." She swallowed. "I like you and I'm attracted to you." She felt the heat rise in her cheeks. "But our relationship isn't going to go anywhere as long as you refuse to do anything about Tessa's behavior."

Taylor drew back and placed his hands on his hips. "What are you talking about?"

Jo took a few steadying breaths, willing herself to ignore the belligerent tone in his voice.

"She's more and more hostile to me every day, and she's abusive to your crew. I don't know how you don't see it."

Taylor started to speak when she noticed the cabinet samples stacked against the wall in the kitchen out of the corner of her eye. She went over and picked up one of the samples.

"What are these for?"

"We have a lot of sponsors interested in the show, Jo. There are several cabinet companies that want to participate, so Tessa and I thought—"

"No."

"Jo, this is business."

"No, this is Halcyon. We agreed that it would be a good idea to use local trades. Jacob Winters is going to build the cabinets."

Taylor's blue eyes locked with hers, and she refused to blink. She realized she had fisted her hands so tightly they were beginning to tingle. But she couldn't let go. If she did, she might fall apart. She held her breath and waited to see what kind of excuse Taylor would use.

"Jo, it wasn't easy to get the network to agree to commit to an entire season on one project. I'm under a lot of pressure to make sure this is a success."

"I'm sorry, Taylor. I'm sorry that you are under so much pressure that you're willing to put the needs of your show before what's best for the house. I'm not."

"You're being unreasonable."

She shook her head, backing away. "I didn't think you would do this."

Taylor threw his hands up. "What am I doing?"

"I didn't think you would go back on your word."

"That's not what I'm doing, I'm just—"

She held her hand up. "It's okay, Taylor. I'm not going to ask you to choose between your partnership and me."

She walked away from Taylor, leaving him with a thunderous expression on his face. Jo waited until she reached her room before she took a deep shuddering breath, fighting to breathe through her disappointment.

WHEN SHE got into bed that night, she whispered in the darkness, "Ada Mae, I need your help. Please. I'm trying to do the right thing and make you proud, but I need you to show me the way."

She squeezed her eyes shut, hoping sleep would take her worries away. She heard the rustle of skirts before she heard the voice. Jo knew the young woman beckoning her to follow was Ada Mae. Her pale blue skirts swished around her as she led Jo through the house into the small parlor.

"She knew, she knew the first time she laid eyes on me. I felt sorry for her. She came to Halcyon, her head held high, so prideful to be the wife of the master and the mistress of the plantation. He made her wait two years before he could bring himself to marry her. His daddy wanted

it—it was business and not love. That was fine by her. She just wanted to be a grand lady. She knew he'd take a mistress, and she didn't care if he took one of us. She didn't know he'd insist on havin' me in the house or that it would be my name he would whisper in the dark.

"I didn't want to be there and she didn't want me there. It was never gonna end in anything but pain and sorrow. I begged Absolem to set me free or to let me work with my brothers and sisters in the field, but he refused. He always thought he could have everything he wanted, just like a spoiled child."

She turned in a slow circle around the room. *"He asked me what my favorite color was. When I told him yellow, he decorated this room for me. I hated it as much as I loved it. I would have always chosen my freedom over his love."*

The sconces and the fireplace flared to life, illuminating the room in a soft golden glow. Jo looked down to see a yellow rug bordered with pink and blue flowers at her feet. The walls were covered in a pale yellow damask stripe and the furniture in a yellow brocade. Everything had a floral motif, making the whole room appear as if it were a bouquet of yellow roses.

"My brother carved the mantel. Absolem was always getting offers to buy Henry, his skill was so great. But he refused to even loan him out." Ada Mae shook her head, and a tear slipped down her cheek. *"He carved a map to freedom that he never got to see. Miss Julia had him whipped to death when she didn't like the jewelry box she ordered him to make. Absolem had been away and that's why. She knew she couldn't touch me, but she could hurt the ones I loved."*

Jo listened in horror. "Why did you want me to come here if there is only pain in this house?"

Ada Mae took Jo by the hand and led her over to the french doors. They flew open and Jo saw the garden as it once was. Yellow roses were in bloom, surrounded by the tiny white flowers she didn't recognize. The garden was framed by a high brick wall with a small arched doorway in one corner.

There were people working in the garden. Their brown skin glowed in the afternoon sun. These were some of the enslaved people owned by Absolem. Ada Mae gently pulled Jo back from the doorway. One by one the slaves would work their way over toward the garden. They never stopped working, but their eyes were trained on the mantel.

"Absolem insisted I learn to read and write but I didn't dare teach anyone else. Miss Julia was always trying to trick us. I couldn't risk it. But I could tell stories and Henry could carve. Absolem thought he was making this place for me. He was so blind. He gave me a place to teach. I made this house into a school and he didn't even know. You're here to make sure the past is remembered. You can make this house a place where people can build a better future."

Ada Mae reached out and gently cupped Jo's cheek.

"He's stubborn, like Absolem, and you're stubborn just like me. Don't give up. Keep fighting."

Jo woke up with a start to bright blue skies and the scent of eucalyptus.

She was on her way to work out in the garden later when she ran into Taylor in the front hall. He started to speak when there was a loud knock at the front door.

When Taylor opened it, Mae's mother and the three sisters known as the Jewels were standing on the doorstep with baskets of flowers and gardening tools.

"We're not here to see you," the oldest of the Jewels—Opal—said.

"We're here for Miss Josephine," said the middle sister, Pearl.

Ruby, the youngest, saw Jo and came rushing over to envelop her in a hug.

Mae's mother stepped forward until she was toe-to-toe with Taylor. "I am Mrs. Colton. I assume you are Mr. Colton." She patted her sleek bob shot through with silver. Although she must have been in her sixties, there wasn't a single wrinkle on her dark brown skin. She oozed elegance and style. "I am here with the ladies from the Colton Gardening Club, and we've come to offer assistance to Ms. Josephine Martin today," she said, as if she were giving a formal address to the state assembly.

It was clear they were putting Taylor in his place. He stepped back and bowed with a sweeping gesture. "Please come in," he said, matching Mrs. Colton's formality.

If he thought he could charm any of them, he quickly learned that wasn't going to be the case when all four sets of eyes gave him withering stares. Ignoring his greeting, they surrounded Jo, taking turns to say hello with hugs and kisses. Jo blinked back her tears and sent a silent word of thanks to Ada Mae. She'd asked her for help, and she'd sent it in the form of the Colton Gardening Club.

As Jo led them through the small parlor to the garden, Opal's footsteps faltered when she saw the fireplace mantel.

"Well, I'll be," Opal whispered. "I can't believe it's real."

"What is it?" Pearl asked.

"Sister?" Ruby put her hand on Opal's arm.

"What do you know about this mantel?" Jo asked.

"Our great-grandmother used to put me on her knee and tell me that there was a mantel in the big house at Halcyon that was a map to freedom. She said it was carved with birds—halcyon birds and trees." Opal frowned and shook her head. "There's more, but I can't remember it."

Jo thought about what Ada Mae said in her dream. She reached for Opal's hand and gave it a squeeze. "I'd like it if we could sit down and you'd tell me what you can remember, so we can make sure future generations know the story."

She opened the doors out to the garden, where sunlight streamed through the branches of an ancient oak. It was a beautiful fall day and the perfect temperature for working outside. Jo had already done enough weeding that a brick path was now visible between the four garden beds. She had found a rosebush that survived being smothered by a morning glory, and she knew now that in the spring it would bloom yellow. The Jewels and Ella Colton all oohed and aahed at how good the soil was. They planted purple asters and pansies in one of the beds they cleared to brighten up the garden for now. Ella and the Jewels came up with a plan for planting in the spring after Jo explained her vision for the garden.

Opal squinted up at the scraggly branches of an ancient crepe myrtle, or at least that's what Ella insisted it was after a heated debate with Pearl. "I'm not sure if that one can be saved."

"We should call an arborist," Pearl suggested.

"There are a couple in Greenwood we can call," Ruby added.

Jo smiled at the women. "I'm so happy you're here to help. Thank you."

Ella Colton patted her hand. "We're happy to help your family."

Opal was still staring at the tree. There was a bright flash of blue and a little bird just like the one Jo saw on her first visit to Colton darted into the sky. "A halcyon," she murmured. Suddenly she stood up straighter and exclaimed, "I remember."

"Remember what?" Pearl asked.

"I remember the story Great-Grandma told."

"What is it?" Ruby asked.

Opal turned to Jo. "Have you been to the cabins yet?"

"What cabins?"

"Come on, honey." Opal took Jo's hand. "I want to tell you the story there."

The women led her beyond the garden out into the cotton field to a small thicket of trees half covered in kudzu vines, obscuring where three small brick buildings sat low to the ground.

Opal held fast to one hand while Pearl grasped the other. Ruby and Ella stood behind her with their hands on her shoulders.

"Most folks have forgotten these are here," Opal said.

"Some work hard to forget," Pearl added.

"And some don't want us to remember," Ruby said quietly.

"Great-Grandma told me about a woman kept trapped like a bird in a thicket." Opal's voice took on a dream-like quality. "Let me tell you, child, about a little bird who could not fly free." Opal began to sing in a low mournful voice that echoed the voices of their ancestors who sang of their sorrows at the end of the day.

> *A bird up yonder'll show the way.*
> *A bird up yonder'll show the way.*
> *Fix my eyes to Zion, Lord.*
> *I'm here on bended knee.*
> *A bird up yonder'll show the way.*
> *A bird up yonder'll show the way.*
> *A bird up yonder'll show the way.*
> *When the hour is early.*
> *Walk me on to glory.*
> *A bird up yonder'll show the way.*
> *A bird up yonder'll show the way.*
> *A bird up yonder'll show the way.*
> *Moses tell the story.*
> *The Power and the Glory.*
> *A bird up yonder'll show the way.*

"It was your Ada Mae, wasn't it?" Mae's mother asked.

Jo choked back a sob and nodded.

Ella took Jo's face in her hands. "Look at us. We are generations of Coltons who have lived, loved, and died in this place. You have the strength of our ancestors. Never forget that," she said, wiping away Jo's tears with her thumbs.

"Granny said there was a woman trapped in this house. I think you were called to come here to finally set her free," Opal said.

The other women nodded in agreement.

Jo gave each of them a hug. "Thank you. I didn't realize just how much I needed this today."

After Jo said goodbye to Mae's mother, she turned to where the Jewels were standing by their car, whispering to each other.

"You tell her, Ruby. You're the one who talked to them," Opal was saying when Jo walked over.

Ruby turned to Jo. "Miss Josephine, I don't want to cause any trouble, but I saw Sam and Minh at the barber shop the other day. I poked my head in to ask how things were going here at Halcyon, and they said they weren't working here anymore."

"What?"

Jo looked at Ruby in shock, her mind racing. She hadn't seen Sam and Minh around lately. She'd been spending most of her days in town working with Dax and helping Mae update the town computer systems. She assumed they were either finished with their work for the day or Taylor wasn't ready for the next phase of the plumbing and electrical work. Ruby twisted her hands in front of her. "They said that woman that Taylor works with told them they didn't look right to be on television."

Jo pressed her lips together. She'd been avoiding spending any time with Taylor for the last week, and clearly that was a mistake. Taylor was trying to get out of using Jacob for the cabinets, and now Sam and Minh weren't working at the house anymore.

"Thank you for telling me, Ruby. I'll take care of it, don't worry."

"We're all really happy to have you here. I mean, one of us... I mean, a descendant."

"I understand." Jo's voice shook. "I promise I'll take good care of Halcyon so other generations can come and learn about Ada Mae and everyone who was enslaved here."

Ruby nodded and pulled Jo into a hug.

Jo said goodbye to the rest of the Jewels and stood in the driveway waving until their car disappeared. She walked back around to the garden to take a minute to admire the progress they'd made.

"It looks beautiful out here," Taylor said.

"Thank you. The Jewels and Mrs. Colton were a big help."

Jo reached down to pull another weed and let out a sharp hiss when a sliver slipped under the skin of her palm.

"Careful." Taylor grasped her hand, gently holding it in his palm. "Just stop and let me get this out," he said as she started to pull away.

"I don't need your help."

"No, you don't, but I want to give it just the same."

He carefully pressed on her palm until the edge of the sliver popped up and he could pull it out. Jo's breath hitched when he rubbed his thumb over the wound before he let go of her hand.

His eyes searched hers. "I miss you," he blurted out.

"We weren't friends long enough for you to miss me."

"Maybe not, but I miss working on the house with you."

She'd missed him too. When Judge Beaumont made his decision, Jo didn't know how much she would enjoy working with Taylor on the house. But the man who she thought she was getting to know, the one she liked, wasn't the man she saw now.

She took a deep breath before she asked, "About the house, why aren't Sam and Minh working here anymore?"

"They were busy working on other projects."

"That's not what I heard."

Taylor rested his hands on his hips. "What did you hear?"

"That Tessa told them they didn't have the 'right look' for television." Jo made air quotes with her fingers.

Taylor shook his head. "I'm sure they misunderstood. Tessa wouldn't have said something like that."

"Are you sure?"

"I get that you don't like Tessa, but making up stories about her is a little petty, don't you think?"

"I'm not making up stories and I didn't misunderstand. Why can't you believe me?"

"Why are you always trying to make it look like Tessa is some kind of villain? She's not trying to hurt you."

"Do you really believe that? Hiring a private investigator and accusing me of being a thief wasn't trying to hurt me?"

"She's not the one being so secretive. You still haven't told me what happened back in Chicago with your ex-boyfriend."

"I don't owe you an explanation, and I doubt you'll take my word for it over the lies Tessa has told you. Lies that, despite what you say, a part of you still wonders if they are true. My ex-boyfriend framed me. He's the one who stole MY program to get a promotion. And while he was stealing from me, he was also cheating on me with my best friend. They're getting married next month. I'll find out where they're registered, maybe you and Tessa can get them a wedding present."

"Jo, I—"

"I never tried to deceive you. I'm not the one who—" She shook her head. It wouldn't matter what she said. Taylor would only hear what he wanted to. She pointed to the door. "Get out of my garden."

She turned her back when he tried to reach for her. She waited until she heard him walk away before burying her face in her hands. How could Taylor be so blind to Tessa's behavior, and how could she have been so stupid she'd almost made the same mistake twice? She refused to let any tears fall. She wouldn't cry; she was done with men who tried to steal from her. Oliver stealing her program was bad, but Taylor almost stole her heart, and that would have been much worse. But damn it, she'd already fallen for Taylor, harder than she'd like to admit. Maybe she wasn't head over heels in love with him, but she was well on her way, and his refusal to believe her… to see her, cut deep.

That night Ada Mae appeared in her dreams again. She was in a room Jo didn't recognize; the light was strange and when she looked up she saw the sky, only it wasn't. Ada Mae sat at a desk in the corner, writing something in a small leather-bound book. She had on a silk dress in yellow with brown trim and her hair was upswept high off her neck. She carefully set the pen back into a crystal ink well and turned to Jo, her dark eyes filled with sorrow.

"He's just like the colonel. He will break your heart the same way Absolem broke mine."

Jo pressed her hands on her heart. "I don't understand how you could have loved him."

Ada Mae let out a long sigh. *"I never said I did."*

There was a long pause and Jo wondered if that was the only answer she would receive, but then Ada Mae continued and she could feel her sadness and vulnerability swirling around her. It was so palpable it made it hard to breathe.

"Did I love him? Mayhap yes, mayhap no—how much can any woman love a man who owns her body and can sell it on a whim or lend it out for another man's pleasure?"

Jo gasped. "No, please don't tell me he—"

"No, child, he didn't share me with anyone else. He was too selfish for that."

Jo swiped away at the wetness on her cheeks.

"He whispered so many wishes. He told me so many things during the night that sometimes I believed I loved him. We would whisper our hopes and dreams in the darkness. In the light of day, my darkness turned any hope I had into despair and shattered my dreams. Even then, sometimes on a sunny day I would have a moment when I thought, maybe, if I loved him enough, he would set me free.

"That boy is going to hold fast to what he thinks is right, the same way the colonel did. When the time comes, he'll have to choose what means the most to him."

"What will he choose?"

There was no answer, just the chirping of birds waking her up.

Chapter Eleven

TAYLOR BARELY caught a glance of Jo for the rest of the weekend. He'd tried to get a hold of Tessa to ask her about Sam and Minh, but she had flown back to LA for a friend's wedding and didn't answer any of his calls.

Monday morning, Tessa blustered in with a smile on her face. Before he could ask her about Sam and Minh Jo walked in.

"Should you be on your way to work? The crew will be here any minute and we need to get started," Tessa said to Jo in a voice laced with contempt.

Jo raised an eyebrow, looking at Taylor expectantly and ignoring Tessa's question.

"Tessa, Jo heard that Sam and Minh aren't going to be working here anymore. Is that true?"

He didn't miss the slight flinch before Tessa smiled. "Of course not."

"Great, then I'll just call and let them know that they can start again," Jo said.

"The thing is, we've already started filming with our subs." Tessa turned to Taylor. "It's going to cause a delay we really can't afford if we have to reshoot with new people who don't have experience being on camera."

Taylor stiffened. Tessa's excuse wasn't unreasonable, but he could tell by the look on her face Jo wasn't happy with it.

"I see," Jo said in a clipped voice.

"Jo, we can—" Taylor started.

She turned her back and walked out of the room before he could finish.

"She is so rude," Tessa huffed.

"Tess, Halcyon belongs to her as much as it belongs to me. Jo has a right to have a say in what happens here."

"Maybe with the house, but not with the show. I'm the producer here, and it's my job to make sure everything runs smoothly. She has no right to tell me how to do my job."

"That's not what she's doing."

"Come on, Taylor." Tessa threw up her hands. "That's exactly what she's trying to do. I'm not going to let her interfere with the show and neither should you. You have a lot riding on the success of this season."

The crew started to come in, and Taylor didn't want to continue the conversation with an audience. "We'll finish this later. I don't want this to interfere with what we need to get done today."

"I'm glad you have your priorities straight."

Taylor ignored Tessa's comment and went to find Jo. He found her in the garden where he knew she would be. She was on the phone with her back turned. Her conversation brought him to a stop.

"I believe you, Sam. Please tell Minh I'm sorry." She sighed. "I don't know what to do. He won't believe me." She nodded, listening. "I will. Take care, Sam."

She hung up and spun around with wide eyes. "I didn't know you were there."

"I just wanted to see if you were okay."

"I'm fine, Taylor," she said in a flat voice.

He glanced down at the gardening tools at her feet. "Are you going to be working out here today?"

"I am. Callie is coming by later this afternoon to pick up the letter from the colonel and Ada Mae's freedom papers to have copies made for the state archives. I talked to Dax, and he agrees that it makes sense for me to work from Halcyon as much as I can from now on so that I'll be here to make sure decisions aren't being made without my input. That was Sam on the phone, by the way. Not that you'll believe me, but he confirmed what I told you."

He bristled at the way Jo was acting—like he was the one who couldn't be trusted.

"I'm sorry about the miscommunication with Sam and Minh, all right. But you're completely out of line acting like I can't be trusted with the house."

"Taylor, I have the wallpaper samples for the—" Tessa interrupted them. "What are you still doing here?"

Jo stiffened. "I don't have to explain what I'm doing in my own home to you."

Tessa glared at her for a moment before turning back to Taylor. "I have the samples we ordered. I think I've found the perfect one for this parlor."

She held up a dark red swatch with a gold leaf pattern stamped on it. Taylor turned and asked Jo, "What do you think?"

Jo glared at him. He looked down at the wallpaper in his hand and back at her. "We wouldn't have chosen anything without your approval."

"The parlor should be yellow."

"This is more historically accurate," Taylor said, looking down at the sample in his hand.

"I want the parlor to be yellow," Jo repeated.

"I hardly think you have the taste level to decorate a house like this," Tessa scoffed.

"That's enough," Taylor said between clenched teeth. "Tessa, give us a minute, please."

Jo watched the rigid set of Tessa's shoulders as she walked away. Her stomach churned with a mixture of anger and frustration. She braced herself and turned to face Taylor. "And that is why I'll be here every day. You may think you know more about what's historically accurate or have better taste than I do, but I have the best interests of this house at heart."

Jo stepped into the parlor and over to a corner where a piece of old painted-over wallpaper had started to lift. She peeled it away and there was a small fragment of yellow. She stabbed it with her finger. "This room will be yellow."

Taylor looked from the patch on the wall to where Jo stood with her arms crossed. He reached out and ran his finger over the small spot of yellow with a look of astonishment on his face.

"I'll talk to Tessa and make sure she apologizes to you by the end of the day."

Jo shook her head sadly. "When my brother and sister and I got into fights when we were kids, my dad used to say, 'An apology you have to demand isn't an apology from the heart.'"

Taylor threw up his hands. "I can't do anything right for you, can I?"

She didn't answer. Instead she said, "I have weeding to do and the crew is waiting for you. We can argue about wallpaper later."

The look of pity in her eyes made him even angrier. She didn't have any right to feel sorry for him. He returned to the kitchen where Tessa and the crew were waiting. He held his hand up when Tessa started to approach him.

"Not now, Tessa."

He went over to the stool where his hair and makeup assistant, Chloe, was waiting for him. He closed his eyes and pinched the bridge of his nose.

"Are you okay?" Chloe asked.

No, he wasn't okay. Tessa's attitude toward Jo was over the top and disrespectful. It was a side of his friend that he'd never seen before. The conversation he overheard Jo having with Sam made him uneasy.

"Chloe, has Tessa ever lied to you?"

Her eyes darted toward the other side of the room, where Tessa was talking to one of the cameramen, and then back to Taylor. She pressed her lips together and continued to apply powder to his face. Her silence made his gut clench.

She worked without speaking until she finished. When Taylor got up, she whispered in a shaky voice, "I need this job."

The anxiety in her eyes drew him up short. Chloe had been with the show for two seasons now, and Taylor enjoyed working with her. What had he missed? He didn't remember any incidents where Tessa had lied or bullied the young woman, but it was clear by her expression that something was going on.

It took a lot of effort to pretend that everything was okay when they started working that morning. He flubbed his lines more than usual, and they had to reshoot him describing the next steps they were going to take to restore the kitchen so many times that was all they accomplished by the time the crew broke for lunch.

He'd just sat down when Jo came into the kitchen with Callie.

"Hi, Callie, it's good to see you again," Taylor said. "Let me introduce you to the crew."

"I'll be right back," Jo said.

Taylor had just finished making introductions when Jo came back to the kitchen. The color had drained from her face and she was shaking, her breath coming in shallow gasps.

He rushed over to her and grasped her shoulders. "Jo, what's wrong?"

"They're gone."

"What do you mean? What's gone?"

Callie came to Jo's side, looking at her anxiously.

"The letter and her freedom papers are gone," she said in a broken whisper.

Before what Jo had said registered with him, Tessa interrupted. "Don't worry, you'll get your letter and papers back just as soon as they've been authenticated."

There were gasps from members of the crew, and Jo went completely still at his side. Callie tightened her grip on Jo, leaning in to whisper something in her ear. She kept one arm around her while she reached for her phone with the other.

"Dax, I need Isiah at Halcyon right now," Callie said in a shaky voice.

"She may have convinced all of you that the private investigator's report wasn't true, but I'm not falling for it. Once the report comes back proving that letter is fake, you'll own Halcyon free and clear."

Taylor couldn't believe what he was hearing. Somewhere along the line, Tessa had gone from being supportive to overprotective and now....

"You had no right," Jo shouted.

Taylor saw the pain and fury in Jo's gaze and started to move toward her, but a sharp look from Callie stopped him in his tracks.

"I had every right. Taylor doesn't know what's best for him, but I do."

A FEW tense minutes later, Dax walked in with a tall Black man wearing a tan sheriff's uniform. Dax immediately went over to his wife and Jo while the sheriff stood by with his hands on his hips.

"Anyone care to explain what's happening here?" he asked, looking around the room.

"I'd like to report a theft," Jo said.

Tessa scoffed. "Oh, please."

"Stop it, Tess," Taylor bit out.

Jo's face was pale and drawn. The sheriff took her arm and led her over to the table. "Let's have you sit down. Can someone get her a glass of water?" he called out. Once she had a glass in her hand and had taken a couple of sips, he crouched down so he was at eye level. "Jo, what happened here today?"

The tension in the room grew when in a low, shaky voice Jo explained how Callie had come by to pick up the letters and how they weren't in her dresser drawer where she'd been keeping them.

"And you didn't give Ms. Caldwell permission to go into your room and remove the documents?" Isiah confirmed.

Jo shook her head, looking Taylor in the eye as if she were daring him to call her a liar. "No."

Isiah stood up and walked over to Tessa. "Tessa Caldwell, you are under arrest for burglary."

When the sheriff started to reach for his handcuffs, Tessa rushed over to Taylor, her fingers digging into his arm. "You can't let him do this. I was only looking out for you."

For the first time he saw real fear in her eyes. He stood frozen, his eyes darting between Tessa and Jo. He had a responsibility toward Tessa, but all he could think about was comforting Jo.

Taylor put his hands on her shoulders and gave her a little shake. "Stop it, Tess. Go with the sheriff. I'll be right behind you. I'll call our lawyer, and I'm sure you'll be out after a few hours."

"That's enough." Isiah put Tessa's arms behind her back and put the handcuffs on while he read her rights.

Tessa swore at Jo and threatened to have the sheriff fired as he started to lead her away.

"She'll be booked in the jail tonight. She'll go before the judge in the morning," he called over his shoulder.

Taylor looked around at the shocked faces in the room. He cleared his throat. "Filming will be suspended for the time being. I have some calls I need to make. I'll give you an update as soon as I can."

"I want my letters back." Jo's voice was strained, and a tear slipped down her cheek.

Taylor started toward her, but Callie stepped between them. "I think I'd better take care of Jo. You have other things you need to do."

Taylor ran his hand through his hair. "I need to call a lawyer and get over to the jail. Jo, I'm sure this is just a misunderstanding. Tessa would never—" he started.

Jo's head jerked up. "Get out."

Dax grabbed his arm and pulled him outside. "What the hell is wrong with you?"

Taylor ran his hands over his face. "I just… she may have gone too far, but Tessa is always looking out for my best interests."

Dax scowled at him. "I'd really like to know how stealing from Jo is in your best interests. When you figure that out, you can let me know. Until then, go deal with your friend."

When he arrived at Town Hall, Tessa was spitting mad, pacing the small cell in the back of the sheriff's office.

"It's too late for a hearing tonight. She can post bail in the morning," Isiah said without looking up from the computer.

"I am not going to spend the night in this hillbilly jail," Tessa screeched.

"I've already called our lawyer. He's going to have some- one here to represent you in the morning."

"You need to make Jo drop the charges right now—she can't do this to me. I had every right to take those letters. These people don't know their place."

Taylor stopped pacing in front of Tessa's cell and stared at her, seeing her for the first time.

The chair crashed to the floor when Isiah suddenly stood up. He picked it up and slammed it back in its place. "You have five more minutes with your friend and then visiting hours are over." He said "friend" as if it left a bad taste in his mouth.

"Tessa, I'm doing the best I can. I'll be here first thing in the morning."

She reached through the bars of the cell, grabbing his arm. "Halcyon is yours. I know when the lab is done with the letters, everyone will see they are fake and she's a fraud."

"Where did you send them?"

"I'm not going to let anyone guilt you into getting them back before they've been authenticated." She went over to the cot and sat down with her arms crossed.

Isiah came back in and snapped, "Time's up."

"I'll be here first thing in the morning."

He rushed back to Halcyon to find both Callie and Mae talking quietly in the butler's pantry.

"How is she?"

Callie glanced at him with a sad expression while she prepared a cup of tea.

"How do you think she is?" Mae glared at him. "I don't know where you're spending the night, but it's not here."

Taylor held his hands up. "Okay, I'll just grab a few things and stay with Uncle Robert tonight."

Mae followed him to his room and stood outside with her hands on her hips, tapping her toe.

"Are you serious?" he said in a hushed voice. "Do you really think I need to be watched?"

"I think I need to make sure my friend is safe from you and your producer."

"Tessa shouldn't have taken the letters. That was wrong, but...."

Mae grabbed him by the shirt and pulled him back into the kitchen.

"I want to make sure Jo doesn't hear you. I don't want her to be upset any more than she already is. You don't seem to understand the bigger picture here, so let me explain it to you." Mae's eyes flashed with anger. "Your friend stole documents from Jo. Your privileged White friend who has been rude to just about every Black person she had come in contact with in this town, and who has fired Sam and Minh from your show because they don't 'have the right look.'" Mae smirked when he flinched. "Yeah, that friend. Pull your head out of your ass and think about how Jo is feeling right now. A White woman who has treated her horribly stole her ancestor's emancipation papers and accused her of lying about them. Think. About. That." Mae poked him in the chest with each word.

A knot formed in his stomach. "I... I didn't realize—"

"No, you didn't."

"Good night, Taylor." Callie's voice was firm as she came over to stand with Mae.

Taylor nodded. There was nothing he could say. Every word Mae said was like a slap in the face—one that he deserved.

Dax was getting out of his truck when Taylor walked out.

"I know I have no right to ask after what just happened, but I need your help."

"What do you need?"

"Tessa wouldn't tell me where she sent Jo's papers. If there's anything you can do to find them and get them back, I'll pay whatever it takes."

"I'll see what I can do."

"Thank you."

He got into his car and gripped the steering wheel tightly, trying to stop his hands from shaking. He drew in a shaky breath and put the car into gear.

He was numb when he pulled into Uncle Robert's yard. He dropped down onto the top step of the porch and put his head in his hands. Tessa's actions had left him reeling. How was he going to fix this? He waited for Uncle Robert to come out and give him words of wisdom the way he always did in the past, but he never came. The house was dark when he finally went inside. There was a dim light under Uncle Robert's door, and he could hear the soft swish of pages turning. He didn't knock. Feeling alone and defeated, he lay down on top of the covers of the guest bed and stared at the ceiling.

Tessa was released first thing in the morning. Taylor picked her up at the jail after a sleepless night. She came out just as angry and belligerent as she'd gone in. Her lack of remorse added to his growing sense of unease. He spent the day huddled in her hotel room fielding phone calls from the network and talking to her lawyer. Each minute that passed, the walls seemed to close in more.

The network and Tessa agreed that the best thing would be for Taylor to ask Jo to drop the charges and have filming resume as soon as possible. He was the only one who wasn't happy about the idea. Jo was the victim and yet the network and Tessa were talking about her as if she were a nuisance instead of a person. He felt trapped between his obligation to the show and his feelings for Jo. It didn't help that Tessa continued to take out her anger by heaping abuse on Jo to the point Taylor's patience wore thin.

"Just shut up, Tess," he said in a terse voice.

She paused her rant and glared at him. "What the hell is your problem?"

"Stop complaining about Jo. You're the one who took those papers; she didn't do anything."

"I did it to protect you. That's my job." She leaned across the small table he was sitting at in her hotel room. "How do you think you've managed to be so successful? Because I shield you. I take care of all the ugly and unpleasant stuff so you can smile and look good on camera."

His frustration morphed into anger. "It works both ways, Tess. You wouldn't be here if it weren't for my smile."

Tessa dropped into her chair with a stunned look at the deadly calm tone in Taylor's voice.

They locked eyes, and for the first time since they started working together, he didn't blink.

"Of course, you're right." She gave him a forced smile. "We're partners. My priority is always the show. I'm just trying to do my job."

"I know that, but this time you went about it the wrong way."

"I had to do something. You were too caught up in your relationship with her to see straight."

"I think I can see pretty clearly right now."

Tessa's eyes narrowed. "Then you understand that you have an obligation to the network to get this season of the show filmed. You can't walk away now, Taylor. You'll never get another chance to prove yourself."

She was right—he had a contract, and he'd worked too hard to get to this point to fail. He would make Jo understand and he'd get Halcyon restored. There was no other option. He thought about Ada Mae, understanding for the first time what it must have felt like for her to be trapped.

CHAPTER TWELVE

HER LETTERS were gone. They were a talisman, the physical connection to the past that brought her to Colton and Halcyon. Thinking about Tessa coming into her room and taking them made Jo's skin crawl.

She ignored the worried looks and words of comfort from Callie and Mae and stumbled into the small parlor, the room where she always felt closest to Ada Mae. She sank down on her knees in front of the fireplace and wept. She cried for herself, she cried for Ada Mae and all of her ancestors who were tied to Halcyon, and she cried for Taylor, for the man she'd thought he was. When she had no more tears, she drew her knees up to her chest and stared at the mantel, wanting to be the little bird who flew away.

At some point Mae brought her a blanket and wrapped it around her shoulders. Both Callie and Mae tried to get her to go to bed, but she couldn't bring herself to leave the parlor.

"Ada Mae is in this room," she said.

Callie crouched down next to her and whispered, "I understand."

Callie left and came back with the eucalyptus plant she'd given her as a housewarming present and pushed it into her hands.

Jo buried her face in the thick silvery-green leaves. Callie did understand. Jo remembered the story Dax told her about the vision they'd both shared. She looked up at her friend, who had tears in her eyes. "Thank you. She's still here." She rubbed one of the leaves between her fingers. "I was afraid if the letters were gone, that somehow I would lose her."

Callie nodded and wrapped her in a hug. "I'll tell you a secret. Ada Mae was there for me when I needed her. She helped me see that I wasn't alone. I have a whole group of people who will be there for me when I need them—and so do you."

Jo nodded and wiped her eyes. She pulled herself up from the floor and carefully set the plant on the mantel. Callie moved to her side and took her hand. She took a deep shuddering breath. She'd taken the time she needed to mourn; now it was time to figure out how she was going to move forward.

THE NEXT morning, Jacob showed up with a new lock for her bedroom door and Dax arrived with a security system both he and Jacob insisted on installing. He also came with the news that he'd located the lab where Tessa had sent her letters, and that Uncle Robert had volunteered to act as a courier and was currently on a flight to retrieve them.

Every time the door opened, she expected it to be Taylor, but the morning passed without any sign of him. Jo appreciated her friends' concern, but by that afternoon their hovering began to feel stifling. After lunch she convinced everyone she would be okay on her own, and they reluctantly left with promises to check in on her later. Finally alone, Jo went to her garden. She stabbed at the dirt with her trowel, muttering curses with each jab, taking out her frustrations on the earth.

The weed she pulled fell from her hands when she heard Tessa's voice.

"Just use your charm on her like you did before. We have too much invested in this season to fail. They've already proposed a two-part special for unveiling of the finished project."

Jo took a deep breath to steady herself. She slowly pulled her gloves off, using the time to gather her thoughts and steel her heart.

She found them standing in the front hallway, speaking in hushed tones when she came in.

"I was wondering when I'd see you again," she said.

Both of their heads jerked up. Taylor gave her a slight smile, while Tessa made no attempt to hide the malice in her eyes.

Taylor came toward her. "We came to talk to you about the show. Tessa and I have been talking to the network, and we can't delay resuming the production."

"I never asked you to do that."

"I appreciate that. Starting production means that Tessa will be working here again, and it would make things easier if you would agree to drop the charges."

"No." She shook her head. "Absolutely not."

"You're just being difficult. What is it that you want, money?" Tessa asked.

"I'm talking to Taylor, not you," she said firmly.

Her eyes met Taylor's, and she forced herself not to respond to the apprehension she saw in their blue depths.

Jo pointed at Tessa. "She is not allowed in this house."

"Tessa isn't just my producer; she's my business partner. She owns part of the show."

"She doesn't need to be in the house to do her job."

"Absolutely not, I need to be here. Taylor can't do this without me."

Jo saw the slight flinch from Taylor. Did he even realize what Tessa's words did to him? Sorrow mingled with her anger. She always had her parents to build her up when anyone tried to tear her down. Who was there for Taylor?

She looked Tessa in the eye. "I disagree. Taylor is perfectly capable of doing his job without you."

Tessa stiffened as if she'd been slapped. "How dare you? You don't know anything about Taylor."

"I know that he's smarter about the show than you give him credit for. I know that he's scared, and I know that someday he'll figure out that he deserves a partner who will support him and not constantly try to undermine his confidence. And most importantly, I know that in his heart he wants to do what's best for Halcyon, even if you don't."

Tessa's face twisted into a mask of hatred.

There was a note of resignation tinged with sorrow in Taylor's voice when he spoke. "The thing is, I put ownership of Halcyon into the production company before I knew about your claim. I thought it made sense at the time. It would mean that we would get more tax breaks." Taylor's shoulders slumped. "It doesn't matter."

Tessa tossed her hair over her shoulder. Her lip curled into a smug smile. "What does matter is that I am also a part owner of the production company, so I also have a stake in Halcyon."

Taylor's head jerked toward Tessa and Jo saw a flare of anger in his eyes. She fought to stay calm through her own rising panic. The idea of Tessa having any kind of claim on Halcyon twisted her insides. No matter what it took, she would defend the house from Tessa.

She hardened her heart against the distress in Taylor's eyes. He needed to make a choice. "You can get out of the partnership."

"I can't dissolve the production company. I'll lose every- thing I've been working for over the last five years." Taylor glanced at Tessa. "We'll make this work. Tessa knows that she can't run the production the way she did before."

Tessa wasn't going to change. How did Taylor not see it? She stood there with her arms crossed, rigid, unmoving, and determined to get her way.

"This time it will be different, I promise," Taylor continued.

"You really are just like the colonel," Jo said quietly.

"I'm nothing like Absolem."

"You make promises you can't keep, and you ignore the truth even when it's right in front of you, and—" Her voice broke. "—you say you love this house, but you don't know what love is."

She refused to cry with Tessa in the room. She would save her tears for later. She'd thought she might have a chance at getting through to him, but it was clear that Taylor was going to choose fear over love.

"You're wrong, Jo. I can make this work. I can make this work for both of us."

"Saying that over and over isn't going to make it true. Since the day we met, all you've talked about is how much this house means to you..." She fought to keep her voice from breaking. "...how much you love it. But Halcyon was just a business transaction to you. I overheard what the two of you were saying about using your charm to get what you want. I know now that every time you acted like you cared, it was nothing more than a lie you were telling to get your way."

Taylor flinched. "I wasn't lying to you, Jo."

"There's nothing more to say, Taylor. You've made your choice."

Jo paused when she started to walk out and turned back to Tessa. "I'm sorry to disappoint you, but I've put a lock on my door so you won't be able to steal anything else from me."

She left on unsteady legs and barely made it to her car before collapsing into the driver's seat. She dropped her head to the steering wheel and let her tears flow. When she saw Taylor come out of the house and head in her direction, she swiped her eyes and jammed the key into the ignition. She sped out of the driveway, watching Taylor call after her in the rearview mirror. She drove on autopilot, ending up in front of the Catfish Café. She took a deep breath and got out of the car.

"Jo, what's wrong, honey?" Tillie asked as soon as she set foot through the door.

"Tillie, I...." She couldn't hold it together anymore. She broke down and started to cry.

"Come on, sweetie." Tillie put her arm around her shoulder and quickly led her to the back of the café.

Instead of stopping at a booth, she took Jo through the kitchen, calling to the cook to take over as she led her out the back to a small cottage across the street.

Tillie pushed her through the front door into a cozy room with warm white walls and wood floors. The fireplace was framed by floor-to-ceiling bookshelves filled with cookbooks and mystery novels. The space was warm and inviting. She instantly felt at home. Tillie gestured for Jo to sit on the sofa covered in magnolia blossoms on a pale royal-blue background while she started a fire. She tucked a soft blanket around Jo's shoulders before going into the kitchen to turn the kettle on. She returned with a cup of tea and a bottle of whiskey.

"Take your pick."

Jo wiped her eyes and took a sip of tea. "I'm sorry, Tillie, I didn't mean to lose it like that."

Tillie leaned back against the cushions, looking at her thoughtfully. "Are you ready to talk about it?"

Jo swallowed past the lump in her throat. "I'm so embarrassed and mad at myself."

She went on to tell Tillie about what happened. When she finished, Tillie had a glass of whiskey in her hand and a thunderous expression on her face.

"The thing is, I wanted him to pick me. I wanted him to choose both of us working together to make Halcyon something really special. Was I wrong to think we could have had that?"

"Any woman in love would expect nothing less."

Was she in love? Meeting Taylor made her think she might be ready to fall in love again. Maybe not the head over heels kind of love that had broken her heart before, but with Taylor she'd started to believe she could have something more. A lover who was also a partner, someone who respected her and made her feel... wanted.

She took a deep breath, fighting a losing battle against another round of tears. "I can't leave and start over this time."

"That's not true—you could sell Taylor your half of the house," Tillie said, bluntly.

She shuddered at the thought. "Oh no." Jo shook her head vehemently. "Leaving Halcyon would break my heart again. I love living here. I've never felt more at home than I do in Colton."

"That's what I wanted to hear," Tillie said with an approving smile.

"I'm just tired. I feel like all I've done since I moved into Halcyon is defend myself and Ada Mae's memory."

"Let's look at this like the smart, savvy businesswomen we are. Tessa and Taylor have a partnership that has given her the idea that she can claim part ownership of the house. Even if that were true—and I doubt that it is—half of Halcyon is yours. Don't think of it as negotiating with Taylor; you're negotiating with the production company. If getting the show filmed is as important as he says it is and they want to film in the house, they're going to have to negotiate with you."

Tillie was right. She had to put her feelings for Taylor aside and safeguard Halcyon.

"You need a plan, honey. What is it that you want? Do you want Taylor to stop filming the show? You could kick him out and insist on hiring another contractor to do the work."

"I'm not sure."

"You can't be all wishy-washy when you meet with him. You have to know what you want."

Thank goodness for Tillie's calm reasoning. Of course she was right—when she saw Taylor again, she needed to be able to state her position clearly and without emotion.

Tillie insisted that Jo spend the night. They sat up late into the night making a list of demands for Taylor while they drank whiskey and overindulged on pie and fried chicken. With a full belly and a confidence boost, Jo headed back to Halcyon the next morning.

Tillie gave her a fierce hug before she left. "There's a whole bunch of folks who are rooting for you, honey, and we've all got your back. Just remember that."

Jo gave her a kiss on the cheek and braced herself to face Taylor. On the short drive from town, she did her best to ready herself for the conversation she was about to have. Jo reminded herself when she walked into the house that while Ada Mae didn't have the freedom to leave, Jo had the right to choose to stay. It was a privilege that she wasn't going to take for granted.

Taylor was sitting at the kitchen table when she got home. This time she noticed how his clothes were rumpled and saw the dark circles under his eyes. She ignored the sympathetic stirrings of her heart and sat down at the table, clasping her hands in front of her.

"Jo, I—"

She held up her hand. "I have some things I'd like to say."

"Okay."

"Since you decided to be careless and sign away your ownership of Halcyon to your production company, and if what Tessa said is true, you may not have an equal stake in the house. If I'm the majority owner of the house, all decisions must be approved by me. I am not going to make you stop production on your show." She softened her voice. "I wouldn't take away something that you love." He gripped the edge of the table, and she knew her words had hit home. She couldn't back down now. She straightened her shoulders and continued. "I understand that Tessa is a part of your production team and will be working on this project; however, she is not allowed to be in this house unless she is under your direct supervision. You may film in the other parts of the house; however, the small parlor and the garden are off-limits." She fought against the tears she refused to let fall. "You should have been honest with me from the beginning and told me that you had put your ownership of the house in the production company."

Taylor remained silent for a few minutes before he took a deep breath and said, "You're right—I should have said something. To be honest, I didn't think…." He grimaced. "Obviously I didn't think about a lot of things." He shook his head sadly. "I don't know if I can guarantee any of your conditions."

"That's your problem, not mine. My terms are non-negotiable."

He looked at her with eyes filled with anguish. Any sorrow she felt for him was smothered by her determination.

"And what about us?"

His blue eyes held hers, searching her face for what—hope? She pressed her lips together and shook her head.

"We are partners in Halcyon and nothing else. I deserve to be with someone who will value what's in his heart over a business relationship. I was foolish enough to fall for a man who lied to get what he wanted once; I'm mad at myself for doing it again, but I'm lucky I found out now before...." Her voice hitched. "Would you have slept with me to get what you wanted?"

Taylor clenched his fists. "I can't believe you would think I would do that."

"And I can't believe that you would think I would be willing to let Tessa back in this house after what she did."

"I don't have a choice, Jo."

"Yes, you do!" she shouted.

"I can't. You're asking me to give up everything I've worked for."

Jo shook her head. "I don't know what to say to convince you that I'm not asking you to give up *History Reborn*. This is about you. I don't understand why you're willing to let Tessa have so much control."

Taylor ran his hand through his hair. "Tessa has always looked out for me; I owe her a lot. *History Reborn* wouldn't be a success without her."

Suddenly, Jo understood. "You're afraid."

Taylor jumped up. "That's bullshit." He stormed out of the room.

His reaction proved that she was right—he was scared. She sat down with her computer and sent an update to her lawyer. When she finished, she went to her room and climbed under the covers. She drew her knees up to her chest and finally allowed her tears to fall.

It was almost unbearable to stay in the house in the days that followed. She and Taylor continued to barely speak to each other. Taking a break from the tension, Jo decided to treat herself with a mocha and some new gardening magazines from the bookstore and coffee shop Callie had opened next door to the library.

The Spring Street Book and Coffee Co. was charming, with walls lined with books and small tables featuring different themed book displays. There were overstuffed chairs scattered around the room where customers could take their time perusing books while they enjoyed a coffee and pastry. One customer in particular caught her eye when she walked in.

She rushed over to where Chloe was sitting crying quietly.

"Chloe, what's wrong?"

"I've been fired."

"What?"

Chloe wiped at her eyes. "Tessa fired me."

Jo sat down next to her. "Tell me exactly what happened."

"She… she said I wasn't a team player and I couldn't be trusted since I talked to you."

"I see." Jo tried to sound calm for Chloe's sake.

"Tessa will never give me a reference, and she said she'd make sure I never got another job. I was sharing a house back in LA and I gave up my room. I don't know what I'm going to do."

Jo put her arm around Chloe's shoulders. "It's going to be okay. We're going to figure something out."

"I just feel so dumb. Tessa kept promising me that she would promote me to be a production assistant. That's the job I really wanted, but she always had an excuse for why she couldn't, and I believed her. I think she knew the whole time."

"Knew what?"

"That I'm mixed. I'm light enough that most people just assume I'm White, and I thought if I didn't say anything…." She buried her face in her hands. "I'm so embarrassed."

"Why would that matter?"

"It's kind of a known thing that Tessa doesn't want any minorities working on the show. Even the homeowners that they feature are always White."

Jo drew back with a frown. It made sense now, why she didn't want Sam and Minh back to work on the house.

"Just when I thought Taylor couldn't be any worse," Jo muttered.

Chloe shook her head. "The thing is, I don't know if Taylor realizes."

"Being willfully ignorant isn't an excuse. Taylor doesn't matter anymore. What does matter is helping you, and I have an idea."

JO TOOK Chloe across the park to the Barton Building. Dax looked up with surprise when Jo walked in.

"Dax, remember how we were talking about hiring an office assistant? Well, I'd like to introduce you to Chloe Michaels. She needs a job, and I think she would be an excellent candidate."

Dax raised his eyebrows. "Okay."

"Chloe also needs a place to stay, and I thought if you haven't leased it already, she might be interested in renting the apartment you let me use when I first came here."

Chloe's eyes grew wide. "I can't. I'm sure I can't afford—"

"I pay my employees a living wage, Chloe. I'm sure you'll be able to afford it." Dax pulled a key out of his desk drawer. "It's the second door on the left. Why don't you go on up and take a look to see if you like it," he said, pointing to the stairway.

Chloe took the key and turned to Jo, her eyes bright with unshed tears. "You don't have to do this."

"Yes, I do. You deserve better than what happened to you, and I'm going to make it right." Jo gave Chloe a gentle push toward the stairs.

As soon as Chloe was out of earshot, Dax looked at her with a raised eyebrow. "Care to share what that was all about?"

"I'm sorry to ambush you like that but I had to do something."

"That's fine, but what happened?"

Dax swore under his breath when Jo shared Chloe's story.

"I can't believe he would do something so stupid," Dax muttered under his breath when she finished with what she'd learned about Taylor's ownership of Halcyon. "I'm sorry, Jo, I wish there was something I could say or do but honestly, I don't know what that would be."

"Neither do I. All I could think about was making sure Chloe was taken care of. Now, I need to do everything I can to protect Halcyon from Tessa."

"What about Taylor?"

"He made his choice." She swallowed, trying to keep her voice from breaking. "I can't fight whatever hold Tessa has on him."

When Chloe returned, Dax said, "Chloe, you're hired. You can start tomorrow and keep the key to the apartment. You can move in anytime."

"Thank you." Chloe's voice broke and she started to cry again.

Jo gave Chloe a hug. "We're happy you're here."

THAT NIGHT her dream was so real and sharp it took her breath away. It was another dream where Ada Mae was pleading with the colonel.

"You refuse to listen." Ada Mae's voice was filled with anguish. She held the colonel's lapels fisted in her hands. *"You can't have everything you want. You'll have to give something up."*

When the colonel spoke, he looked directly at Jo. *"Don't give up on him. He'll learn—I wish I had."*

CHAPTER THIRTEEN

TAYLOR DID a double-take when he pulled up to Uncle Robert's house and saw the other man sitting next to him.

As soon as he got out of the truck, his brother got up and walked toward him with a thunderous expression and shoved him. "What the fuck is wrong with you?"

His eyes flicked toward Uncle Robert. "I guess you heard about what happened with Tessa."

"How could you be so stupid?" His brother shoved him so hard he almost lost his balance.

"Why doesn't anyone understand? You know Halcyon means the world to me, but I have the show to consider."

Uncle Robert got up and strode over. "You got a lot of folks upset with you, son."

His brother muttered an oath and walked back to the house. The door slammed behind him. Growing up, he'd seen his brother annoyed with him and they'd had their fair share of sibling arguments, but he'd never seen Dylan angry with him the way he was now.

He headed to the porch and dropped into one of the rocking chairs with his head in his hands. Uncle Robert went inside, and he could hear the low murmur of voices from the two men. A moment later his brother came out and sat down next to him.

"Explain to me why you think you can bring Tessa back to Halcyon and expect Jo to be okay with it?"

"I don't have a choice. I have a contract with the network and Tessa is my partner in the production company. I can't fail at this. I'm going to prove you wrong once and for all."

Dylan frowned at him. "What are you talking about?"

"You, Mom, and Dad—I know I'm the family disappointment. Restoring Halcyon is my chance to show you that what I do matters. I may not save lives in an operating room, but restoring old homes has its own value."

"Taylor, no one thinks of you as being a disappointment. Where did you even get that idea?"

"Mom and Dad talk about you with so much pride. They brag about you to all of their friends. I can't even get them to come and visit me on the set. The three of you have always spoken this language of medicine and science and I'm sorry I don't understand it, but just once I'd like it if any of you tried to understand the language of history that I speak."

"I'm sorry if you've felt left out, I really am. I can't speak for our parents, but I've never thought of you or your accomplishments as anything less than mine."

"Then what do all the comments about not taking things seriously mean?" Taylor shot back.

Dylan sighed and hung his head for a moment. "Taylor, you've always been the golden child. Let me finish," he growled when Taylor scoffed. "You're one of those lucky people who walks into a room and everyone says *hooray, Taylor's here*. I envy you for that. I've watched you over the years. If there are two paths and one is harder than the other, you always choose the easier one."

"What do you mean by that? I work hard I—"

Dylan held his hand up. "Yes, you do work hard, but I've watched you give Tessa a lot of free rein to take care of some of the more difficult aspects of the show and your life."

"Why is that a problem? She's the producer."

"Because over time she's taken over more than just the show; she practically runs your life. I get that it's convenient for you to have her manage the show, but she's managing you too."

"You're exaggerating. Tessa is a good friend and my business partner. She looks after me, and she's saved me from making some really bad decisions. At least she believes in me."

"Does she? The few times I've been around her, all I hear is her questioning your judgment."

"Maybe if you made more time to visit, you'd get to know her better."

"Every time I try to arrange to see you, Tessa makes sure there's a reason that I can't. She does the same thing with Mom and Dad, Taylor."

"That's a lie. Tessa wouldn't do that."

Dylan's mouth pressed into a thin line as he pulled his phone out. He scrolled through his screen for a minute and then handed it to Taylor.

He stared at the email from Tessa telling his brother that Taylor's schedule was too busy for him to visit when they started their work on Halcyon.

"There's more if you want to see them," Dylan said quietly.

He didn't but he needed to. He swallowed and nodded. When he finished, he looked at Dylan.

"Why didn't they say anything?" he asked in a gruff voice.

"We tried; you wouldn't listen. Anytime I've tried to talk to you about Tessa, you accused me of being biased against her. The thing is, I am. I don't like her and I don't like what you're like when you're around her. You're my brother and I love you, but I'm not going to stay quiet anymore." Dylan looked Taylor in the eye. "If that means that we don't have a relationship going forward, then I'll have to learn to live with that, but I'm not going to pretend like I'm okay with the decisions you've made."

Taylor's gut clenched. He couldn't believe his brother was giving him an ultimatum like this.

He blew out a shaky breath. "I have some things to think about."

Uncle Robert came out and leaned against one of the porch columns. "You are welcome to stay here tonight if you'd like."

"Thanks, I think I'll take you up on that if you don't mind." He looked at his brother. "How long are you here for?"

"I'll be around for a while."

"Don't you need to get back to the hospital?"

Dylan glanced at Uncle Robert. "I haven't taken vacation in a long time. I thought my brother might need some help."

Taylor's gaze shifted to Uncle Robert. "I guess I have you to thank for this."

Uncle Robert pulled his cap down low over his eyes. "I don't know what you're talkin' about. You two are grown men; you make your own decisions."

He stepped off the porch and headed into the barn, leaving Taylor with his brother.

Dylan got up and patted him on the shoulder. "I'm going to unpack. I'll be here if you want to talk some more."

Taylor rested his hands on his knees and stared out at Uncle Robert's empty field. Dylan was right—it had become easier to let Tessa handle the more difficult or inconvenient aspects of his job and his life.

He had chosen the easier path. He hadn't seen how Tessa questioning his judgment had undermined his confidence. How many times had she reinforced his belief that his parents and his brother didn't support him, using the fact that they never came to visit as proof? He felt sick to his stomach knowing that she had been the one keeping them apart.

He walked halfway to Halcyon, lost in thought, before he realized where he was going. When he saw Tessa's car in the driveway, he quickened his pace. He walked in and stood paralyzed when he heard what Tessa was saying to Jo. He quietly moved closer and hovered out of sight outside the door to the small parlor.

"The crew will be back the day after tomorrow and we'll start filming in the small parlor, so you won't have access to this room for a while," Tessa said.

"No, you won't," Jo replied.

"Excuse me? I don't think you're in any position to tell me what to do."

"Actually, I am. As I just explained to Taylor, I am the majority owner of this house. You're going to have to get approval from me for anything you want to do going forward."

"I'm afraid your math skills are a little lacking, honey. The production company owns half of Halcyon." Tessa smirked.

"Yes, and you own half of the production company—as you said, your share is only twenty-five percent."

"It doesn't matter. Taylor will do whatever I tell him to. He knows he can't run the show without me."

Taylor sucked in a breath.

"Because you've convinced him of that. You like having control over him, don't you? You don't want a partner, you want a puppet."

Tessa's eyes flashed with fury. "I've worked too damn hard to let you ruin everything."

"What am I ruining for you by being supportive of Taylor instead of manipulating him?"

Tessa's voice shook with rage. "I know what's best for him. I don't care who he sleeps with, but you need to know your place. I'm the one who made him the success he is today."

"And without him you'll lose all your power, money, and control, won't you? That's why you keep such a tight rein on Taylor—without him you'll be nothing."

"If I can't have control of him, no one can."

He recoiled at Tessa's statement. He felt ill at the thought of how many of her lies he'd ignored. And he'd let it happen, given her control because it had been easier than doing the work himself. That stopped now.

Tessa looked over her shoulder and smiled when he walked into the room. "Taylor, I'm so glad you're here. I have exciting news. I talked to the network this morning and pitched them the idea of having a Civil War ball for the season finale. We can have actors dressed up like the colonel and his wife showing off the restored house. All the men will be in uniform and the women in those big dresses."

"That's a disgusting idea. I'm not going to use this house to celebrate the Confederacy."

"You know you're not good at the promotional stuff—that's my part of the job."

Taylor cocked his head. "Aren't I? Is that true, or do you just want to have control? What is it you just said… If you can't have control of me, no one will? I heard every word you said, Tessa."

Her smile slipped and there was a flash of anger in her eyes. "Taylor, you misunderstood. That's not—"

"Stop it, Tessa, you aren't going to lie and manipulate yourself out of the situation this time."

"That's not what I've been doing. I'm just looking out for you. Jo's the one who is a liar."

"Jo hasn't lied about anything, but this isn't about Jo. This is about us. I can't keep working with you, Tess."

Her eyes grew wide and she shook her head. "You don't mean that—you don't know what you're saying. You've been under so much stress lately. I can arrange for you to take a break and—"

"You're not going to arrange anything for me anymore."

"Don't do this, Taylor. You can't throw away our relationship like this. If you want to change how the production is run, we can do that."

"You're lying. I know that now. You aren't going to change—you don't want to."

"Taylor, you wouldn't have been able to accomplish anything if it weren't for me." Tessa's eyes narrowed. "So you're willing to give up your show and everything we've worked so hard for over a rundown house and some kind of bizarre slave fantasy where you're reliving the past."

There was a gasp from Jo.

Tessa whirled around. "I hope you're happy. You got your reparations or whatever you think you people deserve, but I doubt you will be happy. You people are never content with what you have."

"Stop it, Tessa." Taylor reached out and jerked her out of Jo's face.

She turned on him. "We have a contract. I'll make your life a living hell if you walk away from me. Don't forget I own a quarter of this house."

He locked eyes with Jo. "That may be, but you don't control me anymore. I'm giving up the show."

He backed away when Tessa tried to grasp his arm. Her eyes grew wide. "You're making a mistake."

"Jo was right—I am just like the colonel. I refused to see what you were doing and I made promises I couldn't keep, but I do know what love is. It means being willing to let go of something or someone you love even though it will break your heart because you know that they will be better off without you." He looked at Jo. "Absolem didn't learn that lesson, but I have. I'm sorry it took me so long."

Tessa's face was bright red with anger. "You always were a weak fool. You'll never be successful without me."

"Maybe not, but I'll be happier. Goodbye, Tessa."

Tessa clenched her fists at her sides, and for a moment he worried she was going to strike out at Jo. Instead she walked out with her head held high.

He took a deep breath. "I'm so sorry, Jo. You have no reason to believe me, but I didn't know until now just how much I was allowing Tessa to do my thinking for me."

Jo's lips trembled. "Did you know she was a racist?"

"I've never heard her say things like she just did before."

"Did you know she was keeping minorities from being hired on your show?"

He stared at Jo in shock. "Where is this coming from?"

When Jo finished telling him about what happened with Chloe, he could barely contain his anger. His stomach rolled. Ignorance wasn't an excuse for being willfully blind to Tessa's attitude and actions.

"That poor girl felt like she had to hide the fact that she's biracial to keep her job. Maybe you didn't know, but that's only because you didn't want to."

Every word hit him like a punch, and everything she said was true. He forced himself to look Jo in the eye. "I'll figure out a way to fix this mess."

"I don't want Tessa to set foot in this house ever again."

"I'll make sure it doesn't happen." He sighed and blinked up at the ceiling. "It's going to be messy."

Jo's voice softened. "I never wanted you to quit your show, Taylor."

"I don't have a choice. I can't work with Tessa anymore." His phone vibrated with a text from his brother wondering where he was.

"It's my brother. He came down to visit." He shook his head. "That's not true, Dylan came to try and put some sense in my head."

Jo gave him a sad smile. "I'm sorry you had to hear what Tessa said about you, but I'm glad you know now."

"So am I."

"What happens next?" she asked.

"The network will freak out, and there will be a lot of phone calls with lawyers and agents."

"Is there anything I can do?"

"Can you give me a chance to show you that I can do better?"

Jo nodded. Her eyes were bright with unshed tears. "I can do that."

His phone pinged again. He looked down and groaned.

"It's starting."

He walked back to Uncle Robert's just long enough to grab his truck and drive back into town. Dax looked up from his desk with a frown when Taylor walked into the Barton Building.

He cleared his throat. "I was looking for Chloe."

"She just ran across the park to get some coffee."

"Do you mind if I wait?"

"As long as you're not here to cause any more trouble." Dax was always the one who was considered the troublemaker when they were kids and knew he was the one everyone walking by looked at with suspicion.

"Can I ask you a question?"

Dax propped his feet on his desk and folded his arms behind his head. "Shoot."

"How did you do it?"

"Do what?"

"Make people understand that you weren't the terrible person they thought you were."

Dax took his feet down and sat forward. "The first thing I had to do was be ready to face the people I'd hurt and apologize."

The door opened and Chloe came in. He winced when her face paled.

"Hi, Chloe, I was hoping I could talk to you for a minute."

Her eyes darted toward Dax, and Taylor was relieved when he gave her a reassuring nod.

"Okay," she replied with a note of uncertainty.

He took a deep breath and began. "The day we found out Tessa had taken the letters, I asked you if she'd ever lied to you and you didn't answer. You didn't want to say anything then, but I'm asking you now. What has Tessa lied to you about?"

Chloe hesitated and looked at Dax again.

"It's okay, Chloe, he's ready to hear the truth," Dax reassured her.

"I love working as your hair and makeup person, but I hoped I could move up into a production assistant job. Every time a position comes up, Tessa tells me that she asked you and you had someone else in mind."

Taylor shook his head. "She never said anything to me."

"That's what I figured out. There's more." She twisted her hands. "There was a young man who showed up at the house asking about an apprenticeship, and she told him he didn't have the right look to be on camera. She tells that to a lot of people... a lot of Black people. Not just on this shoot, either. I may not look like it, but I'm mixed and when I saw what was happening, I started to worry she'd fire me if she found out. I needed my job and I... I was afraid."

"How the hell didn't I see it?"

Chloe looked at him with surprise. "I thought you knew."

"So this whole time you believed I thought the same way Tessa did? That I was a racist?"

"You were always nice to me, but everyone knows that you always side with Tessa."

Taylor swore under his breath. "I'm sorry that you were ever made to feel afraid at your job. I'm sorry for everything, Chloe. I'm glad that you have a job working with Jo and Dax."

"Thank you. Honestly, I'm relieved that you didn't know. I didn't want to believe that you were...." She bit her lip.

"A racist?"

She nodded.

Taylor shook his head. "I played my part, and I'm sorry."

He asked Chloe if he could buy her coffee sometime when he said goodbye. It was disheartening to lose a good employee because of his own willful ignorance, but Taylor hoped he could build a friendship with her.

Dax walked him out after he said goodbye to Chloe. On the sidewalk, he paused and put his hand on Taylor's shoulder, looking him in the eye.

"That's how you do it. One apology at a time, and then you'll reach a point where you'll have no one left to ask forgiveness from except yourself."

He choked out his thanks. On the drive back to Halcyon, he contemplated what Dax said. He had no problem apologizing, but he didn't know if there would be a day when he'd be ready to forgive himself for ignoring what was right in front of him. Jo's words from when they were looking at the fireplace came back to him. *Sometimes people don't see things until they want to.*

CHAPTER FOURTEEN

THE NEXT few days blurred into a marathon of phone calls with his lawyer, negotiating the end of his show and his partnership with Tessa. Dylan hovered, trying to get him to eat and take a break. He was thankful to have his brother with him. They spent a lot of time on Uncle Robert's porch in the evening, talking and reconnecting. With his brother's encouragement, he reached out to his parents and shared his feelings about his relationship with them. They were painful conversations, but they also offered a chance for a better future with them. If only there were a chance for him to have a future with Jo.

Taylor finished the dinner Dylan insisted he eat. His hand shook when he lifted his glass of water to his lips.

Dylan frowned at him. "You need to sleep."

"Easier said than done."

Dylan cleared his throat. "Dax introduced me to Jo when I stopped by his office. She asked how you were doing. She's worried about you. Why aren't you answering her calls?"

"I don't know what to say to her," he admitted. "She supported and encouraged me, and I threw it all in her face. I'm afraid I've used up all of my chances with her."

"You won't know until you ask."

Taylor nodded. He didn't want to spend the rest of his life wondering what would have been. He pushed up from the table and said, "I'm going for a walk."

He'd planned to give Jo some space, time to heal before he saw her again. But his feet and his heart had other ideas. The hoot of a barn owl sitting in the oak tree in front of Halcyon greeted him as he walked toward the house.

It was strange to knock on the door. His hand hovered in the air for a moment before it connected with the wood.

Jo opened the door with a slight smile. She was wearing a paint-splattered T-shirt and had a smudge of teal paint on her cheek, her hair covered in a bandanna. He shoved his hands in his pockets to keep himself from reaching out to wipe away the smudge, just so he could feel her skin under his fingertips again.

"Can I come in?"

"Of course you can. You didn't have to knock—you live here."

"About that, I should probably make arrangements to move out. I haven't had time to think it through, but I'll start looking for a house in town."

"Please don't." She bit her lip. "Halcyon hasn't... it doesn't feel like home without you here."

"Once you get this place restored, it will feel like home."

"That's another thing—I can't finish the restoration without my contractor."

Taylor's heart thudded. He hated the idea of anyone else working on the house. He swallowed his pride. "I can make some recommendations, and there's Jacob. He would be the first person I'd call."

Jo shook her head. "I don't want to work with Jacob or anyone else; I want to work with you."

He felt hope for the first time in days, and some of the weight that had been pressing down on him lifted.

"Are you sure?"

"You love Halcyon just as much as I do. I never wanted to take it away from you."

"I wanted to take it from you at first. I was arrogant thinking that I was more entitled to the house than you are. I'm sorry, Jo."

"You wanted to restore Halcyon for a long time. You had a plan, and I came along and ruined it. I would be upset too. I was upset when I found out about you."

"I already asked if we could start over once, I'm not going to ask you again, but can we just... be friends?"

Jo reached out and slipped her hand in his. "Friends."

Taylor looked down at where their hands were joined. He brushed his thumb over her knuckles, wanting so much more but willing to be happy with just this one touch. His voice was hoarse. "Friends."

They stayed hand in hand until her cheeks turned pink and the room grew warm. Reluctantly he let go. He brushed his thumb over the spot on her cheek. "What are you painting?"

"I finally picked a color for my room. Do you want to come and take a look?"

She had chosen a shade of light teal that showed off the original woodwork and wasn't too dark for the room.

"I'm not an expert painter, but I think I'm doing okay."

"I think you've done a great job. I like this color. Can I help you finish up?"

"You've only been back a few minutes. You don't have to start working right away."

He picked up the bucket of paint and paintbrush. "Honestly, I've missed this. It would be kind of therapeutic."

"Thanks, I'd love the help."

Taylor brushed on the last coat of paint around the window trim and stood back admiring his work. They spent the rest of the evening working together on Jo's room. He'd gotten so caught up in the show and Tessa's lies, he'd forgot- ten how much fun he and Jo had when they first started working together on the house.

"Maybe tomorrow we can do some work on the kitchen. I was thinking that we should tear up some of the flooring and see if we can find what was originally there."

Jo grinned at him. "I'd love that."

They had already demoed the old cabinets and the wiring and plumbing work Sam and Minh had done was waiting for the finishing touches. Being back in the house and doing something as simple as painting reminded him that he still loved doing restoration work.

"Taylor, are you okay?" Jo was looking at him with a worried expression.

He'd been staring off into space, thinking about how in some ways the show had held him back from doing what he really loved.

"I was thinking about how much I miss this. When we first started working on the house together, we had fun and then I ruined it. I don't want to take for granted this second chance to work on Halcyon—thank you for that, Jo."

She swallowed. Her eyes were bright with unshed tears. "I missed working on the house with you too."

He put his paintbrush down and slowly walked toward her and took her hands in his. "If we're going to be friends again, there's something I need to tell you."

Her eyes grew wide and she licked her lips. "W-what?"

He let go of her hands and lifted up the tip of one of her braids. "You have paint in your hair."

She looked down, and her lips quirked before she burst out into a laugh.

The next morning he and Jo were just getting ready to start replacing some of the more treacherous floorboards on the veranda when a young Black man pulled up in front of the house. He straightened his shoulders and clutched the strap on his messenger bag tightly as she approached.

"Excuse me, Mr. Colton? I'm sorry to interrupt you like this, but I wanted to stop by one more time. I know I can't be on camera, but I'd still like to work on the restoration. You don't have to pay me. I can get another job, but I'd like to work here and learn how to do restoration work. I graduated from the trade school in Greenwood, and I have good references from my teachers."

This must be the young man Chloe told him about the day before. Jo gave him a warm smile and held out her hand. "I'm Josephine Martin. What's your name?"

He shook her hand. "Adam Freeman, ma'am."

"It's nice to meet you. Would you like a cup of coffee or tea?"

"No, thank you, ma'am."

"No need to call me ma'am—Jo is just fine."

Jo nudged Taylor with an expectant look. "Oh, I'm sorry. Adam, it's nice to meet you." He shook his hand. "You stopped by before?"

"Yes, sir, the lady told me I didn't have the right look and you couldn't use me. But I don't care about being on camera. I'm interested in learning about historic preservation." His jaw ticked. "I'll cut my hair if I have to…If you think that will make me look more presentable."

"God no, I would never ask you to do that," Taylor blurted out.

Adam watched him with a hint of hope in his eyes. It was a gut punch. How many times had he come before and was turned away?

"Did the woman who turned you away tell you her name?" he asked, even though he knew what the answer was going to be.

"It was a Miss Caldwell—she said she was the producer. Mr. Colton, I'm a hard worker, and I'll take on any job you'd be willing to give me as long as I can learn about some of your preservation techniques. Everybody knows that you're one of the top experts in the country. When I heard that you were filming here, I thought maybe you would be looking for help. I couldn't let this opportunity pass, so I had to try one more time."

Taylor squeezed his eyes shut and took a deep breath.

"Are you okay, sir?" the young man asked.

Taylor opened his eyes. "No," he answered honestly. "But I will be. Please, you don't have to call me sir—Taylor is just fine."

"Taylor, why don't you take Adam inside and the two of you can sit down and talk."

"That's a good idea."

Jo touched his hand and gave him a reassuring smile. Adam followed him inside, his gaze darting around. Taylor watched him taking in every detail of the house as they passed through the rooms into the kitchen.

Adam reached into his bag and pulled out a folder and handed it to him. "Here's my resumé."

"You're an electrician, I see," Taylor said.

Adam sighed. "I know I don't have…" He pressed his lips together. "…that I don't have the right look," he repeated, "but I'm a hard worker and—"

"I'm sorry about what my producer said to you. That was wrong." He scanned the rest of Adam's resumé. "You just graduated from the trade school in Greenwood with certificates in carpentry and electrical work."

"Yes, sir." Adam nodded. "But I'm really interested in restoring old houses, just like you do."

"I hate to tell you this, but I'm not going to be doing the show anymore."

"I'm sorry for wasting your time," Adam said, starting to stand.

"Wait," Taylor called out. Adam paused and slowly sank back down in his seat. "Even though I don't have the show anymore, I'd like to offer you a paid apprenticeship to work here with me."

The young man's face split into a huge grin.

It was a spur-of-the-moment decision, but as soon as he said it, Taylor knew it was the right one.

"Good news," he said when Jo came in. "I've just hired my first apprentice."

Adam's eyes grew wide. "You've never had an apprentice before?"

"I haven't, so you're going to have to be patient with me."

"Yes, sir."

"Let's start with a tour of the house, and then we can figure out a schedule, and we'll make up the rest from there."

Jo nodded in approval. "Happy to have you helping out, Adam."

When he finished giving Adam a tour, they sat on the veranda for a while. The young man peppered him with questions, and they discussed a work schedule. Jo came out and plopped down next to him, waving goodbye when Adam drove away.

"You did a good thing today, Taylor."

"Please don't compliment me for something I should have done a long time ago."

Jo put her hand on his arm. "Hey, you didn't know and you're trying to make it right. That's all that matters."

"I talked to Chloe and apologized to her."

"I know, she called to tell me. She was really touched that you did that."

"It's not enough. I was careless and gave away part of Halcyon." He gritted his teeth. "Tessa is going to hold that over my head and use it against us if she can."

"She can't hurt me anymore; she already did her worst."

"I'm so sorry, Jo."

"So am I. When we... I liked it when it was just the two of us getting to know each other and Halcyon together."

"That first night I saw you at the Buckthorn, you were so beautiful I forgot for a moment what I was there to do, because all I wanted was to get to know you. Then I found out about your claim, and I was so angry with you. When we started working together, I was intimidated and amazed by how smart and thoughtful you are." He looked down at her upturned face. His fingers itched to reach out and touch her, but he held back. He didn't want to ask for more than she was ready to give. "I was so damn jealous because you seem to be connected to this house in a way that I'm not, even though I've been coming here since I was a boy."

Jo sighed and leaned against him. "I'm sorry, Taylor. I wish I could explain my feelings about Halcyon to you, but it's.... I've kept something, some secrets so close to my heart and I... I don't think I'm ready to yet. I can see how hard you're trying to make amends. I just need some time to...."

"To make sure that I'm not going to hurt you again." He put his finger to her lips when she started to object. "I don't blame you, and I'm glad in a way. My brother was right—things have always come easy to me. I work hard, but I've never put my whole heart and soul into anything." He slid his finger across her lips and cupped her cheek, looking into the depths of her eyes. "I don't want you to make it easy for me. When I earn your trust again, it will be because I worked harder than I've ever worked for anything before."

CHAPTER FIFTEEN

JO SAT on the steps leading out to the garden and lifted her face to the sun. It was a clear crisp fall day, with just enough chill in the air to remind her that winter was coming. Since the night Taylor asked her to give him a chance to earn her trust, they grew closer every day. And each day it became harder to ignore the attraction that flared back to life between them again. But Taylor had told her not to make it easy on him, and Jo still wasn't ready to trust her heart.

Taylor came out and sat down next to her, handing her a travel mug.

She smiled. "You have to stop trying to feed me and bring me tea."

"I'll stop when you start eating better," he said with a frown.

"Fair point." The stress over the last few weeks had taken its toll, and neither of them had been eating as well as they should.

He got up and held his and handed hers out to her. "Ready to go?"

"Where are we going?"

"It's a surprise. Trust me?"

She didn't have a good poker face, and Taylor's expression fell. "Okay, wrong question. Will you come with me, please? I promise it will be fun."

She got up and looked down where he was still holding out his hand. "Let me get my coat."

Once they were on the road, he gestured to the picnic basket on the seat between them. "There's some fresh fruit, pastries, and a thermos with more coffee—help yourself."

Jo opened the basket and pulled out an apple fritter. "Do you want one?"

She handed him the pastry wrapped in a napkin when he held out his hand. She took one for herself, biting into the sugary cinnamon and apple pastry. She finished her treat, licking the last of the sugar with a swipe of her tongue when she froze, realizing Taylor was watching her out of the corner of his eye. She turned away, focusing her attention on the passing landscape through the window to hide her blush.

"Any chance you'll tell me where we're going now?"

Taylor smiled. "Memphis. Just for the day. There are some salvage stores I wanted to go to. We can look for some period fixtures we need for the house, and then there's one other thing I want to do. That's a surprise," he said with a wink that made her stomach do a funny little flip.

"Have you been to Memphis before?" he asked.

"No, have you?"

He nodded. "We've filmed a couple of episodes of the show there. There are a couple of neighborhoods with great antique and salvage yards we can explore."

"I've never been to a salvage store before."

"Then you're in for a treat. There's nothing better than digging through piles of old hardware and fixtures looking for treasure."

Jo smiled. Taylor's enthusiasm was infectious. "You really do love this, don't you?"

"I can't imagine doing anything else. What about you, is there something else that you could picture yourself doing besides computers?"

"I've never thought about it before. I suppose I'd like to teach and pass on what I've learned to the next generation. Especially to Black girls—I want them to see that they can work in careers in tech that they might not have considered."

"I think you'd be a great teacher."

"I volunteered at a mentorship program at a high school in the city. I miss it."

"Would you do something like that here?"

"I would, but I don't think I'd be welcome. Just because Dax was willing to hire me, if anyone calls to do a background check on me, the lies that my ex told will still be there."

Taylor's face fell. "I'm sorry, Jo."

He had asked her to tell him what happened with Oliver again a couple of nights ago, and this time she told him the whole story.

He kept his eyes on the road, but he reached over and took her hand in his. "He's…." Taylor let go of her hand and gripped the steering wheel until his knuckles started to turn white. "I don't have any right to criticize when I haven't treated you any better."

"That's not true."

Saying the words out loud, she realized she meant it. Tay- lor wasn't Oliver. She thought about how kind and caring Taylor had been over the last week. Yes, there were times when he was a little bit cocky and overconfident, but he wasn't pompous.

He cleared his throat. "Thank you for saying that."

Jo sat back with a smile. "So tell me, what are we looking for at this place?" The two-hour drive to Memphis flew by, while Taylor shared stories about some of his favorite junkyard finds. After a quick pit stop, they pulled up to a large warehouse with Heritage Salvage and Antiques painted on the side of the building.

They'd barely set foot inside when customers and employees mobbed Taylor. As far as his fans knew, *History Reborn* would be back for another season. The reality was much more complicated. The network was trying to save the show and Taylor was still trying to untangle himself from his partnership with Tessa. They didn't talk about it, but they both worried about her owning a part of the house.

Jo stood off to the side while Taylor smiled and posed for pictures and signed autographs for fans. She admired how easygoing he was even with some of the more aggressive people, like the woman in skin-tight jeans with a cut-off T- shirt who was currently climbing him like a tree. That caused a surprising sliver of jealousy to shoot through Jo's heart.

The owner came out greeting Taylor with a warm smile and immediately started to shoo everyone away. When an employee mistook Jo for a fan and tried to usher her out with the other customers, Taylor reached out and grabbed her hand, pulling her to his side. The redheaded woman who had just been fawning all over him glared at Jo as she was ushered away.

"You're really good at that," Jo said.

"At what?"

"Dealing with all those people, being nice even when they're pawing all over you."

"It's part of the job. Most of the time, it's really fun interacting with fans."

Jo glanced at his profile, noticing the faint lines of tension around his mouth and eyes. He made it look easy, but it wasn't. She found herself wanting to reach up and smooth away those lines. Taylor chatted with the owner as he led them toward a corner of the massive space filled with light fixtures—some on the floor and others hanging at different lengths from the ceiling.

Taylor pointed out the different fixtures that he thought would work for various rooms. He indicated one very large ornate chandelier that he thought would work for the grand entryway.

"The light will reflect beautifully through the arched window over the front door, don't you think?"

Jo stared up at the display, but she was completely captivated by a different fixture altogether. It was also a chandelier, but a quarter of the size of the one Taylor was looking at. Delicate enamel flowers in a shade of deep pink with lighter green leaves were tucked among the arms that were made to look like the branches of a tree. At the very top there was a blue bird with a long beak, its red breast puffed out as it viewed the flowers below. Jo followed the bird's gaze to where it was eyeing a tiny ladybug that had been placed on a petal of one of the flowers.

"It's beautiful, isn't it? The craftsmanship is really remarkable," Taylor said, reaching up to run his fingers over one of the leaves. "It's a dogwood tree."

"It's beautiful," she whispered, standing on her tiptoes to examine one of the flowers a little closer.

Taylor stood back, tapping his lips. "I'm not really sure if there's anywhere we could use it. It's not really the right period for the house."

"That's okay, I was just admiring it."

Taylor cocked his head, looking at her with a funny expression. He waved the owner who had been hovering nearby over. "We'll take these two." He nodded toward the large chandelier he'd been showing her and the one she admired.

Taylor put his hand on her shoulder. "I think it would look really nice in your room. If you love it, then you should get it," he said with a warm smile that sent a shiver through her.

They found two more fixtures and several other pieces of hardware, doorknobs, and other items they could use. They spent a couple of hours at the salvage store, wandering through the different areas. Taylor was like a kid in a candy store and, to her surprise, Jo was having as much fun as he was. She found a small dresser in the antique section of the building and before she could ask about it, Taylor had added it to their purchases.

After they arranged to have everything packed and shipped to Halcyon, they headed toward Taylor's car, chatting excitedly about what they had found. Suddenly the woman who had been fawning over him when they first came in jumped out of her car and plastered herself against Taylor. She slipped a piece of paper into the pocket of his shirt before she wrapped her arms around his neck and planted a kiss on his lips. Taylor pushed her away with a scowl.

"You can do so much better than that, sugar," she said in a low husky voice, tipping her head toward Jo.

Taylor's jaw ticked. "Not interested," he said between clenched teeth, pushing her away.

He jerked open the passenger door for Jo, pushing her inside before moving quickly to get behind the wheel, while the woman continued to call out some rather obscene things she could do for Taylor.

"Sorry about that," he muttered, pulling out of the parking lot.

Jo put her hand on his. "Don't be sorry."

He blew out a long sigh. "I just really wanted this to be a nice day for you."

"It is—I'm having a great time. Does that happen often?"

His jaw ticked. "Sometimes, but that was pretty… aggressive. I'm really sorry."

Jo saw the tension around his eyes and reached out to put her hand on his arm. "It's okay, Taylor."

He exhaled and some of the tension eased from his face. "Thank you."

They stopped at two more shops, this time without incident. As they walked out of the last shop with a box filled with period hardware they'd found for the kitchen cabinets, Jo's stomach rumbled.

"Maybe we should stop and eat." She patted her stomach with an embarrassed smile.

Taylor's eyes brightened. "I know a place that serves great hot dogs." He grinned.

It wasn't exactly what she had in mind, but at that moment it didn't matter what they were eating. She was having a good time with Taylor, and she didn't want to break the spell. Instead of heading toward the center of town with all the bars and restaurants, they were driving toward another part of town. When she saw the building up ahead, her jaw dropped.

Taylor gave her a mischievous smile.

Jo's eyebrows shot up. "Is this my surprise?"

"I know it's not your beloved Cubs, but I thought it would be fun. I got lucky—it's the last game of the season."

Taylor parked the car in the lot for the Memphis Redbirds stadium. The Redbirds were a triple-A team, affiliated with the St. Louis Cardinals organization. She had actually been doing a little reading on the team, since it was two hours closer to Colton than Uncle Robert's beloved Biloxi Shuckers.

They made their way to the gate. Taylor pulled up their tickets on his phone, and the usher pointed them toward the entrance along the first base line.

Taylor had gotten them seats right behind home plate. As soon as they were seated, an usher came and took their food order and offered Jo a scorecard. A wave of homesickness overtook her, looking out over the field in verdant shades of green.

"Hey, are you all right?"

She gave him a watery smile. "I'm just missing my dad. I can't remember the last time I went to a baseball game without him."

"How about I take your picture to send to him, or better yet, why don't you FaceTime him?"

Jo didn't trust herself not to cry if she heard her dad's voice, so she agreed to let Taylor take her picture. She struck a couple of poses while he snapped away with her phone.

"I look like such a goof," she complained. "I've never been good at having my picture taken."

Taylor hooked his finger under her chin. "You look beautiful."

Her eyes locked with his and her breath caught. He started to lean toward her when another man suddenly dropped down next to him, clapping him on the shoulder.

"Making moves already?" Taylor's brother said with a raised eyebrow.

She turned away, trying to hide her heated cheeks. Taylor's brother winked at her with a mischievous smile. She liked Dylan. He'd joined them for dinner a few times after his confrontation with Taylor. Without Tessa's interference, the two brothers were slowly establishing the brotherly bond they both craved.

"Behave yourself," Taylor growled. "Good to see you again."

Jo studied the contrast between the brothers, seeing Dylan dressed for work. They had a strong resemblance, but Dylan wore his hair neatly cut and his face was clean-shaven. They shared the same piercing blue eyes and dark blond hair. Dylan always had a more serious air about him compared to Taylor. He was dressed in dark slacks, a pale blue oxford shirt, and dress shoes, and Jo had yet to see him wear a single flannel shirt.

Dylan rubbed his hands over his face and sighed, sitting back in his seat.

"Tough day?" Taylor asked.

"Some days are tougher than others." Dylan frowned.

"When was the last time you had a day off?" she asked, observing the dark circles under his eyes.

"I've kind of lost track of the days, to be honest."

Just then the food arrived. She thanked the server and asked if she could order the same thing again and then turned and handed her food to Dylan. "Here, you need this—you look like you've had a long day."

Dylan looked from her to the food and back again and said, "Thanks," in a rough voice.

Taylor touched her hand and mouthed *Thank you.*

Just before the game was scheduled to start, an usher came over to their seats. "Excuse me, Mr. Colton, if you'll come with me, I'll take you down to the field."

Jo looked at Taylor in surprise.

He leaned over and whispered in her ear, "This is the fun part of the job." Jo and Dylan followed Taylor as he was led toward the field. They stood off to the side while he walked out to the pitcher's mound. The crowd cheered when he was announced and threw the first pitch. He shook the catcher's hand and then jogged back to where Jo waited with Dylan. Someone from the front office handed him a large gift bag filled with Redbirds merchandise and then turned to Jo.

"Ms. Martin, will you please come with me?"

Jo looked at Taylor, but he just grinned and gently pushed her toward the man wearing a Redbirds polo shirt.

She glanced up at the stands where Taylor and Dylan were taking their seats again while she was led to the dugout. The coach greeted her and gave her a jersey and invited her to sit through the first inning. The players took turns signing her jersey, and the ones who didn't have field positions chatted with her while the other team was at bat. At the end of the inning, she returned to her seat beaming. "That was amazing, thank you."

"I'm glad you had fun."

When the usher returned after a few innings, asking Taylor if he would sign autographs for some of the team owners, Dylan moved into Taylor's seat.

"I haven't really had a chance to say thank you for letting Taylor come back to Halcyon. I'm still angry about what Tessa did to you, but if this is what it took for my brother to finally figure out what's been going on, then I'm glad."

"I'm glad you and Taylor have been able to spend time together."

"It's a lot easier with Tessa out of the way. I wasn't as close to my brother as I wanted to be because of her. Some of it's my fault. I'm not the greatest at work-life balance, but when I'd try to make time to see Taylor, she was always running interference, coming up with some reason why he didn't have the time. I suggested once that she was lying to him, and he didn't speak to me for months."

Jo winced.

Dylan gave her a curious look. "So... when did you two start dating?"

Jo's mouth formed an *O* and she began to shake her head. "Oh no, it's not like that. We started to... well, we were getting close, but it didn't work out. We aren't dating, we're just.... I don't want to rush into anything."

Dylan put his hand on her shoulder with a serious expression. "I saw the way he was looking at you just now. Taylor's not going anywhere. He's a different person when he's with you. He's happy—the two of you are good together. I guarantee he wants something more than friendship."

She missed Taylor's kisses and the way he held her in his arms, but she was scared to trust him again. Taylor returned and sat down next to her. She looked up and his eyes locked with hers for a moment, and her breath caught at the flash of desire she saw in their blue depths. The crowd roared, bringing her attention back to the game.

Jo ignored Taylor and Dylan's amused smiles while she sang "Take Me Out to The Ball Game" at the top of her lungs during the seventh inning stretch—she was back in a ballpark and having a blast. Taylor inched closer and closer throughout the game until he had his arm slung over the back of her seat, peering over her shoulder, watching her fill out her scorecard, quizzing about the game. The Redbirds had a massive rally in the ninth inning that had Jo screaming in the stands. When the fireworks went off to celebrate their victory, she threw her arms around Taylor. "We won!" she exclaimed.

"It looks like the Redbirds have a new fan." Taylor pulled back, looking down at her with a smile.

"I hope you'll come back and visit us," Jo said as the three of them made their way through the stands and out of the ballpark.

Dylan embraced his brother. "I'll try to make it down again as soon as I can."

Jo gave him a hug. "Thanks for coming out to the game. Take care of yourself, Dylan. Try to practice some of that work-life balance you were talking about, okay?"

He nodded. "I'll try."

"I'm worried about him," Jo said as they walked back to Taylor's truck.

"Thanks for giving him your dinner—that was a really nice thing to do."

"He just looked so exhausted. I hope he'll be okay."

"Hopefully he'll take some more time off and come back to visit." He reached over and took her hand in his. "Thank you for trusting me. I had a good time today."

Jo looked down at where their hands were linked. Her mind told her to be careful, but her heart had already started to open again. The cab of the truck felt too small sitting next to Taylor in the dark, and she was keenly aware of the spark of attraction that had returned between them.

That night when she went to bed, she didn't dream about Ada Mae. Her dreams were about Taylor, and she woke up with an ache in her heart from missing him. She missed his kisses and sharing secrets as they sat on the step leading out to the garden in the morning or at the end of the day.

CHAPTER SIXTEEN

THE NEXT day, Callie called with the news that she had found a few pictures—one of the colonel and one of him with his wife, and some from the late 1900s that might be helpful for restoring the interiors.

The window of the library was decorated with bright- colored leaves and Halloween children's books. Callie had laid out the pictures on the table in the center of the room when they arrived. Taylor glanced at Jo, trying to gauge her reaction when she saw the pictures of the colonel with his wife.

She looked from the picture to Taylor and back again with wide eyes. "You look just like him."

He looked at the image in her hand. Just like with the picture he found in the attic, he was looking at himself, Taylor thought. Even in the faded shades of dark and light gray, Taylor recognized his own blue eyes looking back at him.

Callie pushed a pair of gloves toward Taylor and a matching pair to Jo before she picked up the first book and put it in front of him. "These are the Slave Schedules from the 1860 census—every man, woman and child in Colton and the surrounding area is listed here."

Taylor drew a sharp breath when Callie opened the book to a page marked with a small slip of paper. *Master Absolem Madden Colton* was written in the large elegant script of the time at the top of the page. He was listed under the heading "Slave Owner" in the first column. There were a series of numbers and letters in the next three columns, the ink faded brown with time.

"These are the slave schedules for the Colton Plantation." Callie went on to explain what each column meant. "The first column is the slave owner and the second is the number of people they owned. The next three list the age, sex, and race—B for Black or M for Mulatto."

"Mulatto?" Taylor asked.

"That was the term used for slaves who were born from the overseers or the masters," Callie said with a slight tremor in her voice.

Taylor clenched his hands in his lap and squeezed his eyes shut for a moment. When he opened them again, the numbers on the page blurred before him.

"One, Male, Black, two years old." Jo's voice shook as she read across the first row.

"One, Female, Black, five years old," Taylor read across the next line.

They took turns reading down the columns. When they reached the bottom, Callie told him to turn the page.

He carefully lifted the yellowed paper and let it fall to the side. Unlike the first page, there was a column filled out differently than the rest. His heart seized when he saw what was carefully printed out on the last row.

Jo gasped. "Ada Mae Colton—she's the only one who is named. He wrote her name. She was more than a number."

"I came here thinking everything was so straightforward." He pressed the heels of his hands to his eyes. "I thought I knew...."

Jo gently grasped his hand and linked her fingers with his.

He took a deep shuddering breath and looked back down at the name on the page. He reached out with a gloved finger, running it over the letters that formed the name from the past that changed his future. He hadn't really thought of Ada Mae as being real until that moment, and he needed to know more.

"Will you share what you know about Ada Mae?" he asked.

"Let's go home and I'll tell you about her."

Taylor nodded. "That seems like the right place."

They walked out of the library with copies of the pictures and the pages from the Slave Schedule that Callie had prepared for them. He was quiet on the way back to the house, and so was Jo. He glanced down to their joined hands while his other firmly gripped the wheel. It was as if they both needed the physical connection to ground them in the present while they faced their ancestors' past.

When they got back to the house, he got out of the truck and leaned against the front, staring up at the house.

"I hate it. I love the house, but I hate what it represents, and it all gets jumbled in my head sometimes and I get angry and sad and I feel so guilty."

Jo came around to the front of the truck and leaned against the hood next to him, her shoulder pressing against his. "History is complicated, isn't it?" She laughed softly, shaking her head. "You want to know something? My sister asked me if I had some kind of slave fantasy when I told her I was moving here," she confessed.

Taylor's jaw dropped. "She said that to you?"

"That, and a few other choice words."

"I... I don't know what to say. That's just... wow." He exhaled, shaking his head, and turned to her. "You don't think that I have...." He pressed his lips together. "You know I don't have those kinds of... I don't... oh hell," he muttered. "I don't have any kind of fetish about you. I mean, Black women. I mean... I'm going to stop talking now," he muttered, dropping his head.

Jo pressed her lips together, trying not to laugh, and failed, tears streamed down her face. She laughed so hard she doubled over, holding her sides. "I'm sorry," she gasped, still chuckling. "I know it's not funny. No, Taylor, I don't think that about you. Some people do and that's just...." She shook her head. "That's a different conversation that I'm not interested in having. You may not be as charming as you think you are, but one of the things I like about you is that you make me feel like you see all of me. Not just a Black woman or a computer geek but me, Josephine Martin."

He gave her a smile that sent her pulse racing. "You think I'm charming?" He raised his eyebrows.

"I said you're not as charming as you think you are."

"But you think I am just a little bit charming?" he asked, holding up his thumb and forefinger.

Jo's lips twitched. "Maybe a little bit."

Taylor's eyes lit up. "Challenge accepted."

"What challenge?"

"I get to do whatever I can to convince you that I'm more than just a little bit charming."

They started walking toward the house when he saw a movement and what looked like the image of a woman in one of the windows. "Did you see that?" he asked, pointing to the second floor.

She squinted at the window. "I don't see anything."

"It must have been a reflection," Taylor said, his eyes scanning the upper floor.

"What did you see?"

"I thought I saw a woman looking out of the window, but I'm sure it was just a shadow. You often hear strange noises and see odd shadows in old houses." He gave her a reassuring smile.

He guided her toward the veranda, but at the threshold, Jo hesitated. He saw the worry on her face and offered to go upstairs and look around. Jo nodded, and he told her to wait in the hall while he ran up the stairs. He did a quick tour of the upstairs bedrooms and didn't see any sign of anyone or anything out of place. Jo was looking up at him anxiously when he came back to the top of the stairs.

"Nothing unusual, not even a mouse," he announced. "I haven't thought about it but we should get an alarm system installed. I'm not really worried about trespassers, but we do have a lot of expensive equipment around here."

"It's better to be safe than sorry."

"I didn't mean to scare you. If you don't want to talk about Ada Mae now, we can talk later."

She gave him a slight smile. "I still want to. Can we talk in the small parlor?"

"How about I grab us something to eat and drink and you get a blanket and we'll have a picnic dinner?"

"Sounds good."

He quickly fixed a plate with cheese and crackers, grabbed a bottle of wine and some glasses, and headed to the parlor. Jo was spreading a quilt on the floor in front of the fireplace when he walked in.

Taylor took a sip of wine and waited for Jo to begin. She stared at the fireplace for a little while, sipping her wine before she spoke.

She started with the first dream she had where Ada Mae showed her the trunk, and her dream of Miss Julia pushing her down the stairs trying to kill her. She sighed and looked up at the ceiling. "I keep dreaming of where the ceiling is painted to—"

"Look like the sky," Taylor finished for her.

Jo froze and slowly turned to look at him with wide eyes.

"I had a dream about the same room. A woman came in—I thought it was you at first, but it wasn't. I think… it was Ada Mae."

Suddenly the air became heavy with a sweet woodsy scent.

"Do you smell it?" Jo asked.

The smell was familiar and yet different. He tried to remember where he had smelled it before.

"Dax told me a story. There was a gas leak at Callie's house, and Dax had a vision. It was an old woman who came to him and told him Callie was in trouble. He'd had a vision of the woman before. Both times when he saw her, it smelled like eucalyptus. I've smelled it too," Jo said.

"I can't believe it," he said under his breath.

Jo's face fell.

He grabbed her hands. "Jo, look at me, I believe you. What I meant is how amazing it is that Ada Mae survived so much. I hate to think what would have happened if she hadn't lived and gotten her freedom so that I could be here with you now. I know you're not making any of this up, not when we've had the same dream."

She swallowed and nodded.

"I wonder why she speaks to you in your dreams but she didn't speak to me," he said.

"Maybe she didn't think you were ready to listen."

"I'm listening now." He jumped up. "Hold on a minute, I want to show you something." He went to his room and came back with the picture of the colonel he'd found up in the attic.

Jo went over and knelt down next to it. "I just can't get over it." She looked at the picture and then at Taylor. "The eyes are exactly the same."

"I… It makes me uncomfortable that I look like him."

"You may look like him, but you're not him, Taylor," Jo said softly.

He blew out a shaky breath. "Thank you for saying that."

Her tongue darted out and his eyes followed its path as she licked her lips. "Sometimes I wonder if we were brought here to… I don't know, make sure the past isn't forgotten. We're not just restoring the house but repairing the past.

"I've been thinking about what Judge Beaumont said about reparations when he split the house between us. I read an article about reparations a while ago, and it talked about it as repairing the breach. Maybe that's what we're here to do, repair the breach."

Jo drew her knees up to her chest and wrapped her arms around them. "I like that idea."

Her eyes darted toward the portrait of the colonel again. "Was there a picture of his wife?"

"That's the funny thing, usually you find pictures like this in pairs, but I didn't find one of her," he said.

"It wasn't a happy marriage."

"How could it be when there were three people in the relationship?"

"Do you think we're going to be able to replace all of the bad memories in this house with good ones?" she asked.

Taylor scooted next to her and put his arm around her.

She sighed and leaned her head on his shoulder. "Do you know why I'm always in this room or the garden?"

"No, why?"

"Because I feel close to her here. She told me the colonel decorated this room just for her. He asked her what her favorite color was, and she said yellow. Can you imagine? As if that would make her happy when she didn't have her freedom."

He shuddered. "We can make the room different if you want."

"No, I want to put it back the way it was. I want people to know what happened here."

"Then that's what we'll do."

Jo shivered. "This house is full of secrets."

He ran his hand up and down her arm. "What did you say?"

"Ada Mae told me in one of my dreams that her mother used to say she was born with a soul full of secrets."

"Do you think we will ever find out what they are?"

Jo looked at him. "Do we want to know?"

He reached up and stroked her cheek with the back of his hand. "I don't want to keep any secrets from you. So I want you to know that I want to be more than friends. I miss you. I miss how close we were becoming. I woke up every day looking forward to talking to you. Your voice is the last thing I want to hear before I go to sleep at night. I miss being able to kiss and touch you. How alive you made me feel when I held you in my arms."

"I'm scared."

"So am I. I'm afraid of spending the rest of my life without ever having kissed you again."

She lifted her face to his. Her lips curved into a suggestive smile. "We can't live our lives in fear."

Taylor met her halfway, his lips brushing against hers briefly before his desire overwhelmed him and he pulled her closer as she wrapped her arms around him so there was no space between them. He moved his mouth over hers, reveling in her softness. Finally, he was back where he wanted to be. He was home.

CHAPTER SEVENTEEN

THERE WAS one apology that Taylor hadn't made yet, and it took a while for him to work up the nerve. Even now they sat in Jo's car, parked down the street from the Catfish Café, while Taylor practiced what he was going to say.

Jo finally leaned across her seat and planted tantalizing kisses in the hollow of his neck before working her way up to his lips.

"Come on, don't be scared—let's get this over with." She laughed when he finally let her go. Taylor swooped in for another toe-curling kiss that left Jo breathless. Every touch and each kiss opened her heart a little more.

"You know there's no way that woman will ever give me another piece of pie again."

She fought the urge to laugh at the plaintive look on his face.

She brushed a lock of hair out of his eyes. "Just be straightforward and honest."

He clutched her hand as if it were his lifeline when they walked up to the door. Jo timed their visit between the lunch and dinner rush, hoping that it would be quiet at the café.

There were still enough customers that it felt a bit like running the gauntlet as they made their way inside. Tillie stopped wiping down the counter and crossed her arms with her mouth set into a thin line when they walked in the door. Taylor's footsteps slowed, but Jo gave him a reassuring smile and pulled him forward until they were standing at the counter.

He cleared his throat. "Good evening, Tillie."

When Tillie didn't return his greeting, Jo frowned. "Give him a chance—he's trying."

She gave Taylor a skeptical look. "Well, what have you got to say?"

"I'm sorry and thank you."

Jo looked at Taylor with a raised eyebrow. This wasn't what he'd rehearsed in the car.

"I want to thank you for being a good friend to Jo when I wasn't. I'll always be grateful to you for that."

Jo stood on her toes to give Taylor a kiss on the cheek.

Tillie chewed on her lip for a minute, looking at the two of them through narrowed eyes, and for a minute Jo was worried she might be the one person who wasn't going to accept an apology from Taylor.

But then she leaned across the counter and pulled down the collar on her T-shirt. "You've got a love bite on your neck."

Tillie let go of her and turned back to Taylor, who had turned beet red. "I wasn't the one you needed to worry about. If Jo can forgive you, that's all that matters."

Taylor blew out a long breath. "Thank you."

"Y'all have a seat, but not in the back. I don't allow any necking in here."

There were curious looks and a few chuckles from the customers in the restaurant when they took their seats.

Minh walked in and headed toward their table.

"Hey, Taylor, I've got those parts we needed ordered, and I can finish up replumbing the kitchen in a day or two."

"That's great, Minh, thank you."

Minh's smile went from friendly to one hundred watts when Tillie came over to their table and slid a plate with a double-size piece of pecan pie in front of Taylor.

"Afternoon, Ms. Tillie." Minh took off his baseball cap and ran his hand through his hair nervously.

Tillie jerked her thumb toward the counter. "Have a seat and I'll get your coffee in a sec. What else can I get you kids to eat?"

"Would you mind packing up some fried chicken and potato salad for us to take back to Halcyon?" Jo asked.

Tillie patted her on the shoulder. "Of course not, honey." She glanced at Taylor. "Stop playin' patty fingers under the table."

Taylor dropped Jo's hand and put both of his on the table. "Yes, ma'am."

Jo kept glancing over her shoulder where Minh was doing everything in his power to get Tillie to have a conversation with him.

"She's completely clueless."

"Who is, about what?" Taylor said around a mouth of pie

Jo leaned over and whispered in his ear. "Minh likes Tillie, and she has no idea."

Taylor's eyes grew wide and he looked over at the counter.

"Could you be a little more obvious?" Jo said in a hushed voice.

"Uh-oh, I know that look." Taylor waggled his fork at her. "That's the look one woman gets when she's fixin' to help another one with her love life."

"Don't be rude."

Taylor leaned over and gave her a quick kiss. "You're a good friend."

"We're due for a girls' night. I'll talk to her then."

Tillie came back over with their dinner when Taylor finished his pie. When he reached for his wallet, she put her hand up. "This one's on the house."

Jo got up and gave Tillie a hug. "Thanks for giving Taylor a chance to apologize."

Tillie held her hand out to Taylor. "You do right by my girl."

"Yes, ma'am." Taylor grinned.

They ran into the Jewels on their way back to Jo's car. "Miss Josephine, you're just the person I was hoping to see," Opal said.

Pearl and Ruby took turns giving her a hug before looking at Taylor.

"Good afternoon, ladies," Taylor said.

"Mr. Colton." Opal lifted her chin.

Pearl and Ruby followed their sister's greeting.

Opal reached into her handbag. "I wrote down the story our great-grandmother told us and the song for you."

"Oh, thank you so much," Jo exclaimed, looking down at the piece of paper where Opal had neatly printed everything out for her.

The sisters started to walk away when Opal stopped and turned around. "That was a generous donation that you made to the Colton Garden Club, Mr. Colton. Thank you."

"We didn't forgive you because of that," Pearl added.

"It was because you came and apologized in person," Ruby said.

There was a slight tremor in Taylor's voice when he said, "Thank you."

Jo blinked back tears. "Thank you, ladies."

"Can I see what Opal wrote down for you?" Taylor asked when they got back to Halcyon.

"Of course."

Jo handed him the piece of paper, and his eyes widened as he read Opal's story.

"In your dream you said the garden was surrounded by a wall."

Jo nodded.

"Have you seen any sign of one?"

"No, but I haven't really looked that closely."

Taylor took her hand, and they went to the garden. Jo made a circuit starting from where the inside wall would be around to the other side, stopping every so often to dig at the dirt with her toe to see if she could find any sign of where a wall would have once stood. On her second turn around the garden she stopped short, staring at the outside wall of the house.

"Jo, what's the matter?"

"This isn't right," Jo murmured, looking at the corner of the house.

Taylor came over to her side. His eyes narrowed as he studied the profile of the house. "Look at where the wall is in the parlor and then look at the corner of the house. They don't line up."

He went back inside the parlor and then looked out the door to the corner of the house with a frown.

"The house extends past where the parlor is by at least six feet," he said.

"How is that possible?"

Jo went into the parlor and stood next to Taylor, staring at the back wall. Taylor started knocking, and she drew a sharp breath when the sound changed.

"It's hollow," she said.

Taylor pulled out his multi-tool, carefully drew a line, and began to peel back the layers of paint and wallpaper. He paused when he reached the layer of pale yellow wallpaper and looked at Jo as if he were asking for permission.

"Go on," she said.

They peeled away the layers until a large patch of the original wall could be seen. Taylor started running his hand over the wall. Suddenly he stopped and pressed down.

There was a soft click and the creak of hinges that had not been used in many years as a narrow door popped open.

"Oh my God." Taylor stood in front of the doorway they had just exposed.

"*My mother said I was born with a soul full of secrets.*" Jo repeated Ada Mae's words again. "She said she left them all behind when she left Halcyon."

Taylor reached for her hand and drew him to his side so they could both look through the doorway together.

Jo peered over his shoulder and gasped. Time stopped. The pale yellow wallpaper and yellow damask fabric on the small chair in front of a petite writing desk all could have been placed there yesterday. Bright blooms in shades of pink, purple, and yellow that appeared as if they had just been picked were woven into the carpet at their feet. They were exactly the same as the furnishings she'd seen in her vision of the parlor and the pieces she had found in the attic.

Shadows blended with the light from the doorway, and Jo realized there were no windows in the room. The ceiling had been painted to look like a bright blue sky on a summer day.

"The ceiling…." Taylor's breath caught.

"This is the room I've been dreaming about."

"It's the same one from my dream too," he said.

Jo nodded, tears blurring her vision, and she could have sworn she heard a woman crying softly. Taylor stepped back and gently pushed her forward, standing behind her with his hands on her shoulders.

"You should go in first."

Jo hesitated before moving just a tiny bit farther into the room, until the sight in front of her brought her to a dead stop. There was a small bed in the corner, the bedding rumpled and decaying.

She repeated the words from her dream.

"*The colonel was so proud of me. I gave birth to our son without making a sound. He was a fool to think he could keep it a secret.*"

"Oh my God." She clasped her hand over her mouth. She turned into the solid wall of Taylor's chest, and her cries blended with Ada Mae's as he wrapped his arms around her.

Taylor rested his cheek on top of her head, pulling her closer. "I'm so sorry, Jo," he said, his voice breaking as he murmured words of comfort. He gently pulled her out of the room.

She let out a deep shuddering breath and wiped her eyes as she moved away from him. "Ada Mae had a baby here. He kept her here in this house, a trapped bird in a gilded cage." Tears streamed down her cheeks.

"I don't know what to say. How could this be hidden away for so many years without anyone knowing it was here?"

Jo wiped at her tears and looked at the small desk in the corner. "This is where the colonel was when he wrote her the letter."

She saw him so clearly in her mind's eye, she could almost hear his pen scratch across the parchment as he wrote.

Taylor kept his arm wrapped around her. "We shouldn't touch anything until we bring in some experts to help us figure out what to do."

"Don't," she called out, her voice hoarse from crying, when he started to close the door. "It's been closed for too long. It feels like we're shutting her away. I don't ever want Ada Mae to be hidden again."

Taylor nodded. "Okay, we'll keep the door open."

Jo started shaking as they walked out of the room, her mind reeling from what they had just discovered. She sank down into a chair when they reached the kitchen.

Taylor knelt in front of her and pushed a bottle of water into her hands. "Drink this. I'm going to make you some tea."

She took a long drink and wiped her mouth with the back of her hand. "Don't go—I don't want any tea. Will you just sit next to me for a while?"

He sat down and then pulled her into his lap. They sat together for a long time, each of them lost in their own thoughts.

"I have a friend who works in the history department at Emory we can call. It will be a good place to start," Taylor said after a while.

Jo nodded. "We have to make sure it's kept safe. I want people to know about Ada Mae and the other people who were enslaved here."

He wrapped his arm around her shoulder and kissed the top of her head. "We will, I promise."

They went back to the room and took a few pictures, then sent an email to Taylor's friend at Emory as well as a few other historians who they thought might be helpful.

"I remember reading where they discovered a room in Monticello a while ago where they believe Sally Hemings bore Thomas Jefferson's children, but it was nothing like this," Taylor said.

Over and over again, Jo kept coming back to the small parlor to stand in the doorway of the hidden room.

"Jo, you can't stay here all night," Taylor said when he found her back there again.

"I'm afraid if I go to sleep it won't be here in the morning."

"I promise it will be here. I expect things are going to get a little crazy when the news about this gets out. You need to get some rest. We're going to have some long days ahead of us."

"Will you stay with me tonight? Not to... I just don't want to be by myself. I can't stop thinking about Ada Mae being locked in that room."

Taylor cupped her face with his hands and wiped away her tears. "Of course, sweetheart."

When she finished getting ready for bed, there was a knock on her door.

"Come in," she called out.

Taylor came in wearing a T-shirt and flannel pajama pants. He smiled when he saw the black tank top and flannel pajama pants in the same blue and gray that he was wearing. "It looks like my fashion sense is rubbing off on you."

She reached up and ran her hands over her head scarf. "Sorry it's not very attractive, but it beats having a tangled mess in the morning."

Taylor came over and rubbed the silk between his fingers. "It's not what you wear that makes you beautiful, Jo."

She took a deep breath, inhaling the scent of lemon and pine that clung to his skin from his shower.

He dropped his hands and rubbed her arms. "Are you sure you want me here? I'm not sure I'm the right person to be with you right now."

Confused, she asked, "Why wouldn't I want you here?"

"I'm afraid I'll remind you of... him."

Jo shook her head. "No, you won't. Don't you see? You're the only one who understands. You know about Ada Mae. No one else knows her the way we do. I... I need you here."

He swallowed and gave a jerky nod. His voice was gruff but tender when he spoke. "You look exhausted. It's been an emotional day. Let's get you into bed."

Taylor pulled back the covers and she climbed in. He turned off the light and got in next to her. She held her breath, not sure what to do until he patted his side. "Come here, sweetheart."

She scooted over and rested her head on his chest, listening to the steady rhythm of his heart, and sighed. "Thank you for staying with me."

"I'm not going anywhere, Jo. I'll be here for you even if you don't need my help or want it. I'll stand by and support you."

Jo lifted her chin and looked up at Taylor's profile in the moonlight. "I don't want you to stand by; I want you to stand with me, and I want you."

He turned so that their eyes met. "Jo, I want you so badly, but I won't make love to you tonight. You asked me to stay with you and I'm going to keep my word. We'll talk some more tomorrow. If we keep talking and sharing our feelings, then we'll know when the time is right."

Jo nodded and put her head back down on his chest. "We'll take it slow."

He pulled her close, rubbing his chin against the silk scarf covering her head. "Go to sleep. Tomorrow will be here soon enough."

CHAPTER EIGHTEEN

THE NEWS of their discovery brought even more pressure from the network to start filming the show again. But first they had to contend with all of the inquiries and requests from historians, preservation experts, and media outlets who were all eager to come and see Ada Mae's room. Jo was understandably concerned about letting anyone near the room, and Taylor felt the same way. They left it untouched until the experts that they had invited could come and document everything in detail. In the end they invited a young woman who was a professor of African-American studies at Princeton, a representative from the Mississippi Historical Society, and an historic preservation expert from the Smithsonian from the numerous inquiries they had received.

One welcome visitor arrived that morning when Taylor's brother Dylan showed up on their doorstep.

"Dylan, what in the world are you doing here?"

"I told you I'd try to visit," he said with a smile that couldn't hide the exhaustion in his voice or the dark circles under his eyes.

Taylor had never seen his brother like this before, and he was anxious to find out what was going on.

"We have a visitor," he announced, leading his brother into the kitchen where Jo was working at her laptop.

"Dylan," Jo exclaimed, pulling him into a hug. "What's wrong?" she asked, looking at his haggard face.

Dylan shook his head. "I just needed a break, and I figured if I was going to take some time off, I might as well come visit my little brother."

"How long can you stay?" Taylor asked.

"For a while, I guess."

"Dylan, come sit down," Jo ordered.

Taylor sat down next to him. "What's going on, Dylan?"

"I took a leave of absence from the hospital," he said, blowing out a shaky breath.

"What happened?"

"I don't... I'm not ready to talk about it right now."

Jo set a cup of tea in front of him with a pat on the shoulder.

Dylan nodded his thanks. Taylor exchanged a worried glance with Jo when he saw his brother's hand shaking as he brought the cup to his lips.

"Do Mom and Dad know that you're here?" Taylor asked.

"Yeah." He started blinking rapidly. "They said they understand, but I can't help feeling like I've let them down."

"Naw, that's my job," Taylor said with a wry smile.

"That's not true," Jo said quietly.

"She's right—that's not true. I know they don't express it well, but Mom and Dad are proud of you," Dylan said.

"Well, we're not talking about me. This is about you, and I'm going to throw your own words back: Mom and Dad are proud of you, and I'm sure they understand if you need to take a break."

Dylan nodded. "Thanks," he said in a hoarse whisper.

"I'm glad you're here," Taylor replied.

"Do I get a tour of all the work you've done?" Dylan asked, looking around the room, clearly trying to change the subject.

"Work on the house has been almost nonexistent lately, but we do have something special to show you." He couldn't wait to see the expression on his brother's face when he saw the secret room.

"Wow," Dylan said in an awed voice. He looked through the narrow doorway into Ada Mae's room. "This is incredible. I can't believe all the times we played in these rooms, and we never knew."

"I know, you always hear about secrets hiding in the walls of old homes, but I never expected anything like this," Taylor said.

Dylan walked over to the desk and crouched down in front of it with his head cocked. "Doesn't this look familiar?"

Taylor narrowed his eyes, studying the elegant lines of the small piece. "It looks familiar, but I can't figure out where I've seen a piece like this before."

"Well, you're the expert when it comes to antiques. I'm sure you'll figure it out sooner or later." Dylan stood up and turned in a circle. "What happens next?"

"We've invited a few experts and scholars to come and advise us on the best way to preserve it," Jo said.

"We've been learning a lot about the history of this house and the people who lived here." He glanced at Jo. "I have to admit I only ever thought about the colonel's story and not about anyone else who lived here."

Jo smiled at him. "You're learning now, and that's what matters."

Taylor and Jo explained what they knew about Ada Mae and the colonel. They showed him the copies of the slave schedule Callie made for them.

"There's more." He hesitated and then told Dylan about how he and Jo had the same dream, where they both saw the ceiling painted to look like the sky in the small parlor.

When he finished, Dylan stared at the two of them with his forehead wrinkled. "I'm a doctor—I work with science and facts. I have to admit, I'm struggling with this."

"I know it sounds crazy, but it's true," Jo said.

"I've never understood what you love about this place."

"And I've never understood why you don't love it," Taylor replied.

Jo put her hand on Taylor's arm. "Not everyone will love the house the way we do, and that's okay."

Their eyes met, and a look of understanding passed between them. They shared a special connection that no one else needed to understand but the two of them. Jo's cheeks flushed a pretty shade of pink as he looked into her eyes. Dylan cleared his throat and looked at them with a raised eyebrow.

When Jo excused herself to take a call, his brother rested his elbows on the table and looked at him.

"It looks like things are going well between you."

"They are. But we're taking it slow this time."

"That look between you just now didn't look slow."

Taylor shifted in his seat. "It's Jo's choice. She decides if and when we sleep together."

"Not that my opinion matters, but I approve."

It was almost a week before Taylor and Jo were able to persuade Dylan to join them for a night out at the Buckthorn. His brother still looked exhausted, but the tension in his face had eased over the last few days, and he was starting to smile a lot more than he did when he first arrived.

Taylor looked down at his side. Jo had dressed in a dark plum silk blouse she paired with skinny jeans. Her hair fell in soft waves around her face that wasn't overly made up. Taylor's eyes zeroed in on the plum lip gloss that tempted him to kiss her.

Reid waved to them from behind the bar, while Mr. Wallace—the owner of the Buckthorn—scowled at Taylor when they walked in. Taylor asked Jo to grab a table while he ordered. Walking away, she glanced over her shoulder to see Taylor offering his hand to Mr. Wallace.

Word had traveled pretty fast about Jo's letters being taken by Tessa, and there were quite a few folks around who had made it known they were upset on Jo's behalf. He'd been doing a lot of apologizing over the last couple of weeks.

"Well, I suppose that could have gone worse," Taylor said, returning to the table with a tray of beers.

Dylan's eyes roamed around the room. "I've always wondered what it was like in here. I always pictured it being like a back room in an old black-and-white mobster movie."

"I used to imagine the same thing," Taylor said.

Jo scooted next to him, and he kept his arm wrapped around her waist, reveling in the feeling of her body against his while the three of them talked.

Mae appeared at their table, looking down at his arm wrapped around Jo. "Okay, this is new."

Taylor squeezed her knee under the table. She looked at him with a smile.

"Be nice," Jacob said, arriving with a handful of beers. "Callie and Dax will be here soon."

Sure enough, Callie and Dax walked in. Dax went over to talk to his brother Reid at the bar while Callie came over to the table.

"It's good to see y'all here." Dax joined them. "The whole town is buzzing about the room that you found."

"We have three experts coming to see the room to start with and advise us on conservation. We don't want too many people coming in and out. It's important to make sure everything is preserved properly."

"That sounds like a sound plan." Jacob nodded.

"Of course, you're all welcome to come and see," Taylor offered.

"It's good to see you again, Dax. I heard you got married—congratulations," Dylan said.

Taylor made introductions around the table. When he got to Mae, she said, "The doctor?" Mae sat up straighter.

"Yes, ma'am," Dylan said.

Mae launched into an interrogation, grilling Dylan about what kind of medicine he practiced.

"We used to have a clinic here, but our last doctor retired several years ago. We need a good clinic for the town," Mae said with a hopeful gleam in her eyes.

"I can keep an ear out for anyone who might be interested," Dylan offered.

Mae sighed with disappointment. "Thank you, that would be great."

"You can't rebuild Colton all at once. It's going to take time, but you're doing a good job." Jacob patted her arm.

Taylor took note of how Jacob's hand lingered before he pulled it away. He'd talk to Dylan about the clinic later. He'd try to get his brother to take a look while he was here and give some guidance on updating the equipment and anything else the facility would need.

"Hey, Ashton." Dax waved over a man who had just walked in. "Dylan, this is Ashton Beaumont. He manages the bank."

"Hey, everyone, mind if I join you? I heard about that secret room y'all found." Ashton leaned forward. "You know, my sister thinks that place is haunted."

"Sometimes I wonder the same thing," Taylor said.

The door opened and Ashton's face fell. "Oh Lord, I'm sorry y'all."

A young woman with brassy blond hair headed their way, bringing a collective groan from everyone at the table. She was wearing jeans with rhinestones, a bright red T-shirt covered in silver stars, silver cowboy boots, and way too much perfume.

Mae leaned toward Jo and whispered, "You know what they say. The bigger the hair, the closer to God."

Jo's eyebrows shot up. "Who in the world is that?" she asked, tipping her head in the woman's direction.

"That is my sister Presley," Ashton said.

The young woman stopped at another table, glancing toward where they sat with a frown and a flip of her hair.

"Presley Beaumont is Colton's resident beauty queen, troublemaker, and all-round fool," Mae said in a loud whisper. Callie poked her cousin in the ribs. "Sorry, Ash," Mae sighed.

"You're not wrong." Ashton took a large swig of his beer.

"Is there a reason why she keeps looking this way?" Taylor asked.

Ashton eyed his sister. "She's calculatin'," he concluded. "She's fixin' to come over and put the moves on you. She just hasn't figured out her plan of attack yet."

"It helps that you're sitting with us. It gives you a bit of cover." Dax smirked.

"Why is that?" Taylor asked.

"Ever since she was a little girl, Presley thought Dax here belonged to her. She wasn't too happy when he thwarted her plans for him and fell in love with Callie. A much better choice, by the way." Ashton lifted his glass in salute toward Callie. "She usually tries to avoid Callie."

Sure enough, after a few moments Presley fluffed her hair, straightened her shoulders, and made a beeline for their table.

"Ash, aren't you going to introduce me to your friend?" she asked, batting her eyelashes at Taylor.

"No," Ashton said.

Taylor coughed a laugh while Jo scooted closer and wrapped her arm around his.

Ashton's sister pouted in a way that Taylor suspected she thought made her look sexy, but only succeeded in making it look like she'd had her lips done by a bad plastic surgeon.

"I am so sorry about my brother's rude behavior—I'm Presley Beaumont." She held out her hand with a limp wrist, as if Taylor was meant to kiss it instead of shake it.

He shook her hand and then waited for her to introduce herself to Jo. But she completely ignored her and kept her focus on him.

"I hear y'all are fixin' up Halcyon." Presley's eyes glittered with excitement under a pound of sparkly blue eyeshadow. "I have a ton of friends who can't wait to have their wedding receptions there. I was thinkin' if you needed help decorating, I have a lot of ideas. Oh—" She clapped her hands. "—and wouldn't it make it so authentic if y'all hired some actors to work out in the field pickin' cotton and to walk around serving mint juleps."

Taylor looked at Presley in horror, while Ashton banged his head on the table.

Mae started to stand up, muttering, "Oh not she didn't." Jacob grabbed her and forced her to sit back down with a look of absolute delight on his face.

"Presley, I don't think I can hold her for long, so I'd suggest you run," Jacob said while Mae struggled in his arms.

"Y'all ain't right," someone muttered in Presley's direction as they walked past their table.

Jo's grip tightened on Taylor's arm while Presley grinned at him, as if she should be thanked for her idea.

He didn't think of himself as a guy with a big ego, but he couldn't help feeling satisfied at the glint of jealousy he saw in Jo's eyes and the possessive hold she had on him.

He was just about to tell Presley exactly what she could do with her idea when a low, deep voice said, "Miss Beaumont, I'd like to have a word with you."

Everyone looked up to see Isiah, still in his sheriff's uniform, standing behind Ashton's sister with his arms folded in front of him, staring at her with a thunderous expression.

Presley gaped at him, but before she could respond he grasped her by the elbow and pulled her out to the patio. Everyone at the table watched through the window while he pointed in her face, clearly giving her the talking-to she deserved. Presley was nowhere to be seen when Isiah came back in and dropped down at the table with a frown.

"My apologies," he said.

"No apology needed." Ashton handed him a shot glass. "If anything, I'd like to offer my thanks."

"I knew there were people who thought that way but... wow, that was awful." Taylor shook his head.

"I hate to say it, but she's not the only one," Dax added.

Jo gave Taylor a worried look.

"You let me know if you have any problems with anyone at the house," Isiah said.

"We haven't even talked about having the house open to visitors. But it's not just my decision, and I'll be happy with whatever Jo decides."

Jo looked at him when she said, "It's our decision."

They were a team, and a good one. But he wanted Jo as more than just a partner in Halcyon. He wanted her as a partner in life.

It was good to see his brother relax and have a good time. Taylor looked around at the group at the table and realized he hadn't had a night out like this in longer than he could remember. He glanced down at where Jo kept her hand on his arm while she chatted with everyone. It was moments like these that had been missing from his life, and sharing them with Jo made them just that much better.

CHAPTER NINETEEN

JO LEANED against the door, watching Taylor show Adam how to create a template to re-create a piece of missing molding. Adam was splitting his time between working with Jacob and helping at Halcyon.

With Tessa out of the picture, work became fun again. Taylor was able to focus on the restoration work that he loved, and a sense of peace settled over the house and the people working there.

Taylor looked at the sketch Adam made and nodded his approval. He was a good teacher. Adam had arranged for him to give a lecture at the trade school the week before, and he'd been invited back to speak again next month. The house was alive with activity again. Sam and Minh were back. The kitchen cabinets were installed now, and the countertops were due to arrive tomorrow.

The historians they had invited to look at the hidden room had made several visits, and they were working on a preservation plan to ensure everything in the room would remain the way it had been found and could be displayed safely for future generations.

They were also contacted by the head of the archaeology department at Emory, who had a group of students who were interested in doing a dig around the slave quarters. Jo had been worried about how Taylor would react to the idea of having the past literally dug up. But he wholeheartedly supported the idea.

Chloe had asked to help, and she divided her time between working with Jo and Dax and working as Taylor's assistant again. Things between Taylor and Tessa were still messy and very ugly. Taylor spent a good portion of his days talking with his lawyers,, and Jo was worried about the toll it was taking on him.

Dylan stopped by every day offering to help out, but Jo knew he was checking in on his brother and was just as worried as she was.

"Try to get him to eat more if you can," he said that evening on his way out.

"I will. I'm worried he's still not sleeping well either."

"He's being so hard on himself." Dylan ran his hand through his hair.

Jo gave him a sympathetic smile. "Both of you are. I hope at some point you'll want to talk about what happened that made you decide to come here."

Dylan's jaw clenched. "I… I can't."

"We're here when you're ready."

Dylan gave her a hug. "I'm glad you're here for him. I'll check in again tomorrow."

At the end of the day, she found Taylor in front of the small parlor. He was crouched in front of the fireplace, lighting a grouping of pillar candles. There was a piece of furniture under a drop cloth set in front.

Taylor jumped up and smiled. "I wanted to surprise you. The fireplaces still need a lot of repair, so it's not safe to have a fire, but I know you like to sit in here and it's getting colder in the evenings and…." He blew out a breath. "I'm rambling."

"What's this?" she asked, pointing to the tarp.

"It's a present."

Jo looked at him in surprise. "Do I get to open it?"

He nodded and stepped back so she could pull the covering off.

"Oh, Taylor, it's beautiful," she exclaimed.

It was a small settee covered in a yellow damask fabric, just like she had seen in her dream.

"I found it in the attic. The original fabric was mostly rotted away, but there was enough that I could find a close match and have it reupholstered."

It was a small piece, delicately carved with roses along the back. The seat was slightly curved and just big enough for two people. The yellow silk began to glow in the candlelight as the last light of the day faded.

"I found some chairs as well. The fabric is completely rotted away, so I thought you would like to choose what you wanted for them."

The wood felt like satin under her fingertips as she ran her hand over the settee.

"I wanted to do something for you to make up for everything Tessa had put you through. I know how much you like this room—now you'll have a place to sit by the fire. Well, sort of a fire until we get the fireplaces repaired."

"Will you sit with me?"

Taylor hesitated for a moment before joining her.

He'd been trying to keep his distance since he came back, but that didn't mean Jo was blind to the heated looks he gave her when he thought she wasn't looking.

The settee was small enough that when he sat down his thigh brushed against hers. Jo realized he was holding his breath as he sat stiffly next to her.

"This is nice, isn't it?"

"Yes." He looked like he was almost in pain, sitting there with this hands clenched at his sides.

She felt a pang in her heart when she saw how uncomfortable he was. Had she waited too long? Had he decided he didn't want to be around her anymore?

Sadness threatened to overwhelm her. She forced herself to say the words, to let him go. "If you don't want to be here, you can leave."

Suddenly he twisted to face her and reached up to cup her face. "I don't want to leave, but I have to. I dream about you every night. About falling asleep with you in my arms and waking up with the feel of your body against mine. I promised that is was your decision, but I want you so much I'm afraid if I don't leave I won't be able to keep my promise. I want to be the kind of man you deserve, one who keeps his word, who respects you as much as he…" He drew in a breath. "…as much as I want you."

He started to get up and Jo grabbed his hand, pulling him back down. "Don't go."

He froze, his eyes searching hers looking for reassurance. In one swift movement she shifted and straddled his lap and brought her mouth down on his, making the decision for both of them.

His fingers dug into her waist. He moaned, his tongue delving into her mouth. She reached between them, placing her hand on his chest and feeling his thundering heartbeat beneath her fingertips.

He tore his lips away, his breath coming in soft puffs against her lips. "Jo, I need to know…, If we keep going, I won't be able to let you go again."

"I don't want you to let me go. I want to be here with you," she whispered against his lips.

He slipped his arm around her waist and pulled her against him until he could feel her body against his. He tugged at her shirt until he could feel the soft skin of her waist against his palm.

She unbuttoned his shirt, pushing it off his shoulders. He pulled back just long enough to pull her shirt over her head before kissing her again. His breath hitched. His fingers traced the line where the lace of her bra caressed her breasts. They became a tangle of arms and legs, lips and tongues. He grasped her hip just as his hip slipped and they tumbled to the floor.

"Bedroom. Now." Taylor cupped her breasts through the pale blue lacy bra that he couldn't wait to rip off of her.

They raced through the house, and at her bedroom door he stopped her from opening it and braced both of his arms on either side of her head. "Are you sure?"

Jo dragged her lower lip between her teeth in a way that made him want to thrust into her right then and there.

"I'm not going to change my mind, Taylor. I know what I want, and I want you," she said, reaching behind her to open the door.

MOONLIGHT STREAMED through the window, bathing them in a pale silvery glow. The first time they made love, it was fast and frantic. The next, gentle and slow. Jo sighed and moved closer, wrapping her arm across Taylor's chest, loving the feel of the hair on his chest against her cheek. It felt so good to be held in his arms, their legs tangled together under the sheets. It felt right being here in this moment, with this man.

He kissed her shoulder. "Do you want me to go?"

She raised herself up on her elbow. "No, I want you to stay."

"As long as you want me, I'll be here."

Jo put her head on his chest, listening as his heartbeat began to match the rhythm of hers, lulling them both to sleep.

SUNLIGHT STREAMED through the window, creating streaks of light and shadow on Taylor's face. She ran her hand over his beard, remembering how those same whiskers felt against her skin in the night.

He stirred and opened his eyes, his mouth turning up into a smile. "Good morning," he murmured. He reached out and cupped the back of her head, pulling her down for a good-morning kiss that quickly turned into much more.

It was late in the morning before they finally stumbled out of bed. They were out on the veranda with their coffee, talking about their plans for the day, when Jo set her cup down and climbed into his lap, wrapping her arms around his neck with an excited gleam in her eye.

"I have an idea for what we should do with Halcyon."

"What do you want to do?"

"I had another dream about Ada Mae," she said.

Taylor nuzzled the side of her head. "I know." Jo looked at him with wide eyes. "You were talking in your sleep."

"She wanted to turn Halcyon into a school. She was going to come back after the war and teach the former slaves to read and write."

"Is that what you're thinking that we should do, turn Halcyon into a school?"

"Not a school, but something similar. What if we worked with the trade school in Greenwood and some other programs and offered apprenticeships for other students like Adam who are interested in historic preservation?"

Jo's enthusiasm was infectious, and Taylor's mind raced with the possibilities.

"So many of those skills are being lost. We could bring in carpenters, stonemasons, and historians to teach the next generation," she said.

"I had someone from the architecture program at Ole Miss reach out to me the other day, asking about bringing some students by to see the house. Maybe we could put together a presentation about what we're thinking about doing."

"We have enough rooms. If we put two beds in each room, we could have as many as a dozen or more students living and studying here." Jo grew serious. "I don't know how it would work with the show, but we can figure it out."

"Honestly, I'm not sure I want to keep doing the show. I love it, but I know now that the show was holding me back in some ways. I was constantly traveling, the filming schedule was grueling, and I didn't realize how burned out I was. I would miss the show, but I don't want to go back to the way I was working before. I like the idea of having a program here that would benefit the community."

"I'll support any decision you make—you know that, right?"

"I do, and thank you." He reached up and cupped her cheek, his eyes searching hers. "I love your idea and I love you."

Jo stiffened and pulled away. She saw the sincerity in his eyes and knew they weren't empty words. But there was still that small piece of her heart that questioned, and it was enough that she couldn't say the words back. It was all too much. Overwhelming.

Taylor kissed her temple. "It's okay if you're not ready to say it back."

"I'm just... I care about you so much. I'm just... afraid."

"And that's my fault."

"No." She shook her head. "It's not your fault, it's Oliver's and mine, for being so naive and trusting. I just... I want the next man I say 'I love you' to to be the only man I say those words to for the rest of my life."

A slow smile spread over his face.

"What are you smiling for?" she asked.

"Now I know when you say, I love you, it will be forever."

Chapter Twenty

TAYLOR SCRUTINIZED the picture on his tablet, comparing the carving on the leg of the desk with the one in the book sitting next to him. He pressed his lips together, shaking his head. It was close but not a match. Where had he seen the desk before? He slammed the book on early American furniture closed and pushed back from the desk he had set up in his room.

"Everything okay?" Jo asked from the doorway.

Taylor held his hand out to her. "Just trying to do some research."

As soon as she was within arm's reach, he pulled her into his lap, nuzzling her neck.

"I'm sure everyone will understand if I bail on them tonight," she said, running her hands across his shoulders.

With a ragged sigh, he gently pushed her off his lap. "You've been looking forward to having a night out with the girls." He took her hand and pulled her close. "I'll be here when you get back. We have plenty of time for it to be just you and me."

Jo's eyes flashed with a mixture of longing and desire that matched his own. Hand in hand, he walked her out to her car and gave her a goodbye kiss that left no doubt about his need for her. He watched her drive away feeling more content than he had in a long time. They were going to be happy here, he thought, turning back to the house. There was just one thing that still troubled him, and if his hunch was right, he could make sure Halcyon would be safe for generations to come.

Back inside, he was pulled toward the hidden room like a magnet. Time and memory mingled together to make the air in the room heavy with sorrow. Taylor took a deep breath and stepped over the threshold. He walked over to the desk, scrutinizing every curve and line.

His breath hitched with a flash of recognition. How could he have forgotten? The desk he stood in front of was a miniature of the one that his father used in his office at home in Atlanta. He thought back to his grandfather's gravelly drawl telling him how the desk had belonged to the colonel. He'd been just a little boy that day, when his grandfather helped move the desk into his father's office. Taylor's heart began to beat in double time as he recalled the rest of the memory from that day.

JO ROCKED gently back and forth in Callie's porch swing, watching the leaves from the big oak tree across the street float to the ground in waves of gold and green. Mae's voice faded into the distance as she shared her idea for starting a farmers' market with the group.

Callie had invited Jo over for dinner with Mae and Emma. As much as she'd been looking forward to it, she'd been reluctant to leave Taylor that night. They had come a long way in repairing their relationship, but there was a fragility that made her fiercely protective of their time together. She treasured each moment as their bond continued to blossom and grow.

She listened with one ear while she imagined walking through the farmers' market hand in hand with Taylor. Her brother and sister always teased her that she was too practical to be a romantic. If they could see her now, they wouldn't know her. Sometimes she didn't recognize herself as the person she was when she first arrived in Colton. She didn't worry so much about what other people thought anymore. It may have been an impulsive decision to come here, but she'd received so many gifts by taking the leap of faith. Family, friendship, and… love.

She swallowed. Love was dangerous. She shifted in her seat. She wanted to trust but something was still holding her back.

TAYLOR SWIPED a path through the dust, revealing the rich reddish-brown hue of rosewood. Just like its larger version, the legs were carved with a delicate curve that ended with a claw balancing on a balled foot. A silver inkwell, its contents long since evaporated, sat in one corner along with a few sheafs of paper.

The room was still just as they had found it. His dream about the colonel and Ada Mae, combined with his recollection of his conversation with his grandfather, overruled waiting to disturb anything until they had a plan from the conservation experts they were consulting with.

Taylor set his flashlight down and studied the small drawer at the front of the desk. He reached out, carefully hooked his finger on the ornate brass handle, and pulled. He expected resistance from so many years without use, but the drawer slid open with a whisper of wood sliding against wood. Taylor drew in a sharp breath, looking down at the papers scattered inside along with a small leather journal that he instantly knew belonged to Ada Mae. He opened the journal and flipped through the pages. He stopped when he recognized the telltale brown color of a daguerreotype tucked inside. Pulling it out, he froze when he saw the image.

His hand shook so badly he was afraid he wouldn't be able to keep hold of it. He picked up the flashlight illuminating the photograph. Absolem Madden Colton stood in the center of the picture. It was taken before the war, and he stood with his head held high by a starched collar and bow tie. His coat fell to his knees, and his pocket watch chain was visible against the paisley pattern on his vest. His mustache and beard were neatly trimmed and his hair just long enough to curl at the nape of his neck.

His wife, Julia Colton, sat stiffly in front of him. The ruffles on the collar of her dress grazed her chin. The dress was a dark color with a full skirt. Even in black-and-white, Taylor knew it was the red dress Jo had described from her dream, when Julia had pushed Ada Mae down the stairs. Her hair was piled high on her head in a severe style that matched the severity of her expression. She stared at the camera, her eyes cold and distant. The third person in the picture explained the hatred in her gaze.

Taylor's heart pounded in his ears when he looked at the woman standing at the colonel's side.

It was Ada Mae.

"Jo... Jo," someone called out.

She shook her head. "What?"

"Uh-oh," Mae said. "I know that look." She pointed at Callie. "You had that same look when you started falling for Dax."

Callie ducked her head behind her curtain of curls. Mae and Emma were sprawled out in wicker chairs, enjoying an unusually warm fall evening. They'd finished their dinner and moved out to the porch for wine and some of Callie's 7UP cake.

"I don't have a look," Jo said. The night air carried the scent of eucalyptus that swirled around her. The minty pine fragrance that usually soothed her made the hair on the back of her neck prickle. She hugged herself.

"Oh yes you do," Mae and Emma said in unison.

Callie nudged her shoulder. "Don't worry, it's going to happen to them one day, and then it will be our turn to give them a hard time when they fall in love."

"I'm not—" Jo gulped. "—I'm not in love."

Even as she said the words, she knew it wasn't true—she had already given her heart to Taylor. He made her cry and he made her laugh, but most of all he made her feel loved. Oliver had always had a comment about the clothes she wore, her hair or makeup. His compliments were always tinged with criticism. She reached up and fingered her hair. She'd stopped using a flat iron and most days her hair fell in soft waves. The only makeup she owned was a tube of mascara and some lip gloss. And every day since Taylor came back, he told her how beautiful she was, and the way he gazed into her eyes when he said it, she knew he was sincere. He saw her for who she really was.

Mae leaned over and said to Emma in a loud whisper, "She's doing it again."

Jo dropped her hand and tried to school her expression. "We're friends, that's all."

Mae's eyebrows rose. "Oh really."

"Quit being ugly," Emma said with a sharp look at Mae.

Everyone did a double-take. Emma Walker was one of the quietest people Jo had ever met.

Emma blushed, the same color as her strawberry-blond hair. "Sorry," she said so softly Jo had to strain to hear her over the crickets.

"But you like him, don't you?" Callie asked.

Jo let her foot drag across the floorboards. "I do," she sighed.

Callie gave her an encouraging smile. "That's a good thing."

"And he likes you, right?" Emma asked.

"He told me he loves me," Jo admitted.

"He screwed up once and you forgave him. Are you willing to give him a second chance?" Mae questioned, looking unimpressed with her declaration.

The women who surrounded her on the porch were real friends. These were women who listened and supported her. One of the best gifts she'd received in coming to Colton was the friendship of the women she was sitting with. In a short time, they had become better friends than the ones she had in Chicago. Her ability to trust was still shaky. Could she share with them what was in her heart?

"It's complicated."

ADA MAE looked exactly as she had appeared in Taylor's vision. She wore the same white lace blouse with a high collar and a dark-colored skirt that fell in soft folds to the floor. Her hair was swept up in a much less severe style than the colonel's wife, and there was a small cluster of roses arranged on one side. She faced forward along with the colonel and Julia, but she wasn't looking at the camera; she looked out of the corner of her eye at the colonel. Ada Mae held her hands clasped in front of her. The skin over her knuckles was stretched taut.

Taylor lifted the flashlight and peered closer at the picture. "My God," he whispered.

The colonel stood with one hand on the back of the chair his wife sat in. At first glance it looked like he held his other hand at his side, but when Taylor looked more closely, he could see that the colonel held Ada Mae's skirt between his fingers.

No one in the picture smiled. The expressions of the three people were at war with each other: fear, determination, and pride.

This was where Jo got her strength from.

He gingerly took out the contents of the drawer and reached inside for the lever his grandfather had shown him in its larger twin. A click and the soft scraping on wood revealed another small compartment at the back of the drawer. A jolt of electricity went through him when his fingers contacted the thick parchment envelope that he extracted from the compartment, the papers heavy in his hand. Whatever the contents, their weight was more than just words on paper.

The light in the room dimmed, and he spun around just as the door closed with a soft click.

"I waited for you to realize you were supposed to be with me," a woman's voice said through the door.

EMMA REACHED over and put her hand on Jo's arm with a comforting smile. "Go on, we'll listen."

Everyone was offering her support, and she had no reason to doubt their sincerity. So why was her stomach in knots?

"You know how sometimes when things are going really well, and you get scared it will all fall apart? That's what this feels like. I… It's hard to give up on the idea of us. I was so happy before, and then when he said he wanted to do the show again and everything fell apart, I was so hurt." She swallowed. "Now everything is different. This might not make sense, but in some ways it's better. I couldn't bear to lose what we have now."

They may have shared the house before, but now they had so much more that connected them. They had shared pain and loss, both their own and Ada Mae's. Jo was connected with Taylor in a way she knew she could never be with anyone else. She sat up straighter. She knew now without any doubt. Taylor was the love of her life, the other half of her heart.

"I can see that." Callie nodded. "They say a couple that has gone through a struggle together often has a stronger relationship. I was really scared to give Dax another chance, but I'm so glad that I did." Callie's face glowed with love for her husband as she spoke.

"That doesn't answer the question. Are you going to do the deed with Taylor again or what?" Mae asked.

"Mae!" Callie and Emma exclaimed in unison.

"Oh please." Mae waved her hand. "Don't act like y'all weren't wondering the same thing."

Three pairs of eyes zeroed in on Jo, making her squirm in her seat. "He said he loves me, but I haven't said it back yet." She took a shaky breath. "I just don't want to make another mistake."

Callie took her hand in hers and looked her in the eye. "What would be worse, risking your heart or losing Taylor?"

The air left her lungs. She couldn't lose Taylor now, not now when she was finally ready to listen to her heart.

TAYLOR RAN over to the door, pressing his ear against it. An icy wave of fear washed over him. For a brief moment, the idea that it was the ghost of the colonel's wife on the other side flashed in his mind.

"You don't want to do this," he said.

"Yes, yes I do. I've been wanting to do this ever since I saw her with you."

Taylor's stomach twisted. He pressed his forehead against the door and chose his words carefully, hoping he could say the right thing that would free him. How many times had Ada Mae thought the same, wondering what she could say that would free her?

"If you let me go, I'll make her leave and it will just be the two of us." He tried to sound convincing.

"You aren't fit to live here—you never should have let her in this house."

He wrinkled his forehead. The woman's voice sounded vaguely familiar. Would Tessa go this far? She'd threatened to take everything from him, and she hated Jo. If it wasn't Tessa, who else could it be?

"Tessa?" he called out softly.

He gave in to his rising panic when he heard her laughter on the other side. He banged on the door, listening as the sound faded away.

"TAKING IT slow." Emma sighed with a dreamy look on her face. "I think that's lovely."

Jo rubbed her hands together and then clenched them tightly in her lap. She couldn't pay attention to what anyone was saying over the sound of her pulse pounding in her ears. She tried to take a deep breath and enjoy the evening and this time with her friends She should be enjoying herself, and she was.

She forced herself to smile at Emma.

Mae's eyes flashed with exasperation. "Let me get this straight, you have a super-hot guy who says he loves you and you're not going to take advantage of that?"

"Mae, everyone comes to love at their own time and at their own pace," Callie admonished her cousin.

"Fine," Mae muttered.

Jo appreciated having friends who truly had her best interests at heart. But she wasn't ready to share what was happening with Taylor, not when she was still trying to overcome her fears and accept that she'd already... fallen in love?

"Well, I'm just glad that producer is gone. She only came into the pharmacy once, but that was enough," Emma said.

It turned out there weren't many people left in Colton that Tessa hadn't offended in one way or another. Taylor had been horrified when stories of her behavior came out, and he was determined to start over again, making amends and apologizing to everyone he'd already apologized to for his own behavior. And that included her. Jo blushed thinking about how he'd woken her up with kisses before bringing her breakfast in bed.

"You're doing it again." Emma's cornflower-blue eyes were studying her.

"What?" Jo asked.

"You keep smiling like you've got a secret," she said.

Jo pressed icy hands to her heated cheeks. Her friends were making her realize how overly cautious she was being. Taylor loved her. And yes, she loved him too.

So what was this weight pressing down on her, making it hard to breathe?

TAYLOR LOOKED around the room frantically for anything he could use to pry the door open. He reached to pull his phone out of his back pocket and realized he'd left it plugged in the kitchen to charge. Taylor banged on the door, calling out until his voice became hoarse. He sank down to the floor and put his head in his hands. There was no way out of the room from the inside. How could the colonel have kept Ada Mae trapped this way, with no way to escape if something like this happened?

"LET'S PICK on someone else. I don't want this to be all about me." Jo zeroed in on Mae. Mostly she didn't want them looking at her. Whatever was happening to her—a heart attack, a panic attack—it must have showed on her face. "Is there anything interesting happening at the hardware store you'd like to share with us, Madam Mayor?" she asked with a raised eyebrow.

Now it was Mae's turn to blush. "I don't date lumberjacks," she muttered.

"Maybe not, but you sure do make eyes at them a lot," Emma said.

Mae's eyes grew as large as saucers, while Callie doubled over laughing and Jo grinned.

Mae glared at them and then suddenly lifted her nose. "What is that smell?" she asked, sniffing the air.

Jo froze. "You... you can smell it?"

Callie turned to Jo, wide-eyed. "Eucalyptus."

The voice was so clear, Ada Mae could have been standing with them on the porch.

"You gotta go to him—he needs you."

It wasn't a heart attack, but her heart knew something was wrong. She flew down the steps to her car, praying she wasn't too late. She should have listened sooner.

Jo FOUGHT against her rising panic as she raced toward Halcyon. Nothing could happen to Taylor, not when she hadn't had the chance to tell him that she loved him. Her car fishtailed, turning into the driveway. She fought for control and put her foot on the gas when she saw the flicker of flames coming from the back, where the kitchen and their bedrooms were. She skidded to a stop in front of the house. Her fingers fumbled with the phone as she punched in 911 and ran inside.

She ran blindly toward the back of the house where she'd seen the flames, screaming Taylor's name. A blast of heat in the hallway pushed her back. She yelled for him again, and when she didn't hear anything, she ran toward the other side of the house, searching for him. As soon as she made it to the library, she heard the distant sound of pounding. Her nose began to burn from the smoke, and the air grew heavy and thick. She rushed through the rooms toward the small parlor, following the faint sound of his voice.

"TAYLOR." HE heard Jo calling his name, her voice growing louder as she came closer to the small parlor.

"Here," he called out, choking against the smoke, pressing his ear to the door and listening to her footsteps coming closer.

"The door won't open," she cried out.

His blood ran cold, realizing that if Tessa was still in the house, she could hurt Jo.

"Jo, you have to leave. It's not safe."

Jo coughed. "I've got to find something I can use to pry the door open. Hold on," she yelled. "I'll be right back."

He listened helplessly as her footsteps faded away. He looked around the room, his eyes stinging, searching again for anything he could use to free himself, but there was nothing.

He couldn't help thinking about something like this happening to Ada Mae. How did the colonel think he could keep her safe by locking her away like this? Absolem's words came back to him. He had left everything Ada Mae needed to keep Halcyon. He had to do everything he could to protect what they'd found. This was how he could finally make amends for the past. He crouched down low and crawled back to the desk, carefully pulling out the journal with the picture, the envelope, and all the other papers inside. As carefully as he could, he tucked them into his shirt. All that mattered now was to make sure Jo had the proof she needed to make sure Tessa or anyone else could never take Halcyon away.

Sirens sounded in the distance. He squeezed his eyes closed and tried to take shallow breaths, lying on the floor as the smoke grew heavier. He heard a crash but couldn't tell where it was coming from.

"Taylor." Jo's voice sounded raspy.

Something scraped against the other side of the door, and he could hear Jo's sobbing.

"Jo, stop, you need to get out," he pleaded, listening to her struggle on the other side.

He fought to breathe through the smoke that became heavier with each minute that passed. He had to convince Jo to save herself, but his body was losing the fight against the fire.

He closed his eyes and the voices drifted away. The room brightened again. He heard the soft swish of skirts and looked up to see Ada Mae standing by the door, with the colonel next to her.

"You'll be safe in here," the colonel said.

Ada Mae shook her head, her eyes filled with tears.

"Please set me free."

"Just give me time."

Ada Mae looked at Taylor. *"You have a lifetime ahead of you—just hold on a little bit longer."*

CHAPTER TWENTY-ONE

SMOKE AND her tears blinded Jo. Her arms strained from the effort, but she couldn't get the door to open. Suddenly a large hand grasped her arm and pulled her back.

Startled, she looked up to see Nate with a large ax and another fireman holding a fire extinguisher under his arm.

"Get out now," Nate yelled at her, pushing her toward the front door. She hesitated and then Dax ran into the room and grabbed her arm, pulling her out of the room.

Fresh air washed over her and she fell to her knees, gasping. Dax crouched down next to her, lifting the shield on his helmet. "You okay?"

Jo nodded. He patted her on the back and rushed back inside.

She looked around and saw men and women from the community pulling up, jumping out of their vehicles. Some were already in their firefighting gear while others were pulling their heavy bunker coats and pants out of the back of their vehicles.

Tillie ran past, shrugging on her coat as she went by. Minh and Sam were hot on her heels, along with Mae.

Callie rushed up and put an arm around her, gently guiding her out of the way as members of the volunteer fire department continued to organize around her.

"He's still in there." Jo looked over her shoulder toward the flames that had started licking out from the roof.

"Nate will get him out," Callie said.

Dylan arrived, jumping out of his car and running toward them. "Jo, are you okay?"

"I'm fine." She coughed. "But Taylor's still inside." He started toward the house with a look of anguish.

"Don't," Jacob yelled, running past them. "Let us do our job."

As if from a long distance away, Taylor heard a crashing sound. The door broke open, but he felt nothing. Then a man stepped through, picked him up, and slung him over his shoulder.

He clutched at his chest. The papers. That's all that mattered. He had to keep them safe. For Jo.

"We need oxygen," he heard someone calling out.

Jo kept her eyes glued to the front door, watching for Taylor. Finally, after what felt like years, she heard the sound of a chainsaw. A few minutes later, her heart leaped when Nate came out with Taylor over his shoulder.

"Put him over here," Dylan yelled, pointing to the back of a truck nearby.

Nate set Taylor down, rushed to the fire truck, and pulled out a kit, handing it to Dylan. "There's O^2 and a mask in there," he said gesturing to the box he'd just handed him. "Just a second and I'll grab the other emergency medical kit."

Taylor moaned, and Jo heard him call her name. She rushed to his side, trying her best to be near him while staying out of Dylan's way.

Nate handed Jo the second kit and ran back to the pumper truck to help the others get the hoses out and hooked up to the well. She set it down next to the other equipment and watched anxiously while Dylan checked Taylor's pulse and started unpacking the oxygen mask and O^2, fitting the mask over Taylor's face.

Taylor kept pawing at his chest until he pulled out a sheaf of papers and a small leather book. He pointed at Jo, pulling the mask off. "For you," he wheezed.

Dylan forced the mask back on with a scowl. "Keep that mask on, dammit."

Jo clutched the papers to her chest without looking at them. She didn't care about anything other than making sure Taylor was okay.

"Papers," he wheezed, his voice muffled by the oxygen mask. "Jo—" He tried to reach out for her. "—must keep promise."

His hands were being held. He opened his eyes to find Jo anxiously looking down at him, tears creating tracks of soot down her face.

"It's going to be okay," she said.

"I need you to take deep breaths," his brother said in a shaky voice. He looked down at Taylor, his face a mask of worry, and he could see the fear in his brother's eyes.

Taylor let his head fall back and closed his eyes.

His brother shook his shoulder, calling out his name. He tried to open his eyes and sit up, but he couldn't make his body follow his command. He felt like he was drowning, trying to breathe.

Cold metal from Dylan's stethoscope pressed against his chest. "I need you to sit up. We need to get this smoke out of your lungs." Dylan lifted Taylor up from under his arms. "Try to take a deep breath."

Taylor did what he was told and started wheezing and coughing until he thought he might throw up.

"That's good—we need to get as much smoke out of your lungs as possible." Dylan pressed the oxygen mask to his face when he tried to remove it. "Stop fighting me and keep this mask on," he growled.

Taylor squinted toward the house, watching in horror at the flames shot up from the back corner where the kitchen was. Sam and Uncle Robert were breaking out the kitchen windows. Dylan patted him on the shoulder and ran toward the fire truck, where Nate was shouting orders.

"Taylor." Jo cupped his face, her eyes searching his. "The house doesn't matter. You're safe and that's all that I care about."

He pressed his face into her palm. He tried to speak but was stopped by another coughing fit.

Jo sat next to him and wrapped her arm around him. Together they watched their friends and family fight the flames. Jo gasped and buried her face in Taylor's shoulder when a plume of flames erupted through the roof at the back of the house.

Dylan came back to check his pulse and listen to his lungs again. "I'd tell you to go to the hospital just to be safe, but I know you won't leave."

Taylor shook his head.

"Keep an eye on him," Dylan shouted over his shoulder, running toward one of the volunteers who came out of the house cradling their arm.

Jo wrapped the blanket that she had around her shoulders over both of them. A second, larger truck arrived from Winona, and they held on to each other, watching helplessly while the firefighters fought back the fire.

The Jewels arrived and within minutes had set up a station with coffee and water in the back of their car. Most of the town had arrived at Halcyon and were trying to help in any way they could.

Taylor was able to drink some water. The cool liquid burned against his throat. "Tessa," he croaked.

"What about Tessa? Is she inside?"

He stared at the house. Could she still be in there?

He started to get up over Jo's objections and staggered. Dylan came rushing over and pushed him back down. "Whoa, where do you think you're going?"

"Tessa." He lifted a shaky finger and pointed at the house. "Locked me in."

Dylan drew in a sharp breath. "I'll let Nate and Isiah know. You stay right here."

They clung together, breaking glass mingled with the sound of chainsaws. Jo whimpered and pressed her cheek against his shoulder. The sky began to glow an eerie gray orange and ash began to drift down on them. Taylor felt just as helpless watching Halcyon burn as he had trapped in the secret room.

His mind was spinning with the reality of what Tessa had tried to do. He knew she was angry, but the things she'd said.... He shuddered.

"Are you okay? Do you need me to get Dylan?" Jo asked.

Taylor pulled down the oxygen mask. "No, I'm okay."

Just those three words made his chest constrict and set off another coughing fit. Jo tried to fit the oxygen back over his nose, but he grasped her hand.

"Wait." His voice sounded foreign to his own ears. "Where are the papers?"

Jo picked up the pile from where they were sitting next to her. "I've got them."

Taylor closed his eyes and sent a silent prayer of thanks to Ada Mae and the colonel.

"I found it, the colonel's will." He nodded to the papers Jo held against her chest. "I just wanted to live long enough to keep the promise to Ada Mae, but now there might not be anything left. I'm so sorry."

She kissed his temple. "It doesn't matter—nothing matters except that you're safe." She choked back a sob. "You could have died! I was so scared. Ada Mae will live on because we will carry her memory with us and pass it on to our children. Generation after generation will remember her name. This house is nothing to me without you here. We can fix the house, but you are irreplaceable to me." She took his face in her hands, making sure he could see it reflected in her eyes when she said the words out loud. "I love you, Taylor."

He reached for her, and they held on tightly. If they lost Halcyon, it would be okay as long as they had each other.

At dawn, Halcyon was still standing. Smoke trailed in the air from the last remnants of the fire.

Nate came over to where they had remained huddled throughout the night. "The fire is out. It's going to take some time to figure out how it started." He paused, and everyone watched in horrified silence as the coroner carried out a body bag.

"Is... is it Tessa?" Taylor asked.

"It's going to take a while to identify." Nate shook his head. "A section of the roof fell from the attic through to one of the bedrooms, and the body was badly burned."

Jo grasped his hand. "I'm so sorry, Taylor."

Isiah took Taylor's statement about how he'd been shut in the secret room and the conversation he had with the woman on the other side of the door. He went back to the patrol car to call it in.

Uncle Robert came toward them. "Callie's gonna take both of you to my place—you'll be bunking with me for the time being. We'll be here for a while watching for any hot spots and helping with the cleanup," he said.

Jo jumped down from the truck and embraced Nate. "Thank you." Her voice broke. "Thank you for saving him."

Taylor got up on shaky legs and put his hand on Nate's shoulder. "Thank you."

After Callie brought them to Uncle Robert's, Jo took him into the bathroom and peeled away his shirt. He did the same for her. They took turns undressing each other and squeezed into the small shower in the guest bathroom.

They gently washed away the dirt and soot, letting go of their fear and embracing their love for each other with each touch and caress. Taylor dug up one of Uncle Robert's T-shirts for Jo and a pair of sweatpants for himself. Jo wrapped her arms around him as soon as they slipped under the covers. Taylor began to shake uncontrollably, the events of the day finally catching up to him.

Jo pressed gentle kisses over his face and along his jawline. "She told me." She looked into his eyes. "Ada Mae—she told me you were in trouble and I needed to get to you."

"She told me to hang on just a little bit longer." He closed his eyes and shuddered. "I didn't know if I could."

"I was so scared trying to get that door open."

"I'll always be thankful to Ada Mae for bringing you to me."

"I can't think about if I hadn't come back to the house. You would have been alone…."

He reached up and brushed away her tears. "I'm not talking about tonight. I'm talking about Ada Mae bringing you to Colton, to Halcyon… to me."

CHAPTER TWENTY-TWO

JO WOKE up wondering if the day before had been a dream, but the faint smell of smoke that still lingered on their bodies brought reality crashing back. She stroked Taylor's hair, watching the rise and fall of his chest, still trying to reassure herself that he was okay. She shuddered remembering how hopeless she'd felt trying to pry the door open. If Nate hadn't gotten there in time....

Taylor's eyes opened and he brushed away the tear at the corner of her eye with the pad of his thumb. "Hey," he croaked, his voice still hoarse from the smoke, "why are you crying?"

"I was thinking about how close I came to losing you," she confessed. "I couldn't get the door open and I was so scared."

"I kept thinking about Ada Mae, and what it must have been like for her every time he sat her in that room with no way out." Taylor closed his eyes and shuddered. "I was thinking about how grateful I am to her for surviving so that I could love you."

"Taylor, I was so afraid."

"It's okay, I'm all right."

She buried her face in his neck and shuddered. "All I could think about is that I wouldn't make it in time to tell you that I love you."

Taylor pulled back, his eyes searching hers. "And all I could think was that I needed to get out to tell you that I love you and give you the colonel's will. Halcyon will always be yours now—it will be protected."

Jo pressed her lips to his, tasting the salt from Taylor's tears. All of a sudden Taylor lifted his head, his forehead creasing. "Where are the papers?" He grasped her arms, looking around the room.

"There, right here." Jo retrieved them from the top of the dresser and handed them to him.

"Thank God." He slumped with relief. "Have you looked at them yet?"

Jo shook her head. "I didn't want to without you."

Taylor scooted up against the headboard and patted the spot next to him. Jo climbed in and Taylor pulled the photograph out of the journal where he'd found it.

Jo gasped. She reached for the photo with a trembling hand. Her eyes darted between Taylor and the picture. "How could he have made them take this picture?"

He pointed to the page in the journal. "She wrote it right here."

"Absolem insisted on taking this picture. He wanted to punish her for trying to hurt me. I begged him not to do it. He was almost crazed when he came home and found out she'd pushed me down the stairs. He was beside himself with worry that I might lose the baby. Absolem knew he had to send us away. Stephen was too dark to pass, and he finally realized he couldn't keep us safe. War is coming and he's going to have to leave Halcyon to fight. He knows he can't leave us here. Julia will sell us or kill us when he's gone. We will not survive locked away in this room. He had the picture taken so that she couldn't forget that he married her because he had to, not because he wanted to."

Jo read Ada Mae's words out loud. She clapped her hand over her mouth and choked back a sob. Her hands trembled while she carefully turned the pages of the journal. "Her whole story is here," she said.

Taylor handed Jo the envelope, and she turned it over in her hands. It was heavier than the first one she'd found. "I'm afraid to open it."

Taylor covered her hands with his. "Whatever it says, just know that I love you."

Jo nodded. "I love you too."

She took a deep breath and carefully broke the seal. She instantly recognized the colonel's handwriting on the parchment.

I, Absolem Madden Colton, being of sound mind and body, do make this my last will and testament, revoking all others. It is my will and desire that all my just debts shall be paid out of any monies due me and any money that may arise to the property mentioned hereafter. I will and bequeath to my wife, Julia Colton, one-third of all that I have left after my estate is settled during her lifetime. I give her the mares Betty and Laurel, bridle, saddle, and the landau carriage. I direct that she shall leave the house and plantation known as Halcyon and permanently move to the house in Jackson where she now resides.

To my beloved Ada Mae, whom I would have lived with as my true wife. You are the only woman I ever loved and our son, Stephen, my only child, is my pride and joy. To Ada Mae Colton, now Mrs. Ada Mae Martin, I give and bequeath the plantation house and contents contained within, along with one hundred and sixty acres of land beginning at the point of Groves Line south of the orchard then running west to Robertson's line at such a point as to cut off one hundred and sixty acres next to William Cullen's farm. This includes all of the buildings contained therein known as Halcyon. She shall have, moreover, two horses, Barney and Bod, and the harness for the two, wheel horses, the plantation wagon. One horse plow, one harrow, one shovel plow, two cows, five hogs, twenty hens, five roosters, and six sheep. Mrs. Martin will also inherit the remaining monies I have set aside to pay any taxes on the house. It will be kept in a safe place until such time as Mrs. Martin is able to return to Halcyon.

In the event that my wife, Julia Colton, passes from the bonds of this earth to the hell she so richly deserves before my passing, the entirety of my assets and estates will pass to Mrs. Ada Mae Martin.

It is my will that the house and land bequeathed to Mrs. Ada Mae Martin be passed on to our son Stephen.

Upon Stephen's passing, after what I hope is a long and fruitful life, the property shall pass to his descendants in perpetuity.

In the unlikely event that I shall have any children with my lawful wife, Julia Colton, those children shall inherit the house in Jackson and any remaining assets that I have bequeathed her.

I hope that this, my last will and testament, will in some small way provide recompense for the pain and suffering Mrs. Ada Mae Martin endured due to my selfishness.

Absolem Madden Colton

"Thank God, Halcyon will be safe," Taylor said.

Jo buried her face in her hands and cried while Taylor held her. She hadn't believed that the will actually existed. Now she held the proof that the colonel had kept his promise.

"He wrote it down. He meant to keep his promise." Taylor reached up and caressed her face. "Halcyon is yours, as it always should have been."

She shook her head. "No, it's ours."

They stared at the document for a long time, rereading it and then reading pages from Ada Mae's journal. Eventually they got up, showering and dressing in quiet contemplation, each of them processing what they'd read.

He reached for the will, frowning he took in the words his ancestor had written.

"What's wrong?" Jo asked, scooting closer she rested her head on his shoulder.

His voice was raspy and raw. "He could have freed them all. The colonel kept his promise to Ada Mae, but he's no hero." Taylor let the parchment fall from his hand and reached for the comfort of the woman he loved. "I'm so angry and ashamed."

Jo reached up and turned his face to hers. "We're going to make sure they're remembered, every man, woman, and child the colonel owned."

He squeezed his eyes shut and nodded.

Pulling him into a hug, she whispered in his ear, "You're a good man, Taylor. You're my hero."

They learned that night that Tessa wasn't the woman who was killed in the fire when she called, frantic to see if Taylor was okay. After Taylor reassured her that he was fine, she started pleading with him to work with her again, but he refused. Jo stood by helplessly while he argued with her in a voice still ragged from the smoke. Tessa grew so angry and her voice got so loud, Taylor didn't need to have her on speaker to be heard. When Tessa started to turn her abuse toward Jo, he hung up on her.

Taylor sat at Uncle Robert's kitchen table, turning his phone over in his hands with a frown. He'd been fielding calls from the network, members of the crew, and his parents all morning. Jo threw him a worried glance while she made him a cup of tea. His voice was still ragged and his face was drawn.

She handed him the tea and reached up to smooth away the wrinkles on his forehead. "Here, drink this and stop talking. You inhaled a lot of smoke last night."

Taylor took a sip and pulled her to his side, resting his cheek against her stomach. She ran her fingers through his hair while he drank his tea.

"What about you, what do you need?" His voice sounded like sandpaper.

"Don't worry about me."

He pulled her into his lap. "Always going to worry."

She put her fingers to his lips. "Rest your voice. Dylan will be here soon to check on you. Yes, he will," she insisted when Taylor shook his head. "You inhaled a lot of smoke last night. Please let your brother give you a checkup. You scared us, and he's worried about you too."

Taylor nodded with a frown while he fingered the cuff of the flannel shirt Uncle Robert had loaned her that morning. It was big enough that it was almost a dress on her.

"I'll go into Greenwood later today and get us some clothes and toiletries."

"Coming with you," he ground out.

Jo pressed her mouth to his and gave him a kiss that left them both breathless.

"If that's the only way I can get you to rest your voice, then I'm willing to make the sacrifice." She smiled against his lips.

He started lowering his face to hers when there was a knock on the door and Dylan walked in.

"Well, I guess you two are feeling fine this morning," he said with a smirk.

Jo gave him a warning look when Taylor started to open his mouth. "He sounds terrible, and I can't get him to rest his voice," she reported.

"I borrowed a few things from Nate. Let me take a look." Dylan set the small bag that he was carrying down and pulled out a tongue depressor and a stethoscope. Jo stood by and watched while he listened to Taylor's lungs and looked at his throat. "Everything looks good. But Jo is right—you need to rest your voice for the rest of the day if you can."

Taylor nodded.

Dylan turned to her. "How are you feeling? Any soreness from yesterday? Nate mentioned that you were fighting pretty hard to get the door open. Any strained muscles?"

"No, I'm fine, just a little tired, that's all."

"That's understandable. Emotional trauma can be just as physically draining as physical trauma. I want both of you to take it easy for the next day or two."

Neither of them made it out of the house that day. Tillie came by after Dylan left with enough food to last them for a week. Callie and Dax stopped by to check in with Mae and Jacob. Chloe had gone into town and picked up some clothes and toiletries for them.

Nate showed up late in the day with his report. The fire was started in Taylor's room. Old construction methods and walls insulated with sawdust and cotton had accelerated the blaze. The flames traveled up the wall and into the space between the floor joists, using holes in the floor to travel up and do most of the damage to the second floor. Smoke and water from fighting the fire caused more damage than the actual fire itself.

The kitchen and back bedrooms were in ruins, and the destruction on the second floor above that side of the house was significant. Thankfully the small parlor and the hidden room escaped with just smoke damage. It was still a great deal of damage and would complicate the restoration efforts.

Nate closed the file folder and clasped his hands in front of him. "I'm sorry for both of you."

Jo reached out and grabbed his arm. "Nate, there's nothing to be sorry for. You saved Taylor's life, and that's all that matters."

"I know it's early, but do you folks know what you're going to do?"

"Rebuild," they both said in unison.

Taylor smiled at Jo, and she slipped her hand into his and gave it a squeeze. It was a relief to know that he felt the same way she did.

"As soon as the house has been cleared for you to go back in, I'll let you know."

"Thanks for everything, Nate."

They walked Nate out and sat out on Uncle Robert's porch, enjoying the last of the afternoon sun.

Jo sighed. "I'm not sure what we're supposed to do next."

"There's nothing much we can do until we're allowed back into the house and we can see the damage for ourselves."

She closed her eyes and felt a tear roll down her cheek. Taylor pulled her out of her chair and into his lap, wiping her tear away with his thumb. "I'm okay, I'm just tired."

He nodded and pressed his forehead against hers.

Uncle Robert came out to check on them. "You two look dead on your feet. Y'all need to go to bed. There's nothing you can do tonight. Rest while you can; there's going to be plenty of long days ahead for you."

He was right. Once they were cleared to go back inside the house, there were going to be long hard days of rebuilding ahead. Jo climbed into bed and snuggled up to Taylor's side. Within minutes, they were both fast asleep.

THE NEXT morning, they took the colonel's will, the journal, and the rest of the papers to the library. Callie invited Judge Beaumont to look over the documents Taylor had found.

When he finished reading the will, Judge Beaumont removed his glasses and looked at the two of them. "Thank you for giving me the opportunity to see this document. Miss Martin, if you would like, I can officially certify the will and put the sole ownership of Halcyon into your name."

Jo reached out for Taylor's hand. "No, that's okay."

"Wait," Taylor said. "Jo, let him do it. This way Tessa's ownership in the house becomes void. Halcyon will be in your hands, and it will be safe."

"I don't want to take it away from you."

He reached up and cupped her cheek. "You aren't. This is the way it was always meant to be. I'm making sure the colonel's word is kept."

"Do you... do you think this will heal the breach?"

"I think it's the right thing to do."

She'd promised Ada Mae she would get her house. She didn't expect it to happen this way, but Taylor was giving her a way to make sure she fulfilled her promise as well as protect Halcyon.

She held his gaze and nodded. "Okay." She turned to the judge. "Thank you, Judge Beaumont, I would like it if you would do that."

The judge got up and came over to shake their hands. "You know, I wasn't sure if I made the right decision when I split the house between the two of you. I have to say I'm pleased you found a way to work together."

"Thank you, sir," Taylor said.

"I'll get these to the state archives so they can be properly photographed and copied. And then you can decide what you want to do with them," Callie said.

"I'd like to figure out a way that we can share them with people when they come to the house, but I think we should keep originals with the other letter and Ada Mae's freedom papers in the safe deposit box, just to be safe."

"I think that's a good idea," Callie said.

She felt a pang of loss leaving the library without the letters. Jo knew they would be well cared for with Callie, but it was hard to let them go after what they'd gone through to find them.

"Jo, are you okay?" Taylor asked.

She slipped her arm around his waist. "I'm okay. It just feels strange.... It's funny—at first, I was okay having half of the house because I figured it was better than losing it altogether, and now I have it all and... I don't want it to just be me. I liked it better when it was us."

He stopped and pulled her against his chest. "Jo, it will still be us. It will always be us."

When his mouth met hers, the truth of his words was in his kiss. The rest of the world disappeared, and it was just the two of them.

CHAPTER TWENTY-THREE

TAYLOR RECOVERED physically quickly, but the two of them were still emotionally fragile from the fire. He had a hard time letting Jo out of his sight, and she was the same way about him. He glanced down at their joined hands. They were walking to Halcyon from Uncle Robert's. Today would be the first time they were going into the house since the fire. They were silent, walking shoulder to shoulder. He needed this contact, the reminder he wasn't alone. She glanced up at him and gave him a slight smile, but there was concern in her eyes. They were both anxious about what they were going to see.

It took more than a week before they were allowed back into the house, while the county fire marshal completed the investigation and certified that the house was structurally sound for people to go back in. Nate had given them a brief report on the damage, but now they could finally see it for themselves. A lump formed in Taylor's throat, thinking about how much had been lost in the fire. Was it too much? Was Halcyon beyond repair?

Soot and debris crunched under their feet as they made their way through the rooms. The acrid smell of burned wood and smoke still filled the air, and there was a layer of ash over everything. Jo looked up through the hole in the ceiling above the dining room at the blackened ceiling of the floor above.

"Where do we even begin?"

Taylor wrapped his arms around her. "We'll just have to go one step at a time. Salvage what we can and rebuild the rest."

She was feeling overwhelmed, but in Taylor's arms she believed they could accomplish anything. They continued through the house, picked their way through the rubble, going from the front of the house to the back where the worst of the damage was. Jo averted her eyes going past Taylor's room. The woman who was found inside still hadn't been identified. A shiver went up her spine thinking about the things she'd said to Taylor when he was locked in the secret parlor.

The pretty teal color on the walls of her room was now an ugly shade of blackened blue streaked with water from the fire hoses. Her eyes flickered to the chandelier Taylor had bought for her in Memphis, and she fought back more tears.

"I think we can have it restored," he said.

"This may sound corny, but it was the first present you ever gave me." Jo wiped her eyes.

Overwhelmed, she turned and buried her face in Taylor's chest.

"I don't care about the chandelier. Every time I think about how close I came to losing you, I...." She choked back a sob.

Taylor held her face in his hands. "We're both okay, and I love you—that's all that matters."

His kiss was slow and deliberate and sent a different kind of shiver down her spine. They were interrupted when Adam called out, "Taylor, Jo, are you here?"

They rushed to the front of the house and found Adam and Chloe with a group of young men and women wearing work clothes, gloves, and goggles. Some carried shovels while others had brooms in their hands.

"Adam, what's going on?" Jo asked.

"These are some of my classmates from the trade school. We came to help you start the cleanup."

"Thank you," she cried, looking out over the smiling faces.

Taylor cleared his throat. "I.... Thank you."

She moved closer to Taylor's side and wrapped her arm around him. She knew Taylor was just as touched as she was by the gesture.

"I called and ordered a dumpster. I hope that's okay. Chloe said you wouldn't mind if I said they could bill you," Adam said.

Taylor shook his head. "Of course it's okay—thank you for taking the lead."

"We're a bit overwhelmed right now, but we'll go change and come back and help," Jo added.

"Nah." Adam shook his head. "We've got this. You guys come back when you're ready."

Taylor put his hand on the young man's shoulder and looked him in the eye. "You're in charge, and thanks again. I don't know what we would do without you."

Adam drew himself up. He turned and shouted to the students. "All right, y'all, we've got work to do. If you have any questions, I'm in charge."

They stood by and watched while Adam organized everyone into groups and started handing out assignments.

"He's a great young man. I'm so thankful he came back and asked to work with me again," Taylor said, watching him with pride in his eyes.

They walked hand in hand back to Uncle Robert's, drawing up short when they saw the sheriff's car in front of the house. Isiah and Nate stood on the porch talking to Uncle Robert.

"Jo, Taylor." Nate nodded in greeting. "How are you folks holding up?"

"We're good, thanks," Jo said.

Jo eyed the manila envelope in Isiah's hand. "This isn't a social visit, is it?"

The sheriff frowned. "I'm afraid not."

"Let's take a seat at the table and get this over with." Uncle Robert held open the door for everyone.

When they were all seated at the kitchen table, Isiah pulled a photograph out of the envelope and set it in front of them. "We've ID'd the woman we found in your room. Do you recognize her?"

Jo gasped. The woman in the picture was the same one who had approached Taylor in the parking lot at the salvage store in Memphis.

Taylor's hand shook when he picked up the picture. "I don't know her, but she approached me when Jo and I took a trip to Memphis. She was pretty aggressive, but I…. It happens with fans sometimes."

"It turns out she'd been sending emails and letters to you at the network for months. They escalated recently. Didn't anyone forward them to you?"

"Tessa usually took care of fan mail—anything threatening, she reported to the authorities."

Isiah and Nate shared a look of disapproval. "These weren't reported," Isiah said quietly.

Jo put her hand on Taylor's arm. He pushed the photo away. "I see."

It was petty, and by not reporting the threats, Tessa had put Taylor in danger. Jo wanted to wring Tessa's neck for her selfishness.

"I'm sorry she didn't have anyone around her who could see how unstable she was and try to get help for her," Jo said after Nate and Isiah left.

Taylor had just finished making calls to his lawyer and the network, all the while furiously pacing on Uncle Robert's porch as Jo watched his growing anger with concern.

He hung up the phone with a muttered curse, running his hands through his hair. Jo came over and wrapped her arms around him. "Do you want to talk about it?" she asked.

He kissed the top of her head. "Not really—can we just sit for a while?"

Jo led him over to one of the rocking chairs that lined the porch and pushed him down. She climbed into his lap, resting her head on his shoulder. "I'm not going anywhere. When you want to talk, I'll listen."

They rocked for a while, listening to the birds start to sing their evening song and the shadows lengthen over Uncle Robert's yard.

"I'm scared," he said after a while. "I had such a clear vision of what I wanted, or what I thought I wanted, when I came here, and now everything is different. It's good, but it's also overwhelming."

"I came here without any idea of what I was really doing. All I wanted to do was get away from my old life and the embarrassment of being fooled by Oliver. It wasn't even about the house at first, but then when I came here and saw Halcyon, I just knew this is where I was supposed to be. I'm so glad I listened to Ada Mae. But I'm scared too."

Taylor kissed the corners of her eyes before any tears could fall. And then kissed each cheek, making his way across her face until he captured her mouth. They rocked and kissed until Taylor tore his mouth from hers, panting. "We need to figure out a place to live. As much as I appreciate Uncle Robert's hospitality, I want to be able to make love whenever and wherever we want."

"We'll figure it out." Jo nuzzled his neck.

THEY TOOK each day as it came, thankful that they could face it together. They worked in other areas of the house, but they avoided the secret room. The memory of being trapped inside had given Taylor more than one nightmare over the last couple of weeks. Jo had been there for each one, loving him through each memory.

That morning Taylor had announced that he was ready to go and look at the damage to the secret room. Adam had taken down what was left of the door and they would have it restored, but with a different mechanism so it could be opened from both sides. No one would ever be kept against their will at Halcyon ever again.

Jo had a large flashlight with her. The room was even darker with the blackened mirrors. Everything was intact but covered in soot, and it reeked from the smoke. She almost wept with relief when they learned that there was minimal water damage to that part of the house.

"Where do you want to begin?" she asked.

Taylor looked down at the rug they were standing on. "Let's roll this up so we can send it out to be cleaned."

They started to roll it up from one end, revealing a patch of wood below that was untouched by the smoke and any sunlight. Taylor stopped and ran his hand over the boards. "Look at this color. It's—" He stopped and frowned. "Help me roll the rest of this carpet up."

When the rest of the rug was out of the way, they could clearly see a small panel, the width of two floorboards and about a foot in length. He pressed on the seam, and Jo drew in a sharp breath when they heard a click. Whoever built the compartment must have been the same person who designed the door, with the same spring-loaded mechanism.

Jo handed Taylor the flashlight and peeked over his shoulder as he looked inside. There were small canvas bags stacked neatly, one on top of another. He reached down to pick the first one up and grunted from the weight. He set it down and pulled on the drawstring at the top.

Jo gasped. "Gold coins."

"The taxes he put aside for Ada Mae," Taylor said in an awed voice. "He said he put it in a safe place for her return to Halcyon."

"Jo, these are liberty coins. Each one can be worth more than a thousand dollars."

They peered down and counted the bags. There were twenty that they could see, with even more underneath.

"That's thousands of dollars' worth of gold," Jo whispered.

"Maybe more."

They sat back on their heels and stared at each other in shock.

"What do we do?"

"We need to get it out of here and to the bank first, and then you can figure out what you want to do with it," Taylor said.

"Me?"

"Halcyon belongs to you, Jo. This is part of Ada Mae's inheritance, and now it's yours."

Her whole body went numb. "I...." She shook her head. "I can't believe this."

Taylor wrapped his hand around the back of her neck and drew her close enough to press a kiss on her forehead. "Do you remember what Ada Mae told you?"

"This house is full of secrets," she whispered.

Taylor called out for Adamm who came running into the room.

"Everything okay?"

"Adam, we need your help. I need you to get a wheelbarrow, and then I want you to get Jo's car and back it up to the doors right here," Taylor said, pointing to the french doors leading out to the garden.

Adam looked between the two of them with a worried expression.

Jo waved him over. "Adam, the colonel said in his will that he left Ada Mae the money for taxes on Halcyon." She put the flashlight on the bags in the compartment and then reached into the bag Taylor had pulled out and held out her hand.

Adam's eyes were as big as saucers. "Holy shit," he whispered.

"I want to get these out of the house and to the bank without drawing a lot of attention. If anybody asks, we're going to move the furniture out of the secret room so it can be restored," Taylor said.

Adam stood up and nodded. "Got it."

THEY PULLED fifty bags out of the compartment. The look on the bank manager's face was priceless when Taylor and Jo opened a bag in his office and told him there were fifty more.

Ashton Beaumont stood in front of the open hatchback, staring at the pile of bags. "Well, slap me silly," he said.

"You think you've got a deposit box big enough?" Taylor asked.

Ashton shook his head. "It's gonna take more than one, that's for sure."

The three of them went to work loading the bags into the safe deposit room. When they finished, Ashton brought in one of the tellers, and they started counting. There were about two hundred and fifty coins in each bag in denominations of five, ten, and twenty dollars. When everything was locked away, Ashton offered to reach out to a bank customer who was a coin collector to get the names of some reputable coin shops who could take a look and help them figure out the value.

Jo shook Ashton's hand. "Thank you."

"Y'all let me know if I can do anything to help out at Halcyon. I'm not the best with a hammer, but I'll do what I can. A lot of folks around here were relieved to hear that you were rebuilding and not just tearing the place down. Everyone was worried you were going to give up and move back to Chicago."

"They were?"

"Everyone has been talkin' about how you've been helping out Mae with new computers. You're just the kind of person we've been hoping would move here."

"Thanks, Ashton, I appreciate that."

INSTEAD OF going to her car, Jo walked over to a bench in the park. She burrowed her face into the collar of her coat against the brisk winter air and laughed softly at herself. People in Chicago would have been wearing short sleeves on a day like today. She'd already acclimated to winter in Mississippi. She watched a group of children playing tag around the gazebo for a few minutes before a flash of blue caught her eye and a little bird, just like the one she saw on her first day in Colton, swooped down and landed in front of her. It hopped back and forth, cocking its head and looking at her before taking flight again. A feeling of rightness settled over her. This was her home, her community. She remembered the first time she'd dreamed about Ada Mae.

"Your future is here," she'd said.

"You were right," she whispered with a smile.

"YOU'RE THINKING so hard you're keeping me awake." Taylor ran his fingers across her forehead.

"I've been thinking about the money that we found."

Taylor pulled her on top of him and gently tucked a stray hair back under her scarf. "How does it feel to be an heiress?"

Jo wrinkled her nose. "You make me sound like a character in one of those old black-and-white movies."

Laughter rumbled through Taylor's chest. "What's troubling you, sweetheart?"

"If we can get the apprenticeship program going, I think I'd like to have a scholarship program to go along with it. I want to use half of the money for a scholarship and give the other half to the Colton Foundation. What do you think?"

"I think you are a very wise woman, and I'm so thankful to have you in my life. Loving you has made me a better man."

CHAPTER TWENTY-FOUR

"WHAT DO you think?" Taylor watched his brother anxiously after presenting the new offer he'd negotiated with the network. He was shocked when the network reached out to him a few days ago with another offer for his show. They were sitting in a booth at the back of the café. He'd called Dylan a few days ago and asked if he would be willing to come back down to Colton to meet with him. To his surprise, his brother told him that he was already planning a trip down and wanted to meet with him too.

History Reborn would become *Colton Reborn*. There would be no more than six episodes per season, and they would all be filmed and produced in Colton. The show would focus on restoring the area's historic homes as well as helping new businesses rejuvenating the storefronts in town.

"What does Jo have to say about this?"

"I haven't told her yet." Taylor held up his hand when Dylan frowned. "I'm not keeping this from her, I swear. I wanted to see what you thought. If you didn't think it was a good idea, I'd turn it down."

"I don't think you've ever asked me for my opinion before."

"Probably not, but I'd like it now."

Dylan rubbed his jaw. "Well, you can start by renovating a house for me."

Taylor did a double-take. "Wait, what?"

"I've decided to leave the hospital and reopen the clinic here."

Taylor's jaw dropped. "Working in a big hospital is all you've ever wanted."

"Lately I've begun to realize that's what Mom and Dad always wanted for me. I don't get to know my patients working in the ER, and since I've been coming down here to visit, I really like the sense of community everyone is working on here. I've started rethinking what matters to me, and I've begun to wonder if I'm missing out on too many moments in my life that matter. I need more balance in my life, and I want to be here to give my nieces and nephews their checkups someday."

Taylor grinned. "I haven't asked her yet."

"But when you do, she'll say yes."

"I hope so too, and if she does, I like knowing that you'll be here to be my best man."

They finished their lunch at the café and walked over to a little house Dylan had already found that he was interested in, just a couple of blocks away from the clinic.

"Well, what do you think?"

It was a wreck, but Taylor could see the potential. It was a classic single-story cottage with the most important thing for any Southern home, a front porch.

"I know you have your hands full with Halcyon, and I'm not in any hurry. Reid offered to let me stay with him until the remodel is finished. There is some work that needs to be done at the clinic right away so I can get it open, though."

"Between Adam and I, we'll make it work."

"Thanks, Taylor."

He looked at his brother. "Thank you. It means a lot to me that you've asked me to help you with this. It feels—" He shrugged. "—validating."

"I'm sorry that you didn't think I appreciated your work, Taylor. I do, and I'm really proud to have you for a brother and proud of the work that you're doing."

He swallowed past the lump that had suddenly formed in his throat. "Thanks, man, I appreciate that. When will you be moving down here?"

A slow smile spread on Dylan's face. "Today."

"You're not wasting any time, are you?"

"I started talking to Uncle Robert about it after my first visit here. After the fire, I knew this was where I wanted to be. This town needs a doctor. I already gave my notice at the hospital, and I've put my place in Memphis on the market. I'll be working on getting my license transferred and getting the clinic updated equipment. Mae mentioned that there's a grant program through the Colton Foundation that Callie and Dax started. They're going to provide funds for new equipment, supplies, and any remodeling that the clinic will need. While I'm waiting, I thought I could help you out at Halcyon."

"Now that you mention it, I do need a favor. Can you come by the house first thing in the morning?"

Taylor left Dylan and returned to Halcyon, anxious to talk to Jo about the new offer from the studio. He'd been willing to give up his show, and he still was, but this new offer had him thinking about a different future where he could do even more to help revitalize Colton. When he got home, Jo and Adam were bringing out more burned lumber.

Most of the demolition was finished, and they were already starting to rebuild. The echo of hammering filled the air as a roofing crew along with a few carpentry students from the trade school in Greenwood were making repairs on the roof.

Jo came up to him with a streak of soot on her cheek and a big smile on her face.

"Think you can take a break?" he asked, dropping a kiss on her forehead.

"What's up?"

He walked her over to the veranda and pulled her down next to him. "I had a phone call from the network the other day."

Jo's face fell.

Taylor turned so that he could look into her eyes and held her hands in his. "We're a team. I'm not going to do anything that you don't agree with, okay?"

She nodded, but her eyes were filled with uncertainty.

"The network has offered me a new show." He held fast when she started to pull away. "It would be based here in Colton and only six episodes a season."

"What about Tessa?"

"I signed over my half of the production company to her when we found the will. I should have told you when I did it. I just… I didn't want you to worry." He smirked. "I also made sure word got out about what Tessa did to you and her racist hiring practices. The network has severed all ties with her."

"You shouldn't have given up your half of the company. You should have made her pay you."

"It doesn't matter—I gave her half of nothing." He huffed a laugh. "All this time, she told me I wouldn't be successful without her help. I'm embarrassed that I believed her. Now that people are starting to hear about what she's really like, no one is going to want to work with her. The company is worthless now. I can start over with a new production company here in Colton."

Jo blew out a shaky breath. "I don't know how I feel about this."

"That's understandable after everything that happened. And if you don't want me to do it, I won't. I turned them down when they first called, but then I started thinking about it and I called them back. I told them that I would only do the show if I could use local talent, and we would feature homeowners from diverse backgrounds. I'll be picking out the projects and the trades I want to work with. I also had a talk with Chloe. I asked her if she would be interested in running the production office if we ended up doing the show."

"I like the idea, I really do. I just…. It was so awful when you were working on the show before."

"I know, and I'm sorry. I'm not trying to make excuses, but a lot of that had to do with Tessa and my unwillingness to see past our friendship to the hurt she was causing. I'm not going to let that happen again."

Jo sighed. "I had a call too. From my old job—they want me to come back. They figured out Oliver stole my program." She gave him a wry smile. "He made a mess of it and lost one of their biggest clients because of it."

"Do you want to go back?" His heart hammered in his chest. Did Jo want to move back to Chicago?

"No, I don't. But the client who left reached out to me, and they want to hire me directly as an independent contractor. I could continue to work with Dax and take on other projects of my own."

Taylor took a deep breath. "Do you think we can make this work?"

"I'm not going to lie and say I'm not worried. But I never wanted you to give up your show, and moving the production here could do a lot of good to help the town." She looked up at the house. "We have a lot going on. I don't want to get so caught up in our jobs that we don't have time for each other."

"Weekends are just for us." He pulled her closer and nuzzled her neck. "And every night," he whispered in her ear.

Her lips met his, soft and warm. It was a kiss that reassured them both that they were going to face whatever the future had in store for them together. When they finally broke apart, he swiped his thumb over her swollen lips and whispered, "I love you."

"I love you."

"That's the only thing that matters," he said.

Her eyes were dark with desire. "The only thing."

"Hey, I have more news."

She wrinkled her forehead. "What else?"

"Dylan is moving to Colton, and he's going to reopen the clinic."

"That's wonderful," she exclaimed.

Taylor wanted to ask her right then, but he was determined to make everything just right. He pulled her up and tugged on her braid. "Come on, Ms. Martin, we have a house to rebuild."

She grinned up at him, and they walked back into the house arm in arm.

DYLAN WAS on Halcyon's doorstep the next morning along with the members of the Colton Garden Club.

"You want to let me know what's going on?" Dylan asked, watching the Jewels file past with their arms full of flowers.

"Come on back and I'll show you."

He led Dylan out to the garden, where Sam and Minh were stringing lights back and forth from the house to the tree in the corner to create a canopy across the garden. The Jewels, along with Callie, Mae, and Mae's mother, were filling the garden with flowers.

"We don't have much time. Tillie and Jo are having a spa day."

"Is this what I think it is?" Dylan raised his eyebrows.

"Yep, I'm proposing to Jo tonight."

Dylan clapped him on the shoulder. "What do you need me to do?"

"We've got two deliveries coming. Jacob will be here any minute with the first one, and then we've only got about an hour before the next one should arrive."

Just as he spoke, Jacob arrived with a truckload of gravel, followed by Uncle Robert with his tractor. Taylor put Dylan to work helping to create a gravel pad at the end of the garden. They finished just in time when Adam and Dax pulled up in Taylor's truck with the second delivery.

"Oh, it's adorable," Callie exclaimed.

Hitched to the back of his truck was a vintage Airstream camper. He and Jo had been talking about where they were going to live while they rebuilt Halcyon. As much as they appreciated Uncle Robert's hospitality, they were craving a place where they could be alone. When Taylor had suggested finding an RV they could rent, Jo loved the idea. But when he stared looking, he stumbled on the vintage camper and knew it would be perfect for them.

They got it placed on the gravel pad. Everyone pitched in to turn the camper into a temporary home that he and Jo could live in until they could move back into the house. By the time everyone left. the garden glowed from all of the string lights. The camper was positioned at the end of the walkway, with more twinkle lights set up under a green-and-white awning. On the inside, the bed was made up with fresh bedding, and there were flowers on the little table at the front of the camper. There was a bottle of champagne chilling in the refrigerator. Taylor had moved their clothes over from Uncle Robert's that afternoon.

Freshly showered and changed, he paced the veranda, waiting. When Tillie pulled up and Jo got out of the car, his heart threatened to leap out of his chest. Tillie had taken her job of decoy seriously. He didn't know what story she'd told her, but Jo got out of the car wearing a pale lavender sweater dress that hugged every curve. The gold necklace that nestled in the deep vee neckline glowed against her dark brown skin. She'd paired the dress with a pair of knee-high brown boots and had a plaid shawl in shades of purple and brown around her shoulders. She'd gotten her hair cut, and it brushed against her shoulders in soft deep brown waves. She was absolutely stunning, walking toward him with a smile.

Jo's back was to Tillie so she didn't catch the wink and wave she gave to Taylor as she drove away.

He held his hand out to her. "You take my breath away, Ms. Martin."

Her eyes sparked in the evening light. "Thank you." She looked him up and down. "What's the special occasion?"

He'd tested out the tiny bathroom in the camper, showered and changed into a pair of khakis with a blue dress shirt under a navy-blue cashmere sweater just before Jo got back.

He held out the bandanna. "It's a surprise."

She took a deep breath and closed her eyes. His hands shook as he tied the bandanna over her eyes. Her unquestioning trust humbled him.

Taylor carefully led her through the house toward the garden. The smell of burned wood and smoke had slowly been replaced with the scent of new wood and drywall over the last few weeks. To Taylor, it smelled like hope. He positioned Jo at the top step leading out to the garden and untied the bandanna.

He pressed a quick kiss to her lips. "Keep your eyes closed until I say so."

He pulled the small box out of his pocket and got down on one knee in front of her and opened the lid.

"Open your eyes."

Jo's eyes opened and her hands flew to her mouth with a gasp.

"Josephine Martin, you are my home and my heart and I love you. Forever is a long time, but it won't be long enough for me to love you. It took generations for us to come to this moment, and I believe in my soul we were brought to this place, in this lifetime, for a reason. We're here to heal the past, to fill this house with love and children, and to be a family." He looked up, her face blurred with his own tears. "Will you marry me?"

"Yes." She nodded. "I love you so much, and I can't imagine my life without you a part of it. I want to make Halcyon a home filled with family and friends, and I can only do that with you by my side."

He jumped up and kissed away the tears that had gathered at the corners of her eyes.

"Oh, Taylor, it's beautiful," she said, looking down at the emerald-cut diamond he slid on her finger.

He wiped away his own tears and held her face, looking at the love reflected in her eyes. Together they had finally found the way home.

AUTHOR'S NOTE

HISTORY IS not always convenient. Sometimes the narrative does not fit what we want it to be.

The relationship between Ada Mae and Colonel Colton is, in no way, consensual. Any relationship where one person claims ownership, and the other has no agency, and where noncompliance means death, cannot be consensual.

But the existence of a place like Tawana House, a resort on what is now the grounds of Wilberforce University in Ohio, where masters would take their slave mistresses on "vacation," force us to ask some tough questions.

Why didn't these women run away? How did the women endure these relationships? Sadly, we do not know. We have lost the voices of the women subjected in the winds of history. A slave narrative from one of these "wenches," as they were known, has not yet been found. We can only hope that one of these histories is still hidden, waiting to be discovered.

My DNA and stories passed down through generations provided the inspiration for Ada Mae's story.

There are many terms used for where enslaved people were housed. I used "cabins" because that is what I grew up calling the small wooden structures where several of my great-aunts and -uncles lived.

And, finally, a word about the song Opal sings. My dear friend Donn Thompson, who performs as Donn T and wrote this song, has graciously provided this breakdown of how the enslaved people of Halcyon would have used the song as a coded message.

"Bird Up Yonder" was a way to communicate the path to freedom. It provided a way to pass information in code that would not have been obvious to the overseer or the master.

"Bird Up Yonder"

A bird up yonder 'll show the way.
A bird up yonder 'll show the way.
Code: Bird up at the main house has the details. Find the bird.

Fix my eyes to Zion, Lord.
I'm here on bended knee.
Code 1: Be on your knees and look up. Wherever this bird is in the house, it's not very high.
Code 2: Pretend you're cleaning on your knees, don't draw attention. Don't get caught. Be discreet.

To white slave owner, slaves are singing about praying (on their knees) to God and being subservient.

A bird up yonder 'll show the way.
A bird up yonder 'll show the way.
A bird up yonder 'll show the way.
When the hour is early,
Walk me on to glory.
Code: It's best to see the bird early in the morning, natural light makes it readable. Will lead you to freedom.

To white slave owner, my slaves love God, they don't mind dying (glory, the afterlife), I got good slaves.

A bird up yonder 'll show the way.
A bird up yonder 'll show the way.
A bird up yonder 'll show the way.
Moses tell the story,
The Power and the Glory,
Code: Moses, let my people go. Everyone, this is an escape song. Find the bird and take direction to leave tonight. Harriet Tubman (aka Moses) or someone like her is meeting us. Power & Glory repeated (to simplify) also representing Almighty God (the King of Glory) will go with us.

Meaning of "Go Down Moses"

—"Go Down Moses" is a spiritual phrase that describes events in the Old Testament of the Bible, specifically Exodus 8:1: "And the LORD spake unto Moses, Go unto Pharaoh, and say unto him, thus saith the LORD, Let my people go, that they may serve me," in which God commands Moses to demand the release of the Israelites from bondage in Egypt.

—Sarah Bradford's authorized biography of Harriet Tubman, *Scenes in the Life of Harriet Tubman* (1869), quotes Tubman as saying she used "Go Down Moses" as one of two code songs fugitive slaves used to communicate when fleeing Maryland. Tubman began her underground railroad work in 1850 and continued until the beginning of the Civil War.

—"Bird Up Yonder" used Moses in the third verse to represent Harriet Tubman and the Underground Railroad. Moses = it's time to escape.

To white slave owner, I have good submissive slaves; they know the Bible (Moses, power and the glory).

A bird up yonder 'll show the way.

Keep Reading for an excerpt from
The Way Beyond
Mockingbird Bridge Book Three
by Eliana West

THE WAY
Beyond

MOCKINGBIRD BRIDGE

BOOK THREE

ELIANA WEST

Mockingbird Bridge Book Three

When she finds out his secret, will he lose her for good?

Jacob Winters has a secret: he's come to Colton undercover as an FBI handler. He didn't plan to stay, but the small town has charmed him with a sense of community that he hasn't felt in a long time. And his attraction to the beautiful Mae Colton complicates things even more. Jacob doesn't do relationships—he won't risk making memories he might regret.

Mae Colton loves her little town of Colton, Mississippi, and doesn't want to leave. In fact, instead of moving on to bigger things—namely a political career in DC like she'd planned—she wants to run for a second term as mayor of Colton. But not everyone in town supports this choice, including the commitment-phobic Jacob Winters.

Mae is ready to make their secret relationship official and go public, but that would break Jacob's one rule. When a threat against Mae's life forces him to admit the truth of his feelings, he has to race to save the woman he loves before it's too late.

Scan the QR code below to order

CHAPTER ONE

THE LATE spring air was filled with the scent of honeysuckle, jasmine, and lavender. Mae Colton stood under the gazebo in Colton Park, watching her friends exchange their vows. There were so many flowers under the canopy, there was barely any room for the bride and groom. The rest of the wedding guests sat in white folding chairs that ringed the gazebo. Almost all of the small town of Colton had turned out to wish the bride and groom well.

Mae glanced over at the groom's side, where Jacob Winters stood in his gray suit with a sage-green gingham tie that matched the sash on the strapless bridesmaid's dress she wore. Her breath caught when their eyes locked for just a fraction of a second, and the heat that flared in his let her know that she'd be gazing into them longer at the end of the night.

She turned her attention back to the bride and groom, who were following local tradition and getting married under the gazebo in the town square surrounded by their friends and family. Mae was happy to see the bride wanted to follow local custom. Mae never thought much of the legend that Colton brides who married under the gazebo would have a long and happy marriage. But standing in this special place, watching another friend say her vows, she wondered if maybe there wasn't just a little bit of magic at work. She eyed her best friend and cousin, who'd become a Colton bride just a year before. She was looking at her husband standing across the aisle, her face practically glowing with love, and he was looking at her with the same intensity.

Country star Lucas Monroe, a friend of the groom, walked down the aisle strumming the first chords of Stevie Wonder's "As" on his guitar. Tillie, the owner of the Catfish Café, came next, with her head held high, wearing a sage-green silk suit that had a matching gingham camisole under the jacket. Her freshly dyed bright red hair was styled into an elegant updo, and she was beaming from ear to ear. She'd been crowing about being the maid of honor for weeks now. Jo came up the stairs, and Mae swallowed the lump in her throat, seeing her on her father's arm. She wore an ivory lace fitted blouse with a high-necked lace collar. The blouse was tucked into a full silk skirt with a train. Her hair had been swept up with yellow roses and white camellias clustered on one side. The dress and hairstyle matched the picture of her ancestor that was found during the restoration of the plantation house Halcyon.

Mae observed the groom wiping his eyes as his bride approached. As Jo walked up to him, the scent of eucalyptus overpowered all the other flowers that surrounded them. Watching them, Mae felt a slight twinge of jealousy at how open and honest they were with their love.

Judge Beaumont cleared his throat and began the ceremony. There was a lovely reading of the Paul Lawrence Dunbar poem "Invitation to Love" before the judge asked them to repeat the traditional vows. Mae had been busy sneaking glances at Jacob and almost missed the moment when the groom's brother handed him a simple platinum band that he slid on the bride's finger, next to her beautiful diamond engagement ring. Mae blinked back her tears as they were pronounced man and wife.

A broom was placed in front of them, decorated with flowers and gingham ribbon. Taylor Colton took his bride's hand, and they both jumped to cheers and applause, and the DJ started playing PJ Morton's "Only One." Each groomsman escorted a bridesmaid, dancing down the aisle. When it was her turn, Jacob held out his hand for Mae with a smile. For a large man, he could move surprisingly well. He swiveled his hips and spun her around, making her breathless before they descended the gazebo steps.

Tilly insisted on hosting the reception, so the street in front of the park was closed off, lights had been strung in a zigzag down one half of the block in front of the café, and a large tent was set up at the other end. Mae watched with amusement while the café owner directed the students from the culinary program at the trade school in Greenwood as if she were the conductor of an orchestra. She waved her arms around while the students scurried about, bringing out platters of food. The culinary students presented the three-tiered cake covered in confectionary flowers in yellow and white as their wedding present to the newly married couple.

There were the traditional toasts and speeches, and then it was Mae's turn to come to the microphone. She'd been working with the governor's office for months to arrange this moment, and she'd managed to keep it a secret, wanting to surprise her friends.

She stepped up to the microphone and cleared her throat. "Ladies and gentlemen, I'm happy to be here with you all tonight. Although my role on this occasion is a bridesmaid, I hope y'all will indulge me for just a minute while I put my mayor hat on."

She reached down and pulled out the plaque she had hidden earlier by the podium. "Will the new Mr. and Mrs. Colton please come up here with me?" They came forward, looking at her with curiosity. "Taylor and Jo, it is my great honor as the interim mayor of Colton to announce that the governor of Mississippi has signed an executive order renaming Colonel Absolem Madden Colton Park, the Ada Mae Riley Park." There were gasps and murmurs of approval as she held up the plaque so everyone could see.

Jo pulled her into a hug. "I don't know what to say. Thank you. This is an incredible gift."

Taylor was next to wrap her in his arms. "Thank you, Mae. Just when I thought this day couldn't get any better."

The three of them stood with their arms wrapped around each other, posing with the plaque for the photographer. The bride and groom took the plaque over to show their parents while Mae made her way back to her table.

Her mom and dad came over when she was finished. "Oh honey, I'm so proud."

"Thanks, Mom."

"That's a pretty big secret," her dad said. "How in the world did you pull it off?"

Mae gave her dad a wry smile. "I didn't let any email or phone calls go through the office, so my office manager didn't know."

Joseph let out a hearty laugh. The same woman had been running the office at Town Hall since the days when they were called secretaries. The woman was a notorious gossip, and in a small town where secrets didn't stay secrets for long, she transmitted information faster than the new high-speed internet they'd just brought to town.

"Well, good job, baby girl."

"Excuse me." Jacob came over. "I thought the mayor might like a glass of champagne to celebrate both the wedding and her hard work."

His hand briefly touched hers as he handed her a glass, sending a shiver of desire through her. As much fun as the evening was, she couldn't wait for it to be just the two of them.

Her parents drifted away to visit with Jo's parents. Jacob drained the rest of his glass and set it down on the table. "May I have this dance?"

Mae set her glass down and slipped her hand into his. He pulled her onto the dance floor just as the tempo changed. He drew her closer and clasped her hand to his chest, while her other hand rested on his shoulder.

"You smell like summer," he whispered in her ear.

"People are staring."

"No, they aren't, they're watching the bride and groom."

"Behave yourself, Mr. Winters. It was your idea to keep our relationship on the down-low."

"It was both our idea."

Mae pulled back and scowled. He was right, but he didn't have to remind her about a decision she was beginning to wonder if she regretted. Looking around at the other couples dancing and occasionally kissing, she wondered why she thought she couldn't have what they had.

"Is there a problem, Pixie?"

"Children, don't fight," Dax admonished as he danced past them with Callie.

Jacob looked down at her, his lips curling into that smile that always made her stomach dip. He leaned forward and whispered one word in her ear that set her entire body on fire.

"Foreplay."

"We can't leave yet. It would be too obvious."

Jacob nodded, the song ended, and the tempo changed again. Mae watched Jacob break out some serious dance moves that she honestly didn't think a White man could be capable of before she met him. She already knew the man had mastered the electric slide from his performance at Callie and Dax's wedding. Jacob was full of surprises. Mae cherished the brief glimpses of carefree moments when he let his guard down.

Her dad came over when the next slow song started. "Do you mind if I have a dance with my little girl?"

Jacob nodded. "Of course."

Joseph Colton clapped his hand on Jacob's shoulder. "You'll understand one day when you have a little girl of your own."

Mae looked down just in case there was a hole nearby she could jump into. She watched helplessly as Jacob walked away while her dad twirled her around the dance floor.

"You shouldn't have said that, Dad. What if Jacob doesn't want to have children?"

"He'll settle down one day, just like you will once you've established yourself in DC."

"Can we take a break from talking about my future and just enjoy the party?"

"All right, all right, I'll stop." He chuckled. A minute later, he looked toward the gazebo. "Just promise me when it's your turn, you'll come home from Washington and get married under the gazebo."

"Of course, Dad."

Mae added her dad's request to the impossibly long list of her sister's failings she'd have to make up for.

The song ended, and he let her go. She stood on tiptoe and gave him a kiss on the cheek. He could be annoying sometimes, but he was her dad, her hero. He was the first man she'd ever danced with, standing on his shoes in the living room, giggling while he waltzed her around. No matter how hard it was to carry the weight of her parents' expectations sometimes, she loved them.

Suddenly, it felt like there were too many people around her, and the air was too hot, too sweet from all the flowers and the spring air. She backed away from the dance floor and headed into the park and the gazebo.

She stepped under the canopy adorned with flowers, reaching up to caress one of the cherry blossom branches that had been artfully arranged to become part of the ceiling. When it was her turn, she didn't want so many flowers or people; just her with the man she wanted to wake up to every morning and create a lifetime of memories with. The truth was, Mae never thought she'd be a Colton bride; she'd always pictured herself single, living in the big city. But just over a year ago, a giant of a man who reminded her of an angry lumberjack the first time she saw him walked into her life. Now, she had a job she loved and a relationship that held promise. Her life had changed, and now she wondered if her hopes and dreams were really hers or what other people expected her to do.

"Hey, Pixie, what are you doing out here?"

The nickname Jacob gave her on the first day they met wasn't as annoying as it used to be. She'd grown to like it as much as she liked the man who made it sound so sexy when it came from his lips.

She turned around, and Jacob was leaning against one pillar of the gazebo with his arms folded in front of him. How long had he been there watching her?

"I just needed a break from all the people."

He poked his thumb in his chest. "I'm the one who's antisocial. You love this stuff."

"You're not antisocial, you're just... grumpy."

"You didn't think I was grumpy the other night," he said with a cocky grin.

Mae glanced around to make sure they were alone before she stepped toward him and kissed him, nipping at his bottom lip before she moved away.

"I happen to like grumpy."

He reached out, linking her pinkie with his. "I don't understand why."

His gaze was filled with sadness and something that she could only think of as longing.

"Because you may have fooled some folks around here, but I know your secret." Jacob's eyes widened just a fraction. "Grumpy is just an act. The real Jacob Winters is a thoughtful man, who can be a romantic when he wants to be."

"Mae, I—"

Whatever he was about to say was interrupted by a *pop* and then a burst of color overhead.

"Come on, let's go watch the show," Jacob said, letting go of her hand and shoving his into his pockets.

Mae walked alongside him, wondering how they had made their relationship so complicated when it was supposed to be so simple. *A summer fling*, that's what she told herself when Jacob roared into town on his motorcycle. From the very beginning, he'd told her he didn't know if he'd be staying, and he wasn't a commitment kind of guy. That was fine with her; she wasn't looking for two-point-five kids and a white picket fence. But now here they were, a year later, and Jacob had bought the hardware store and put down roots.

She glanced at his profile, lit up with a rainbow from the glittering lights in the sky. His jaw was set, and his eyes were locked straight ahead. Jacob always had a way of moving like he was headed toward a target. Most of that came from his years in the military, but some of it was just a part of who he was. Just one more part she'd given her heart to.

Thoughtful and *romantic* weren't the words she'd use to describe him; she wanted to say *loving*, but she couldn't bring herself to. That was a bridge they'd agreed not to cross. Summer flings didn't end with her under the gazebo in a white dress, but summer flings weren't supposed to last once the leaves turned from green to gold and back to bright again, either.

JACOB BURROWED deeper under the covers, wrapping his arms around the warm body pressed against him. Mae turned with a soft sigh, reaching up to cup his cheek.

"I'm sorry," she said, brushing her thumb over his lips.

No other woman could bring him to his knees with a simple touch the way she could. He grasped her hand and pressed a kiss to her fingertips.

"I'm sorry too."

It was a silly argument over whether they had left the wedding party too early or not. They both liked to push each other's buttons. He did it just because he liked to see the fire in her eyes. Deep-brown eyes that were filled with so much life. Humor, passion, pain, everything Mae experienced was reflected in her eyes. He'd become addicted to looking into them, as he had everything else about her.

"We have to stop," she said, pulling her hand out of his. She sat up and started looking around the room for her clothes.

Jacob ran his hand through his hair and sat up, leaning against the headboard. "I'm not being rude. I'm being honest."

Mae scooted back until she mirrored his position. "We can't keep sleeping together when we both know nothing is going to come out of it."

He hated the way she spoke with a tinge of sadness. He didn't want to hurt her, but he'd made it clear from the first night their fighting escalated into something more that he wasn't interested in a relationship. He didn't want to make memories he'd never be able to forget.

Mae jumped out of bed and began gathering her clothes that were strewn around the room. She glowed in the morning light. Shorter than average, when he first met her he thought she was all sharp angles. Over time, that opinion had changed. He relished how soft and warm she felt in his arms every time they were together. His fingers itched to reach out for her and pull her back into bed so he could run his hands over every inch of her dark brown skin. He couldn't keep her, but he didn't want to let her go. These were the only moments he regretted taking the assignment that brought him to Colton.

ELIANA WEST, the recipient of the 2022 Nancy Pearl Award for genre fiction, is committed to embracing diversity in her writing. That means she doesn't limit herself to a single genre. Instead, Eliana welcomes every story that comes her way with open arms. She aims to create characters that reflect the diversity of her community, with a range of social backgrounds, ethnicities, genders, and sexual orientations. Eliana loves to weave in historical elements whenever she can. She believes everyone deserves a happy ending.

From small towns to close-knit communities, Eliana West loves stories that bring people from different backgrounds together through the common language of unconditional love and acceptance. Eliana is a passionate advocate for diversity within the writing community. She is the founder of Writers for Diversity and teaches classes and workshops, encouraging writers to create diverse characters and worlds with an empathetic approach.

When Eliana isn't plotting her characters' happy endings, she can be found embarking on adventures with her husband, traversing winding country roads in their beloved vintage Volkswagen Westfalia, affectionately named Bianca. Whether it's traveling abroad or exploring locally, Eliana and her husband are always willing to get lost and see where the adventure takes them.

Eliana loves connecting with readers through her website: www.elianawest.com.

Follow me on BookBub

THE
WAY
Forward

MOCKINGBIRD BRIDGE

BOOK ONE

ELIANA WEST

Mockingbird Bridge Book One

The small town he couldn't wait to leave is calling him home....

Dax Ellis returns to Colton, Mississippi, a changed man. He traveled the world, earned a fortune, and made a lifetime of memories, but now he longs to put down roots. Time hasn't been kind to his hometown, and Dax wants to help—if only he can convince everyone he's not the same petulant boy he used to be. Especially the one woman who has every reason not to trust him.

Librarian Callie Colton cherished summers with her grandparents, in the town her ancestors helped build, in spite of the boy who called her names. Now that Colton is her home, life is quiet until Dax returns... and, along with him, threatening letters on her doorstep. He may still have the power to hurt her, but she's not the same scared little girl she used to be.

But as the danger escalates, Dax will have to face his past to find a way forward for the relationship they were cheated of once before.

Scan the QR code below to order

A
HIDDEN
Heart

MOCKINGBIRD BRIDGE

BOOK FOUR

ELIANA WEST

Mockingbird Bridge Book Four

Rhett Colton has spent the last two years working deep undercover for the FBI. He's forsaken his friends and family to keep his community safe, but now that his mission is over, he's haunted by what he's done and is having a hard time returning to his previous life. Only two things are keeping him from becoming totally lost—his dog, Rebel, and the beautiful new town veterinarian.

Jasmine Owens is ready to start over in the charming town of Colton, Mississippi, by opening her own veterinary practice. Jasmine knows what it's like to constantly have her abilities questioned, but she's strong enough to persevere. When she agrees to board Rhett's dog while he's away in DC, they begin talking every night over the phone and she realizes Rhett isn't the man she thought he was. He's so much more and sparks quickly fly on both ends.

But when new threats surface, Jasmine and everyone in Colton's safety are threatened. Rhett will need to make a decision. He's always sacrificed everything for his job, but is he willing to risk their relationship too?

Scan the QR code below to order

Four Holly Dates

ELIANA WEST

An Emerald Hearts Novel

Four dates
A chance to reconnect
A different way to embrace the magic of the holiday season

Soccer star Nick Anderson is new to Seattle. He's thrilled to see the shy girl he remembered from high school when he visits the local Children's Hospital. Unfortunately, his excitement is one sided. With the help of her friends, he's got four chances to show Holly another way to celebrate the holiday season.

Holly Williams had worked hard to become a pediatric nurse at Seattle Children's Hospital. The only problem is she hasn't taken the time to enjoy it. Now the popular guy she secretly crushed on in high school is asking her out not just for one date but for four.

As Holly and Nick get to know each other again, they each learn what the holidays are really all about.

Scan the QR code below to order

Summer of Noelle

of Noelle

ELIANA WEST

An Emerald Hearts Novel

Star midfielder for the Seattle Emeralds, Hugh Donavan looks forward to his visits to Children's Hospital and spending time with the young patients. What he looks forward to the most is seeing one nurse who's captured his attention.

Noelle Williams is ready to open her heart again, but she isn't interested in dating a professional athlete after a disastrous marriage to one, no matter how kind and charming Hugh is.

With encouragement from friends and one special little patient to live her life to the fullest, Noelle agrees to one date with Hugh.

Will the magic of summer in Seattle lead to love?

Scan the QR code below to order

An Emerald Hearts Novel

A senseless accident leaves Ryan Blackstone a single father. His son, Leo, survives, only for the hospital to discover he has leukemia. Ryan's only hope to save him is a bone marrow donor.

A donor registry reveals a perfect match for Leo but unearths an unsettling family secret: Ryan's wife's brother isn't dead. Then they meet, and Ryan realizes Dylan could save him as well.

Dylan McKenzie stopped thinking about his family's betrayal when they kicked him out twelve years ago. They would rather say he is dead than gay. So the news of his sister's death comes as a shock. Dylan is afraid being pulled back into the family will hurt him again, but meeting Ryan *and Leo upends his plan to keep his heart closed.*

Ryan almost lost everything. Now he must decide if he can gamble losing his family to have everything he's ever wanted. Together, he and Dylan could be the perfect match.

Scan the QR code below to order